cvlg

June 2020

DEADLY DIARIES

DEADLY DIARIES

C. E. WATERMAN

THORNDIKE PRESS
A part of Gale, a Cengage Company

LIBRARY OF CONGRESS CIP DATA ON FILE.
CATALOGUING IN PUBLICATION FOR THIS BOOK
IS AVAILABLE FROM THE LIBRARY OF CONGRESS

ISBN-13: 978-01-4328-7731-6 (hardcover alk. paper)

Published in 2020 by arrangement with Harbourlight Books, a division of Pelican Ventures, LLC

Printed in Mexico
Print Number: 01   Print Year: 2020

This is dedicated to Dean, Niki, Jenny, and Denise, who read my many early versions, and encouraged me all along the way. Thank you.

1

The body rested where she fell, and he stared at her, bile rising in his throat. Why wouldn't she listen? In the adjoining room, a jagged piece of a china cup sported an unbroken pink rose, smirking up at him, taunting in its simplicity. He ground it under his heel, and wiped the dust on the rug. Everything had to be perfect; nothing could be left here to identify him. He itched to leave, jumping out of his skin, but haste now would prove disastrous.

A thud echoed through the house. He froze, his heartbeat elevating. Was someone upstairs? There couldn't be. His palms began to sweat. Maybe it came from outside. If someone was up there, they would have peeked down the stairs by now, it was human nature. Which meant they could identify him. With a shaky hand, he grabbed a knife and started for the stairs. Only one way to be sure.

Footsteps tromped on the wooden front porch. He jumped, knocking against a chair. Cursing under his breath, he positioned the knife handle in his closed fist, an extension of his hand. Why hadn't she told him she was expecting company? The visitor fumbled around until the doorbell rang. Maybe they'd go away. Or if someone was on the floor above, it would draw them out. Either way, he couldn't risk any witnesses.

He forced his body to still. The bell rang again. Tiny windows next to the front door guaranteed he wouldn't reach the stairs unseen. He edged farther back, listening hard, but the ticking of a stupid cat clock in the kitchen drowned out any small sounds. Were they leaving? He needed more time. Shuffling swished beyond the door, and a key clattered in the lock. No time to finish. If a witness lurked upstairs, he couldn't do anything about it now. He moved back behind the body, put his toe against it, and shoved. It might slow them down.

Fine Designs was not as crowded as Maggie Schreiber expected for a Saturday morning, but there was still a line at the checkout counter. Balancing two elegant crystal lamps, one on each hip, she waited in line, taking in the ambience of her favorite store.

8

Gleaming wood floors and artistic furniture placement inspired her.

The tan sofa off to her left paired with black striped pillows and orange accessories would be ideal for the ultra-modern design she'd planned for the Linden, one of the larger houses in Edward Blake's new development. Or the same sofa with blue pillows and a comfy quilt fit perfectly in the homey country setting of the Spruce. Did she dare believe in a chance to snare a major design project like Star Lake? Eleven show homes. It could vault her little business into stardom. Well maybe not celebrity status, but rent on a storefront for sure.

"Can I help you, Maggie?"

Tori, the owner, smiled at her from the open till. The three people in line ahead of her had vanished.

Maggie blinked and, with a laugh, strode forward to deposit her purchases on the counter. "I'd better pay for these and get out of here before I buy out the store."

"In that case, stay." Tori waved an arm, indicating the entire store. "Peruse to your heart's content."

Maggie reached for her purse. "I'm afraid my eyes are bigger than my wallet."

Tori laughed and lightly stroked one silk shade. "What classy place are these babies going to?"

"They're a surprise for Aunt Esther." Maggie pictured the lamps next to her aunt's overstuffed couch. They'd be perfect. "I'd also like to put a pair in a show home I'm decorating for Edward Blake." Maggie fingered the delicate silver bauble dangling at the end of a pull chain. "Can you order more if I get the bid? I'll want some like these, plus a few others in the series."

"You bet." Tori eased a lamp down and rolled it in elegantly printed tissue paper, taping the side. "When will you know?"

Scrolled purple writing repeated Fine Designs, Distinctive Furnishings on the creamy-white packing sheets. Maggie's fingers yearned to help, but she slid her debit card out instead. "I'm submitting next week, so I should know sometime after. Edward seemed in a hurry. I guess he lost his interior designer just as they were breaking ground."

"How weird." Tori placed the lamp into a box filled partway with packing peanuts. "Do you know what happened?"

"No. I was afraid to ask."

"You'll get it." Tori's voice rang with certainty. "Your designs are fantastic." She winked. "And you use such quality materials."

10

Maggie grinned. She couldn't help herself — she wanted to sing or dance or jump. Esther would love these.

Tori smoothed packing paper over the second lamp and nestled it into the box. "Not to change the subject, but you said these were a surprise?"

"She admired them when we were here last week, but you know how she is. I can't get her to buy anything she deems frivolous."

"I won't tell her. But I warn you I'm not good at keeping secrets, so you'd better not wait long."

"I'm headed over there now, so you're safe. They're perfect for her living room. I can't wait to see the look on her face." Maggie bounced on her toes, unable to stop smiling. "She has great taste if she'd loosen the purse strings a little."

Tori laughed. "My grandmother is the same way. She'll spend thirty dollars on gas to save ten in groceries." She snugged the shades in next and stuffed crumpled paper around them. "Can I help you carry it to the van?"

Maggie eyed the tall carton. "That'd be great, thanks." The two of them balanced the ungainly box between them, secured it in her van, and slammed the doors. Giving

11

Tori a quick wave, Maggie skipped to the driver's side and hopped in.

The summer sun radiated off the pavement, promising another hot day. Even here in the mountains, temperatures had been hitting the low nineties all week. She reached for her sunglasses, tuned to her favorite radio station, and all the way to her aunt's house, she belted out the songs she knew.

She turned down the music near the empty driveway and nudged her sunglasses atop her head. Had Esther parked in the garage, or did Maggie beat her home?

Maggie parked on the street in front of the pretty white house, leaving room for Esther's car either way. A large front porch held a hanging swing — her favorite reading spot when Maggie was young. Next to it, a blue door showed through a decorative screen. She wrestled the lamps out of the back, wishing she had Tori's help. It wasn't heavy, just tall and awkward.

Unable to see where she was going, Maggie felt her way up the porch steps and groped for the doorbell. The box was too big to maneuver. Her arms didn't reach around it, and one hand flailed in space, not connecting with anything even close to the door. Finally, she pointed to a corner toward where she thought the bell should be, and shoved. The resultant ringing loosened her shoulders in relief.

Her foot tapped to the beat of the song playing in her head. What was taking so long? She tried to see her watch. Not possible. The box slid easily to the porch. Much better. She tipped her wrist — twelve o'clock, right on time. Where was Esther? Maybe she got held up at the club.

After ringing the bell one more time, Maggie dug the key out of her purse and unlocked the door. The box seemed even more awkward when heaving it up and maneuvering it through the small opening, but she succeeded and shuffled left toward the couch. Her foot caught on something solid. The box flew out of her hands and landed with a thump.

The offending obstacle turned out to be a leather-covered ottoman Esther used as a coffee table. What was it doing in the middle of the room? And why was the TV on the floor?

Maggie rotated on her toes, a knot forming in the pit of her stomach. The drawers on the beautiful old secretary had been ripped out and their contents spilled. In the adjoining dining room, the hutch gaped open, and pieces of broken china littered every surface. Her heartbeat elevated. It must have been a burglary. Was he gone? And where was her aunt?

She moved toward the kitchen, her tennis shoes crunching on broken glass. The swing door blocked her view, and a chill raced down her spine as she approached. She should leave and call the police from a safe distance. But what if Esther was hurt? The burglar wouldn't be here after all the noise she'd made, right? She had to know. "Esther?" she called out and hesitated, listening.

He must be gone.

Her hand shook, and her heart pounded as though trying to beat out of her chest as she placed her hand on the door and pushed.

It didn't budge.

She pushed harder.

It still didn't move.

Prying her fingers around the edge of the door, she eased it toward her.

Esther was lying on her side, a carving knife sticking out of her back.

2

Maggie fought the urge to yank out the knife as she dropped to her knees. "Oh, no, please, God, no," she murmured, her voice tearful. She shook an unresponsive shoulder. "Esther?" She shook again, harder this time. "Esther!"

"Please wake up." Tears dripped from her chin as Maggie placed trembling fingers at the base of Esther's neck. No pulse.

Maggie smoothed silky white hair from a mostly unlined brow. No trauma showed in the beautiful face, at least on the side she could see. Her aunt's features were composed as though she were sleeping. Maggie grasped Esther's hand and brought it to her lips. It was cool. She sat back on her heels, the tears now gushing down her face. An ambulance. She needed an ambulance. After tenderly placing Esther's hand on the floor, Maggie stumbled into the living room, scooping her phone from her purse. First she called 9-1-1, and then her fiancé, Detective Greg Williams.

"Hi, sweetheart, what's up? Did Esther like her surprise?" His warm tones caused a lump to form in her throat.

An answer wouldn't come. A sound she didn't recognize gurgled out.

"What's the matter?" His tone sharpened. "Are you all right?"

She cleared her throat and explained in halting tones what she'd found.

"Did you call an ambulance?"

"Yes, they're on their way."

"Are you sure you can't do anything to help her?"

A hiccup escaped. "No, she has a huge knife sticking out of her back. And no pulse."

"Then I want you to go outside and wait for the ambulance. I'll be there as soon as I can; I'm leaving now."

The swing called to her, but she wouldn't be able to sit still. Leaning against the porch railing, she tried to relax, but every sound startled her. Sirens wailed in the distance, but it was impossible to tell how far. Restless, she wandered down the porch steps, through the yard, and paced along the sidewalk. Why weren't they here yet?

A few minutes later, an ambulance

screeched to the curb behind her van. The doors flew open, and a man and woman sprang from the cab.

She pointed. "In the kitchen."

The man nodded, and they ran straight into the house, slamming the screen.

Maggie continued her pacing until Greg's truck rounded the corner. The police lights in his grill flashed, and his siren whined to a whimper as he slid to the curb in front of her van. Relief washed through her as he and his partner jumped out. And then the tears came.

"I'll be right back," he called as they sprinted past her. A few minutes later, he came out alone and folded her in his arms.

"Are you all right? You're not hurt?" Greg rocked her until her sobs subsided to hiccups. Then he leaned back and gazed into her face. "Will you be OK for a bit?"

She nodded, and he gave her a final squeeze before jogging to the house. His truck provided a barrier from the elderly neighbors watching from their porch across the street. They were nice people, but she didn't want to talk to them right now. More police arrived, including her best friend's husband, Mark, and his partner, Peter.

"Are you all right, Maggie? Are you hurt?" Peter asked.

She shook her head. She wasn't all right, and physically, she wasn't hurt. "Greg and David are already inside."

Mark patted her arm and hesitated until his wife, Robin, parked at the end of what was becoming a long line of vehicles in front of the house. He waited for her to hurry over, and followed the other officers.

Robin, her best friend and former business partner, held her close.

Maggie stepped back, releasing her. "How could this happen? Pinon Heights is supposed to be a safe neighborhood!"

Robin frowned. "Let's sit in the shade. It's supposed to hit ninety today." She led the way to the porch swing and lowered herself into it. "You're not hurt, are you?"

As Maggie sat, she glanced down. No wonder everyone kept asking her that. Blood stained the knees of her white capris and smeared her shins. Smudges marred one tennis shoe, the dark red violent against the crisp white. "I'm OK. It's Aunt Esther's blood."

The kitchen scene flashed in her mind, and her stomach churned. She leapt to her feet. "I think I'm going to be sick." She took a few steps and doubled over the railing before what was left of her breakfast erupted all over Esther's prized yellow roses. She straightened and wiped her mouth with the back of her hand. "Whoa, I didn't see that coming."

Robin handed her a pack of tissues, and they moved to the grass under a tall oak. Maggie wiped her face, wishing for some water to rinse out the nasty taste. "What could have made someone kill her?" she asked. "It's not like Esther was wealthy. This is a nice area, but not ritzy."

"So it was a robbery then?" Robin tucked the rest of the tissue pack into her purse.

"Yeah. There's a huge mess inside — glass everywhere." A few blades of grass remained around the tree trunk, missed by the weed whacker. Maggie gathered them in her hand and yanked, loosening her hand and watching them drift to the mowed yard. "We were supposed to meet for lunch after her golf game. She must have surprised someone when she came back."

Compassion shone in Robin's eyes. "Thieves are getting so bold. Mark says they've hit two other houses in this neighborhood in the last three months."

Maggie winced, trying to push the picture of Esther out of her head. "Thank you for coming so fast. You must have dropped everything. I assume Mark called you?"

Robin nodded.

"Now I remember why I like him." Maggie tried to smile. "Where's the baby?" She glanced at the car as if Robin would have left him in there. The sun glinted off the windshield, masking the interior.

"Libby's watching him. She wanted to come, but Jake should be getting home from school soon, so she volunteered to watch Tony for me."

The mail truck passed, stopping to feed the boxes of Esther's neighbors. Life carried on. School busses dropped off their charges, and mail delivery never stopped. She sighed.

The screen door slammed, and Maggie twisted toward it.

Peter stepped off the porch, flipped a page in his notebook, and cut through the yard. He dropped to the grass, sitting cross-legged, in front of her. He reached for her hand and gave it a light squeeze.

"First of all, I'm so sorry. You know how much we love Esther."

Maggie bit her lip to stop its trembling.

His eyes grew gentle. "Can you answer some questions for me?"

Could she? Her stomach did another flip. She could say no. Maybe they would let her leave. The safety of her home beckoned. It wouldn't get any easier. She just needed to get it over with. She nodded.

"So talk me through your morning, right up to when we arrived."

A deep breath cleared her head. "I bought some lamps at Fine Designs this morning. We were supposed to meet here at noon, and they were a surprise." Tears welled up and overflowed. Wiping them away seemed useless.

"When you drove up, was Esther's car parked in the driveway?"

Her gaze shifted to the empty driveway. "No. I didn't park there either because I thought I might have beaten her home. In fact, when she didn't answer, I went inside to wait for her."

"So the front door was unlocked?"

She shook her head. "I used my key."

"Can you remember if there were other cars on the street?"

So many vehicles surrounded her van now, Maggie had difficulty picturing it earlier. "The Johnsons' red car was across the street — they've lived there forever." She closed her eyes, trying to concentrate. "I don't know the neighbors on the right. But they had a black car in front of their house, and a white one was in the Carsons' driveway." She opened her eyes and pointed to the left. "I'm sorry. I'm not good at makes and models."

"It's OK. Picture the street. Are there any pedestrians?"

She stared at the Sunshine Interiors logo on her van, remembering her excitement when she'd parked. Another tear pooled in the corner of her eye and slid down her cheek. "I don't recall seeing anyone, but I wasn't watching."

Peter nodded and jotted some notes on his pad. "Now lead me into the house. What did you see?"

Maggie thrust the image of Esther, lying in a puddle of blood, out of her mind and described what she'd seen.

"Did you hear anything?"

"No, but I was making a lot of noise."

"Did you touch anything?"

She described what she could remember touching and answered a few more questions.

Peter scribbled on his pad and grunted as he stood. "Why don't you let Robin drive you home? We have enough to go on for now." He reached down and helped her to her feet.

Robin scrambled up beside her, her dark curls bouncing. "I'd be happy to take you."

"Thanks, but I'll be OK. I just need some time alone."

Robin walked her to the van, holding the

door while she climbed in. "Promise you'll call me if you need anything?"

Maggie agreed. "I'll be OK. Don't worry."

Robin furrowed her brow as if she didn't quite believe it, but she pushed the door shut and stepped back.

Maggie maneuvered past the police cars and sped off. The taste in her mouth, and the smell drifting up from her pants sent her stomach into flutters again. Rolling down the window, she gulped fresh air as she made her way home. The car seemed to drive itself into the alley behind her house and into her detached garage.

Honey jumped on her the minute she went through the door to the backyard, gluing her nose to Maggie's legs. "Down, girl." Maggie shooed the golden colored cocker spaniel off her knees. "Why don't you stay here while I get out of these?"

She hurried across the yard and slipped into the house, ignoring the sad whine when she shut the little dog outside. Resting against the door, she exhaled. For the first time since she'd walked into Esther's house, she felt safe. Familiar maple cabinets and cool black, granite countertops soothed her, but the fresh, clean scent of her kitchen was losing the fight against the stench drifting up from her clothes. She wrinkled her nose and dropped her purse on the small wooden accent table by the door. Her keys slid into their accustomed spot in the tulip-patterned dish next to her purse.

A shower was mandatory, but before going upstairs, she grabbed a garbage bag from the pantry. Even if they came clean, she never wanted to wear this outfit again. Using two fingers, she stripped to her undies, bagged her bloody clothes and tennis shoes, and set them next to the island. The bag could wait to go outside later. Her feet slid on the wood floor as she headed for the stairs.

In the shower, she took extra time sudsing up, wishing she could scrub the memories from her mind as well. Feeling better, Maggie took the bag outside, leaving them there to take to the garage garbage can later. At Honey's whimpering, she let the dog follow her inside. Some company would be nice right about now. Hoping to sleep, she lay on her bed and closed her eyes. Her furry friend curled up beside her, offering the only comfort she knew.

Maggie's brain wouldn't shut down, replaying the morning events, culminating with Esther on the floor. Giving up, she hauled herself to her home office to clear the clutter from her desk. If she worked on the Star Lake designs, maybe she could replace the horrible images with better ones. She flipped on some soft music. Comparing fabric swatches with color chips, she kept trying until she produced the right effect and pinned her choices to the design board.

Honey yipped a few seconds before a tap sounded at the back door.

Maggie lowered the fabric sample she'd been studying, rubbed her eyes, and pushed to her feet. She shuffled around the staircase, skirted the dining room, and hurried through the kitchen.

Greg stood on the stoop, holding a large bag from Wong's Mountain Terrace. He placed the Chinese food on the counter. "I took a chance you wouldn't have eaten dinner yet."

Maggie's stomach growled as she reached into an upper cupboard for plates. "I didn't think I was hungry, but something in there smells good."

He fished the individual boxes out of the bag and arranged them on the table. "I didn't know what you wanted, so I got sweet and sour chicken, sesame beef, and egg drop soup."

She leaned back against the black granite countertop, cradling the plates against her stomach as he opened the cartons. "What did you find out? Is it the same guys from the other robberies?"

Greg upended the sack and shook out the napkins and chopsticks. "It appears so at first glance. Her car's missing — do you know if she had any trouble with it? Could it be in a shop somewhere?"

Maggie pictured the empty driveway and shook her head. "It wasn't there when I arrived, and she should've driven it home from the club this morning unless someone gave her a ride." She cocked her head and eyed his profile. "And what do you mean, 'at first glance'?"

He wadded the bag and shoved it into the trash. "Nothing. You should be able to go into the house soon. But for now, please ask if you need anything, and I'll get it for you. Once we finish, I would appreciate it if you could go in and list what's missing."

Was he avoiding the question? Maggie tilted away from the counter and set the plates on the table, scrutinizing him. "I'm still stuck on 'at first glance.' What did you mean?"

The tantalizing smell became stronger when he opened the cartons. "We found some disparities between this crime scene and the other robberies, but they might be explained by her interruption. Since we

26

don't know if anything's missing, we're not positive, but burglary is our assumption for now."

"What disparities?"

He stopped fiddling with the take-out and gazed into her eyes. "I'm sorry. I know this is hard, but that's all I can tell you for now. I'll let you know when we have more."

Maggie busied herself plucking serving spoons out of the drawer, trying to stifle a sniffle. She couldn't handle sympathy right now. If he trained those gentle baby blues on her again, she'd lose it for sure.

"By the way, the back door was unlocked, and one of those collapsible ladders was hanging out of an upstairs window." He kept his voice brisk, as if he knew the fragility of her control, and he smiled as he took the spoons from her and stuck them in the containers. "It hung all the way to the ground. She didn't keep it there, did she?" He dished a portion from each onto his plate, picked up a fallen piece of chicken with his fingers, and popped it into his mouth.

"No, but I remember when she bought them. One summer a house a few blocks away burned down, and she worried it could happen to us, so she bought one for every bedroom." Maggie chuckled at the memory of her aunt swinging from the ladder. "We tried them out, and they moved so much, Esther said the ladders might be more dangerous than the fire."

"Do you suppose she was testing one of them again? If it was down, the burglar could have climbed right in."

He waited for her to sit before sinking into the chair across from her. After saying a quick blessing, he chased a piece of beef around his plate, pinching it between his chopsticks. "The guy could have lowered the ladder to get out, but it doesn't make any sense unless he was caught upstairs when you came in. Did you hear anything?"

She scooped some rice into her mouth and searched her memory. Images of her aunt lying in a sea of red flashed front and center. She blocked them again and cleared her throat. "Peter asked me that, too. I made so much noise I wouldn't have heard an army leave the house. She wouldn't have tested the ladders again, I can tell you that. I remember her reaction the first time." She offered a wry smile. "Saying she hated them would be an understatement. I have to tell you the thought of him being in the house when I came in seriously creeps me out."

"I know. I didn't mean to upset you. He was probably long gone by the time you arrived." Greg opened his mouth to take a bite, and a sloppy piece of beef fell off the chopsticks and into his lap.

She laughed and handed him a napkin.

They finished the Chinese food, and Greg cracked open a fortune cookie. "I hate to ask, but what did you do with the clothes you had on?"

Her mind went blank. "My clothes? I put them outside."

"Can I have them? They need to be tested."

"Tested? Tested for what?" They didn't suspect her, did they?

"We need to check for anything you may have picked up on your pants or your shoes."

"Oh. They're in a trash bag. I haven't taken it to the garage yet, so it'll be right by the back door." Her chair slid across the wood floor. "I'll get it."

He rose in a fluid movement, and his arm caught her halfway to the door. He swung her into a hug. "No. Don't worry. I'll get it on my way out." He kissed her then cupped her cheek, gently stroking with his thumb. Her mind went blank and her body relaxed into his.

"I want you to get some rest, OK?"

She waited at the back door while he

picked up the bag of clothes, and then trailed him outside. Warm air caressed her bare arms while brilliant stars sparkled against the dark sky. The light of a full moon shone on a statue of a woman spilling water from a pitcher, causing the face to glow. Crickets thrummed until Honey growled and flew into the bushes, chasing some shadow Maggie hoped wasn't a skunk.

Greg gave her another quick kiss, crossed the yard, and exited out the gate and into the alley.

Flipping on the fountain, she sank into a lounge chair, enjoying the sound of water splashing from the woman's pitcher into a basin. The scent of lilacs lingered in the air. "Lord, I know I haven't been serving You long, so maybe I'm speaking out of turn, but I don't understand why You didn't protect Esther. You know how good she was. With so many bad people in the world, why her? It doesn't seem right. I hope You're not mad at me for asking, but I can't help it." She lay silent, waiting for . . . what . . . a billboard to appear in the sky? She dozed off.

A ringing woke her. What was it? Oh, her business line. Too many dropped calls in the mountains made having both a cell phone and a landline easier. She hauled

herself up and switched off the fountain. "Time to go in, Honey-girl. Come on."

The dog ran toward her.

Inside, Maggie plucked the phone out of its holder, glancing at her watch. Eleven o'clock, who'd be calling at this hour?

"Where is she?"

Maggie jerked the phone away from her ear, fully awake from the screaming voice. "Where's who?"

"Don't try to hide her from me — I'll find her." The voice was no longer screaming, but violence vibrated through the handset.

"You must have the wrong number."

He started cursing, and she hung up. The phone rang again. She checked the caller ID, wishing she'd done so the first time. It read Unavailable, as did the number above it. She stared at it for a second, and then flipped the ringer off.

In bed, staring at the ceiling, the voice played again in her head. Just a kid's prank. But his voice sounded older, deep enough to be an adult. Maybe a wrong number. But what if it wasn't? Could it be Esther's murderer? And who did he think she was hiding?

3

A few days later, Greg called to tell her they were finished with the house, and she could go inside.

Maggie held the phone long after he'd disconnected, reeling as it hit her again. The woman who'd taken her in when her mother couldn't be bothered — the woman who'd loved her when she was a horrible teenager, the woman who'd taught her how a Christian should act — was dead.

She'd just returned from the lawyer's office, and nothing felt real. She didn't know how long she stood there, phone in hand, until a knock at the back door dragged her from her thoughts. Every movement felt sluggish as though she was deep in a dream. She staggered to the door. Another of her close knit group of friends, Peter's wife, Libby, stood on the porch, a picnic basket swinging from her arm and her brows furrowed.

Maggie swung the door wide. "Who sent you, Greg or Robin?"

Libby laughed, and the lines in her forehead smoothed. "Both. I had to fight them off, but I wanted to see for myself if you're OK."

Would she ever be the same again? "I wouldn't say I'm OK, but I'll make it."

"Is this a bad time? Were you going out?"

"I just got back." She beckoned Libby into the kitchen. "I had an appointment with the lawyer this morning." Tears she thought were dried up spilled down her face. "She left me almost everything, Lib."

"Oh, wow. That's a lot, right?"

Maggie nodded. "Yeah. Uncle Ron had no children, so she inherited his fortune."

Libby placed her load on the table and brushed the fiery red hair out of her face. "What about your dad?"

"I asked, but the lawyer said she took care of him earlier. Whatever that means. She probably didn't want my mom to get it."

Libby shrugged. "I brought lunch. Have you eaten anything?"

"I haven't been very hungry."

"When was the last time you ate a meal?"

Maggie pictured the sporadic energy bars she'd consumed in the past few days. "Greg brought Chinese food Saturday night."

Libby shook her head, her hair falling in her face again as she removed tortillas, tomatoes, and a carton of eggs from the basket, and reached inside for more. "You must be starving. Why don't you relax while I fix us something to eat? Food will make you feel better."

"Are you sure? I can help."

"No, you relax. It'll only take a few minutes."

Maggie allowed Libby to take over the kitchen. Upstairs, she changed out of her business suit into jean shorts and a cotton blouse. Her bathroom's cool colors soothed her as she drew a comb through her hair and twisted it into a ponytail. A wonderful aroma wafted up from the kitchen, making her stomach growl. As she started to leave the room, she noticed her engagement ring glittering next to the sink. She'd forgotten it again this morning. Placing the heavy stone on her finger, she headed downstairs.

"You're right. I am hungry," she said as they sat down to breakfast burritos. The egg and potato melded with the bacon and cheese. She wiped bacon juice from her mouth before she could talk. "Mmm, these taste fantastic."

After they finished, Libby pushed away from the table and carried her plate to the sink. "Did Greg call you yet?"

Maggie rose to help. "Yeah."

Libby waved her off. "Please, let me do this."

Maggie settled back.

"So he told you? Peter said you can go in now," Libby continued.

The maple cabinets in front of her faded to white, and her aunt lay in front of them. A red pool enveloped Esther's body, and the black handle of a knife extended from her back as if to wind her up. Maggie shivered, and her kitchen came back into focus.

Libby must have observed the shiver, because before Maggie knew it, she stood beside her, one hand rubbing her back. She reached for Maggie's plate. "Greg sent someone in to clean the kitchen, so you won't have to face that again. Whenever you're up to it, we can get started. If you don't want to do it tomorrow, we can wait a few days."

Maggie's gaze trailed her to the sink. "Doesn't Peter need to know what's missing?"

"Yes, but he can wait 'til you're ready."

"I'm ready." Once the words were out, Maggie wondered what prompted her to say them with such conviction. She wasn't ready, not now anyway. Warring emotions tugged at her. An almost physical need to be in her aunt's house chased away the desire to escape. How could she distance herself from the pain, yet feel the comfort of Esther's house? There may not be a way to do both. Did her conflicted emotions show on her face?

They must not have, because Libby shifted her gaze and flipped on the water. "As soon as I leave, you're going over there, aren't you?"

Normally she would have. But now she wasn't too sure.

Libby rinsed the plate and tucked it in the dishwasher. "OK, let me call Robin, and we can all go now."

What? Now? Panic surged into her chest then settled as dread in her belly. "No, y–you both have your kids," she stammered. "I can call Maria and get her to meet me over there later." Much later.

Libby stopped cleaning. "Funny." The corners of her mouth curved up. "You thought we'd let you do this alone? That's not how we roll, baby." She wiped her hands on the dishtowel and picked up her phone. "Asking Maria to join is a good idea though. With four of us, we should be done in no time."

She called Robin, and Maggie listened to her agree to meet at three. Once Maggie's kitchen was clean, Libby paused at the door, empty basket in hand. "I know you'd like to get in and get things done, Maggie, but I don't want you to face this alone."

Maggie didn't want to either.

"Promise you won't go early?"

Maggie nodded. Not likely. What had she been thinking? She wasn't sure she wanted to go at all. If she just said the word, everything would slow down, and she wouldn't have to face it yet. But waiting wouldn't make it easier.

A couple hours later, Maggie hauled herself out of the car and stood in Esther's driveway, facing the familiar rose bushes. Thankfully the bath she'd given them didn't seem to hurt them any. Her keys jangled as she twisted them in her hands. She wasn't prepared for this. Tomorrow would have been better — or the next day even. Trembling, she forced herself up each porch step and drew the screen door toward her. Memories of the last time she was here flooded in, and her breath came faster. She fought the urge to run. Squaring her shoulders, she turned the key in the lock and shoved the door open.

The box she'd been carrying that day

waited in a corner of the living room, the lamps still inside. It'd be a miracle if they were undamaged. Someone had taken the Persian rug from the dining room and swept up the glass, but black fingerprint powder covered every surface, including some on the wood floor. Dreading what she would find in the kitchen, she stepped along where the rug had been and placed her hand on the cold swing door. She stilled for a moment, gathering her courage, before pushing at it.

The sun streamed through the window above the sink, highlighting white cabinets and countertops and bouncing off bright yellow walls. The cheery room gave no sign of the violence that had taken place in here. Even the fingerprint powder was gone, and the white tile floor gleamed. The pungent smell of a cleaning agent burned her nose. Unconsciously stepping around the area where Esther's body had lain, Maggie opened the window over the sink, relishing the breeze. She threw open the back door, making sure to lock the screen. How long would it take to feel safe here again? Was it possible a killer had lurked in this space when she'd stumbled in with the lamps? She shuddered.

Maria arrived first and sucked in her

breath at the mess. She sought Maggie's face with a bewildered gaze. "Such beautiful things. Your aunt had so many beautiful things. Why did they have to ruin them?" Tears slid down her cheeks.

Feeling helpless, Maggie patted her shoulder.

Robin and Libby arrived, and the four of them worked together in comfortable silence. Robin and Libby cleaned fingerprint powder from every surface imaginable, and Maria and Maggie sorted through the broken items, attempting to catalog what remained. They tried to identify the broken versus the stolen, but in the end, Maggie couldn't be positive anything was stolen.

When she waved her friends off, convincing them she'd be fine, Maggie closed the front door and sighed. She listened for any sound as she hurried through the kitchen, shutting and locking the back door before going upstairs.

The master bedroom looked beautiful as always. The same elegant spread covered the bed and contrasted the soft green walls. A framed picture of Uncle Ron smiled at her from a side table. Her own picture rested on the dresser next to a small pink dish she'd made in pottery class as a child. She picked up the dish and flipped it over in her hands, running her finger over her initials scratched in the bottom. Esther placed her rings in it at night, but it lay empty now. The mortuary had returned her wedding set to Maggie.

Esther's jewelry case stood in its place, impossible to tell if anyone had opened it. Her favorite necklace and earrings were still inside, a sapphire and diamond set given to her by her late husband. Maggie eased the box closed and moved to the bookcase, her fingers grazing the supple leather of her aunt's diaries. They were all there, years of her life cataloged in their pages. The sluggishness she'd shaken off this morning seeped back into her soul like sludge. Even her bones felt tired.

She chose the year she was born, hugging the volume to her chest and carrying it into her old room. The well-remembered lavender comforter smelled fresh as she slipped under it. The words in the diary sounded familiar, as if her aunt sat on the end of the bed telling her a story.

"Her name is Margaret," it said. "They call her Maggie. She's the sweetest little bundle I have ever seen. I hope my brother is up to the responsibility. He's still very young."

Mom used that excuse when she wanted

to ignore her first marriage. It never occurred to Maggie it could be true — they
were too young to know what they wanted
in life. Maybe it's why her dad bailed when
she was nine.

He would have been twenty-seven when
he left, younger than she was now, and
Mom a year behind him. If youth was the
problem, she could understand their marriage falling apart, but why all the ones her
mom had after? Shaking her head, she read
on. Any other time it might have bored her,
but now, it felt as if she were sitting at Esther's table dipping cookies into her milk.
She skipped ahead to the first mission trip,
the one that started Esther's lifelong passion for the children of Africa:

We got off the plane, and it was so hot I
couldn't breathe at first. They picked us up
in an open vehicle, and by the time we got
to the orphanage, I was covered in dirt.
I'm sure I have half the desert in my hair
and the other half in my teeth, but they tell
me there isn't enough water to bathe every
day. I guess I'll use the washcloth Cara
gave me to clean up, do my best to shake
the dust out of my hair, brush my teeth
and make myself presentable for dinner. I
haven't met any of the children yet, but

tomorrow I'm supposed to sit in on a classroom. I pray I am up to this.

A week later:

The kids are so wonderful! I don't speak their language, but many of them have been able to learn some English from the other teachers, so we're communicating with their limited English and a lot of hand signals. For the most part, it's funny, and we laugh a lot. They're very accepting of me, for which I'm grateful. Seeing the level of their poverty is quite sobering. We feed the children who live here, but for the ones who attend day school, we're unsure of their home environments. I've seen a couple of them save food to take home. We assume it's to feed family members, so I give them a bit extra if I can.

Maggie relaxed her arms, and the diary fell next to her. She closed her eyes and dreamed of Africa.

The sun slanted in the window on its way down when she opened her eyes. Remembering where she was and why she was here took a minute. Tears threatened again, but before they could surface, she stood and smoothed the comforter into place. The spare room still needed to be checked for

missing items.

It looked as neat and clean as ever, a sign of Libby and Robin's diligence. The fire ladder lay folded on the blanket chest. When she picked it up, the awkward metal rungs clanged to the floor, making her jump. She raised the lid and dumped the ladder in where it belonged, the sound deafening. How would a burglar know this was in here? And how could he have gotten it out without Esther hearing?

She dropped the lid, relieved. No way would she have missed such a racket. Esther must have had it out for some reason, but why would she leave it hanging outside? Were the police right? Had the killer climbed in? Didn't make sense. The rest of the room was untouched, nothing in here worth stealing. Time to go.

Wanting to continue the Africa story, Maggie chose the diary she'd been reading, and the year her dad left. It'd be interesting to see Esther's thoughts on abandonment. The latest diary was in the nightstand, so she took it as well. A thought occurred to her. How did Esther feel about getting married so late in life? She was forty when she'd married Uncle Ron. Did she have any doubts? Her steps faltered. Was it too personal?

43

She shook her head. It didn't matter now. If she couldn't talk to Esther, she could at least listen. She tried to remember what year they'd married. She'd been the maid of honor while in high school . . . she flipped through a couple of them until she found what she was looking for, hurried with it downstairs, and out to her car. Taking them out of the house felt strange, almost like stealing, but at the same time, they were comforting and familiar.

The drive home was dark, and headlights from the car behind hit the rearview mirror and blinded her for a second. Her thoughts reverted to the diary, and Esther's passion for the children of Africa. She'd been jealous once, and her face burned with shame now when she thought of it. As she neared her driveway, her cell phone rang.

"Maggie, it's Mark. I'm at the station. Ah . . . you'd better come down here."

She slowed. "Why? Did you guys find out anything?"

Mark cleared his throat. "We're questioning someone."

"Oh, good, but why do you need me? I never saw him."

"Yes, but she's asking for you. It's Allie."

Maggie held the phone away from her ear, stared at it, and then snugged it back. "Al-

lie? Here? In jail?"

"She was found with your aunt's car. Apparently, she's been living in it for the last couple days. We haven't arrested her, but we can't get a hold of her dad. The chief thought she might feel safer with you for now."

Questions swam through Maggie's head. "I'll be right there." She sped to the station, and Mark met her on the sidewalk. She nodded at the desk sergeant as they wended their way past him to the conference room, embarrassed at not remembering his name.

Allie stood facing the window. It'd been a long time, but Maggie would have known the petite blonde anywhere. Her long, straight hair slid half out of its habitual ponytail and hung down her back. Her arms hugged her waist, and she rocked from side to side. She looked about twelve years old in her jean shorts and rumpled white blouse, but she must be seventeen or eighteen by now.

"Allie? Are you all right?"

Allie turned, and the familiar tear-streaked face tugged on Maggie's emotions. She bent to retrieve her purse from the chair.

Maggie hurried to her and drew her into a hug. "What's going on?"

Allie hugged her back. "Can we just

45

leave?" she asked in a small voice. "I'll explain on the way."

Mark led them out of the station and watched while they slid into Maggie's car. He waved as she drove from the lot.

A light blue truck passed slowly.

"Now tell me what you're doing in town and how you ended up being questioned by the police."

Allie wiped her eyes. "I came to stay with Aunt Esther for a while. I showed up at her door Friday night, and she took me in, no questions asked. Well, she did ask some questions as she was making up my bed, but even though she isn't technically my aunt, I knew she'd take me in."

"Why? What were you running from?"

"I wasn't running. You sound just like my dad." She paused for a minute. "OK, I was running away from my dad."

"George?" She pictured the short, round man her mother had made husband number two, remembering his kind blue eyes. The same eyes staring at her now. She couldn't imagine him doing anything to make Allie leave home. "What happened?"

"Nothing happened, but he's driving me crazy. I've accepted a tennis scholarship to the University of California, but I don't want to go. And he won't leave me alone

46

about it."

Maggie glanced in her rearview mirror as a light blue truck passed under a streetlight. Was it the same one she saw when she left the station? It turned off. Guess not.

"I stayed overnight," Allie went on, "but Aunt Esther was gone when I got up. I waited so we could talk, but when she got back, someone came to the door. They were yelling downstairs, so I grabbed my clothes and threw the ladder thing out the window. I tried to be quiet, but it made a horrendous racket."

Maggie lips curled, remembering the clamor when she'd put it away.

"I could see her car in the driveway, so I grabbed the extra key. You know the one she keeps in her dresser, climbed down the ladder, and left." She turned in her seat. "I didn't know she was in trouble, honest. When I came back, there were police and an ambulance. I got scared and took off." Tears streamed down her face. "If I'd known Esther would get hurt, I would have helped her. I swear!"

Maggie steered into her garage, shut off the engine, and lowered the door, feeling better with it down. The motion detector clicked on as they stepped into the back-yard, flooding it with light. They hurried

47

into the house, neither speaking until they were inside with the door closed and bolted.

Allie reached down to pet Honey, who was wild with joy at her presence. "Now they think I lowered the ladder so my boyfriend could rob her. They assume we fought, and I killed her and then stole her car."

Maggie's mouth fell open. No way could Allie have stabbed Esther. She was athletic, true, but she was only five two and a hundred pounds at most. She forced her jaw closed. The boyfriend, however, might be a different story.

"I didn't mean to steal the car. Aunt Esther always lets me use it when I visit." Twisting a few strands of loose hair around her finger, Allie faced her. "What am I going to do? You know I wouldn't hurt her, don't you?"

Maggie tossed her keys in the dish and moved into the kitchen. "Of course, you wouldn't. Who's the boyfriend?"

Allie studied the garden picture on the wall next to the door, her back to the room. "Just a guy I hang around with. He wouldn't hurt anybody."

"Are you sure?" Maggie's voice rang with accusation.

Allie stiffened.

"Why didn't you go home?" She softened

her tone.

Allie turned to face her. "I was afraid. What if he saw me?"

"Who?"

She rolled her eyes. "The killer. He might think I saw him."

"Did you?"

"No, but he doesn't know that. Can we ask your boyfriend to help? Isn't he a cop here or something?"

"Yeah, but how did you know?"

"Aunt Esther brought you up all the time. I couldn't help it."

A warm glow formed in Maggie's chest. "She mentioned you a lot, too."

Allie covered her face with both hands and sobbed.

Maggie tugged a few tissues from the box on the small table and handed them to her. When she reached the hiccup stage, her words were almost indecipherable.

"Aunt Esther can't be gone. She was the only mother I had."

Any judgment Maggie might have felt melted. "I understand. I felt that way, too."

Allie dropped her arms to her sides, her hands balling into fists. "How could you? You were the favorite. Mom didn't send you off the first chance she got; she kept you. Even with Aunt Esther, you were always the

49

favorite."

The revelation stopped Maggie cold. Surely, Allie couldn't feel as unwanted as she did. "You thought Mom wanted me but not you?" Allie's face reddened, but Maggie ignored it. "You couldn't be more wrong. You were the blessed one; your dad wanted you."

Maggie gripped Allie's shoulders and peered into her face. The blue eyes staring back didn't flinch. "Mom kept me because she had to. There wasn't anyone else. My dad left when I was nine."

Allie's posture relaxed and her fists slackened. It seemed she was listening, so Maggie loosened her grip. "Then she and George got married, and you came along. I thought I had a family, but you know how that worked out. There were a few more guys, and I ended up living with Aunt Esther when Mom picked one of them over me." She shrugged. "It's why Aunt Esther and I were so close. But she loved you, too. I used to hear a play-by-play of every tournament and every win." Maggie gently placed her arms around her half-sister.

Allie's body stilled. Then she hugged her back. "Aunt Esther talked about me?" Sobs shook the thin frame.

Maggie held her tight.

Allie's sobs dwindled to a sniffle. "Why couldn't we have had a mother like her?"

Maggie stepped back and slid her fingers down to Allie's hands, giving them a squeeze. "Believe me. I've asked myself the same question a thousand times. In her way, Mom loved both of us, but she had no idea how to raise children. Don't let her weakness affect the way you feel about yourself."

Maggie wasn't talking to Allie anymore — she was talking to herself. Maybe she wasn't at fault for her mother's rejection. Tucking Allie under her arm, she led her upstairs to make up the bed in the guest room. Why did it take her so long to understand? Maybe she could look at her mother differently now. Maybe . . . well, she could work on it.

They talked long into the night, laughing and crying. Maggie wanted more information on the boyfriend, but Allie changed the subject every time she brought it up.

As she flipped off her bedside lamp, Maggie considered the situation. If the police thought Allie was involved, they would have arrested her. And if she wasn't afraid of the boyfriend, why didn't she go home? Could the killer have seen her? Was she a target now?

Maggie would have to keep an eye on Allie and keep her safe.

4

Greg sipped his coffee, studying Esther Campbell's file. The Gunderson folder rested on the desk next to it. Excluding the murder, the robberies had similarities. Both happened during the day, and broken glass and china littered both scenes. But the breakage in the Campbell case was over the top. Had the thief wanted something he couldn't find? Why so much destruction? The fury of it screamed out from the pictures.

He drained his mug, placed it next to his computer, and withdrew a magnifying glass from the drawer. Leaning forward, he compared the images emailed from Esther's insurance company with the crime scene photographs. Thank heaven there were pictures, since he wouldn't know a valuable piece of art from an army boot. In fact, an army boot might be prettier than some of the art in the Gunderson robbery. The paintings consisted of shapes and splatters — nothing he would have considered valuable. The insurance company disagreed.

In the Campbell case, each insured piece corresponded to a picture from the crime scene, and so far, Maggie hadn't come up with anything missing. So either Esther's murder disturbed the thief so much he panicked and left, or Maggie interrupted before he could finish. A sudden chill caused the hair on his arms to rise. Allie said Esther let someone in, so if she was telling the truth, the thief or thieves thought she would stand there and let them rob the place. They must not have known her at all.

Could he assume Allie was telling the truth?

Not finding anything obviously missing, he read the officer's notes from the area canvass. The neighbors on either side weren't home, and the Johnsons across the street didn't notice anything until the police and ambulance showed up. He flipped through the crime scene photos again, hoping something would pop. Nothing did.

Moving on to Esther's calendar, he started with the day she died and copied every appointment she'd had in the past month. Amazing how active she was when she was supposed to be retired. She played golf and tennis every week, volunteered at Children's Hospital in Denver, and then went to other functions in the evenings or on weekends. Had she always been this busy or did it start after her husband passed away?

Her golf partner the day she died had been Monica Tate, and she'd played tennis the week before with the mayor. A pattern asserted itself, and he wondered if someone else had noticed she was at the Black Bear Country Club every Saturday and Wednesday and at the hospital every Tuesday. It wouldn't be hard to know when she'd be out of the house.

Monica was the last to see her, so she would be his first visit. He called and was told Mrs. Tate was having breakfast at the club. He swiveled to the desk behind him, but David wasn't there. Across from him, Peter hunched over his computer.

"You see David this morning?"

Peter glanced up. "He must be getting coffee."

"He'd better get it to go. We're calling on the BB club."

"You're taking David to the country club? Isn't that a bit like taking a Rottweiler to a tea party?"

Greg grinned. "Yeah, it should be entertaining. But hey, he is my partner, and maybe if he shakes the trees, some nuts will fall out."

Peter shook his head. "Just remember, some of those nuts can get you canned."

Driving through the club gates was like entering another world. A riot of colorful flowers burst from every direction, and huge old trees shaded the lush grounds. The Mercedes in front of him glided around the curved driveway past the brick and stone building. It drifted to a stop, and the trunk popped open. A clean-cut kid around sixteen or seventeen rushed to unload two golf bags, stood them in a nearby stand, and closed the lid. The Mercedes drew away toward the sign, which read Member's Lot.

David glanced over. "Swanky."

Greg parked his truck on the other side of the drive and stepped out. The kid appeared at his side.

"Can I help you, sir?"

Greg flashed his badge. "I'm here to see Mrs. Tate. I understand she's having breakfast."

The young man smiled and backed away.

Greg and David strolled toward the entrance.

A kid in a golf cart screeched to a stop beside the stand, and the two of them loaded the clubs from the stand into the cart.

Inside the cavernous foyer, a pretty red-head waited behind a counter along one side. In her matching golf shirt and skirt, she was the perfect model, selling the club's clothing line. "I believe Mrs. Tate is in the dining room, Detective." She rose and came around the counter. "I'll show you the way." The woman led them down a long hallway to the back of the clubhouse, her sandals clicking on the stone floor.

Pictures of lush, green golf holes in front of snow-covered peaks hung in ornate frames along the walls, and they passed a huge bronze sculpture of a golfer. David posed next to the statue and grinned. "Look, this could be me!"

"Yeah, if you could golf." Greg laughed.

"Hey, I play a mean putt-putt."

The woman ignored them and passed through a double doorway into the dining room. More intimate than the grand entrance, the room was no less impressive for its smaller size.

Monica Tate glanced up from her table in the corner. Her son-in-law, Edward Blake, rose as they approached, a half-eaten pancake in front of him.

"Please sit down, detectives. Would you

like to order something?" Monica lifted a hand, and a server immediately started toward them.

"No, thank you, Mrs. Tate," Greg said. "We have a few questions. It shouldn't take long."

"Something to drink perhaps, coffee or tea?" Monica flashed him a smile. "Maybe some lemonade. It's going to be hot outside today. And sit down. I'm getting a crick in my neck."

They seated themselves, and he ordered lemonade. David chose iced tea. The server nodded and disappeared.

Monica smoothed her short, salon styled, white hair away from her temple. "What can I do for you? I'm sure this isn't a social call."

David's gaze seemed fixed on the attractive server, and Greg was thankful he was too distracted to make a smart-aleck remark. "I came regarding the last time you saw Esther," Greg said. "I understand she played golf with you the day she died."

Tears filled Monica's light green eyes, and she looked away.

Edward patted her hand and answered for her. "Yes, we were here at the club."

"The three of you? Was there a fourth?"

The tears spilled over, and Monica bent for a tissue to dry them. "Luther golfed with

58

us. We played nine holes because Jonathan had a tennis match right after, and we wanted to watch." She sighed. "I wish we'd gone longer, maybe then she wouldn't have interrupted the burglary." A fresh set of tears threatened. She dabbed at them, careful not to smear her makeup.

"By the way, is Maggie OK?" Edward asked. "It must have been horrible, finding her aunt."

Greg hesitated. Was she OK? She'd been acting different lately, but that was understandable. Aloud he said, "It was hard on her, but she's doing pretty well. I know she would like to put it all behind her."

The perky brunette server placed their drinks on the table and bounced back to the kitchen.

David's gaze continued to pursue her.

Monica reached for a fruity drink. "Poor dear. I can imagine what she's going through. Are you investigating? Was it tied in with the burglaries we've been having?"

The server stepped out of sight, and David's attention returned. "Burglary is one assumption," he said. "But we have to cover our bases. For example, do you know anyone who might have wanted to kill her?"

"No, of course not. You knew her, Greg. She was the kindest woman alive. Too kind, sometimes."

He noted the change from Detective to Greg. Was she trying to remind him she was older and more respected? Or maybe establish a rapport? It could be just a slip of the tongue — she'd known him from boyhood, after all. "What do you mean by too kind?"

Monica glanced down and wiggled the manicured fingers on her left hand to straighten the huge rock of a wedding ring given to her by her late husband. "If you don't show some people a firm hand, they'll take advantage of you."

David tensed and opened his mouth.

Greg glared at him.

David closed it, sliding a notebook from his pocket.

"Someone was taking advantage of Esther?" Greg asked.

Monica looked up. "Not necessarily, but her maid was awfully forward. I came over one day to drop off fundraiser material for the hospital, and the woman was eating with her in the dining room. In fact, Esther served her tea and cookies!"

What a sin. "Do you think Maria had something to do with her death?"

Monica frowned. "I'm just saying unscrupulous people might have taken advantage of her good nature, and when she stood up

60

to them, it might have been too late."

David kept his head down and wrote something in his notebook. It probably wasn't complimentary.

Greg leaned back in his chair and crossed his ankles, hoping to relax Monica enough to gossip. "So she stood up to someone, and they killed her?"

"Have you seen some of the people she called friends? Her gardener, for instance. He was a criminal or something. You might want to start there. If she caught him stealing, he might have killed her to keep from going to jail again."

David gripped the pen so hard his fingers paled, but to his credit, he kept silent.

Greg spoke into the gap, "Do you have any reason to think he did something to land him back in jail?"

She sipped her tea. "Don't they always? Once a criminal, always a criminal, is what I say."

"So much for second chances," David mumbled.

Greg ignored him. "Is there anyone else we should investigate besides the maid and the gardener?"

Monica fiddled with her diamond watch, twisting it so the clasp lay centered on the inside of her wrist. "No, but I'm sure other unsavory people ingratiated themselves into her life. I tried to warn her concerning the people she associated with, but she wouldn't listen."

He drank his lemonade, trying to formulate more questions. He didn't dare ask if David had any for fear his responses would be less than polite.

Monica placed her fork in the middle of her plate and pushed it aside. "Now let's talk about you, Greg. I've known you since you were a boy, so I'm dispensing with the formality of Detective."

Wonder what she would say if he dispensed with the formalities and called her Monica? Never mind. He knew what she'd say, and it wouldn't be pleasant.

"Why don't you come back and play some golf?" she continued. "You can be my guest. We could use some young blood in this stuffy old place, and I'm sure Jonathan could use the competition."

Greg stood, and David sprang out of his seat. Greg tried to ignore his eagerness to leave. "I wouldn't be much competition, I'm afraid. I haven't played much since Dad passed away."

Edward rose with them.

Monica remained seated. "Yes, but it's like riding a bike," she said. "You never forget.

And bring your pretty fiancée. You know I've always liked her." Her eyes misted again. She blinked the haze away and cleared her throat. "I'll miss playing golf and tennis with Esther. She was my favorite partner." She looked frail, swallowed up by the large chair.

He found himself wanting to offer comfort, but he couldn't. The wall she lived behind was too thick to cross. He started to leave, David already halfway down the hall, when he thought of another question. "Mrs. Tate, how was Esther's state of mind when you saw her? Did she seem upset?"

A faraway look softened Monica's eyes. "You know, she did seem flustered when she arrived, and she didn't score as well as usual. She didn't say anything though, so I didn't want to pry."

He glanced at Edward. "Did you notice anything? Did she say why she was flustered? Was she late?"

Edward drummed his fingers on the table. "No, I didn't notice anything wrong, but I'm not as observant as Monica." He settled back into his seat.

"If you think of a reason she may have been worried or upset, would you call me?"

Monica smiled, good manners trumping emotion. "Yes, of course. And, Greg, come play some golf here. I promise you'll love it."

Greg caught up to David already sitting in the truck, with the window down. "In a hurry, are we?"

"This place gives me gas." David clicked his seatbelt in place. "So are you going to sign up?"

Greg laughed, navigated out of the country club, and hooked a right onto the street. "Not likely."

"I wouldn't be so hasty if I were you. I've heard the golf course here is spectacular, and there are tennis courts and a huge pool."

"So, what are you, the travel brochure?" He made the next left and set off for the station. His friends would never be welcome here, even if they could afford it, which they probably couldn't. "And who would I play, Monica? Or worse, Jonathan? No, thanks."

"I can't see you playing with that weasel Jonathan, but you never know, your fiancée may want to join up. Don't you want to put on your monkey suit and take your best girl to the club for dinner?"

"Nah."

"At least, you were asked. You didn't see her inviting me to join. In fact, she didn't talk to me at all."

Greg shrugged. The only reason he was invited was the money. If he hadn't inherited it, Monica Tate wouldn't be calling him Greg like he was a relative, or offering a membership into her exclusive club. "Speaking of my fiancée, I have to pick her up for the funeral. Are you going?"

"Yes, of course. You know, it's amazing Esther got along with the country club set."

"I know. She was nothing like them. Maggie says her Uncle Ron had the membership before they got married. Then Esther took up tennis after he died to keep busy. She seemed to enjoy it though, and from what he'd heard, she was pretty good." Would Maggie want to keep the membership? He doubted it. Although she could afford to — married to him or not.

"Back to the interview. What impressions did you get?"

"Besides the obvious?" David sneered. "Monica Tate is just as snooty as I remembered. The only people who could have murdered Esther are those beneath her station."

Greg nodded. "What I don't understand is how she keeps her staff happy enough to stay with her. It's obvious what she thinks of them." He drummed his fingers on the wheel. "She must pay well. Anyway, you questioned Maria and Joe already, right?"

"Yeah. They come in once a week, and since neither was scheduled to work there the day she died, they didn't see anything. Their other clients verified they were working at the time of the murder."

Greg pulled into the station lot. "The timing would make sense if the thieves knew everyone would be gone, but if they were watching the house, wouldn't they have seen Allie?"

David slammed the door and spoke through the open window. "Unless Allie was in on it."

5

As Maggie waited with Greg and Allie in the room off the sanctuary, a hum from the packed church drifted toward her.

Mom insisted on staying with the family, even though she wasn't related to Esther. Her shining brown hair swung as she tossed her head, glaring at Dad, as usual.

Maggie peeked around the door again. All the pews were full, including what she could see of the balcony. The entire town had gathered to pay their respects. She imagined her funeral, when it came, would be very different — a few people in an otherwise empty church.

The pastor interrupted her musings by ushering them into the sanctuary. Dad led the procession into the first row. Maggie urged Greg forward, and she filed in between him and her mother. Allie was next, and George, Allie's dad, sat on the end. He leaned in and gave Maggie a warm smile.

The church quieted when the pastor stepped to the podium. "We're here to celebrate the life of a woman who knew the meaning of the word *service,*" he said. "Esther gave to others every day, not considering the cost. We're here to honor a life well lived."

He detailed her aunt's many works of charity, addressing big things like teaching in Africa, and many smaller tasks even Maggie didn't know.

A doctor from the hospital spoke of her generous donations and how she read to the children every week. He choked up when he described how the kids looked forward to her visits.

Familiar faces and new friends attempted to share what Esther meant to them, and pride and shame battled in Maggie's heart. How could she have been so close to someone so good and not have any of it rub off? Her life had been lived in selfishness, despite her aunt's example.

She cringed as she remembered Esther asking her to go to Africa. A teenager then, she'd been horrified by the thought. Esther smiled. "I thought it would be good for you to see how much you have to be thankful for," she'd said.

Maggie had countered with something

rude, and Esther never mentioned it again. Now Maggie wished she'd shared that important part of Esther's life. She sat in the pew, miserable, as each person got up to speak. Then her turn came.

Her throat was dry. She couldn't do this. Why did she agree to it anyway? Gripping her notes in one hand, she clenched the other into a fist as she wobbled on shaky legs up the podium steps. Panic stirred in her chest, and her breath came in short gasps. She prayed for courage as she smoothed out the pages.

"I began reading my aunt's diaries in order to feel her with me again," she said. "And while it did, they allowed me to know her in a more personal way." Maggie surveyed the audience and nearly froze when she locked gazes with her mother. She moved on, meeting Robin's eyes instead.

"Esther called the children at the African school her little ones. Never having had children, she loved them all as if they were her own." Sniffles from the congregation accompanied, and she choked up for a second but struggled on, her voice trembling. "The pastor said she lived her life well, but what does it mean?"

She focused her gaze on Greg and spoke only to him, as though no one else was in the room. Her voice smoothed out. "To me, she was a second mother. She stepped up when my father left, and she took me in when I needed a home. She gave of herself, consistently, over a lifetime. I loved her deeply, and I'll strive to follow the excellent example she set."

Ignoring the guilt on her father's face and the rage on her mother's, she reminded everyone of the reception at Esther's house then left the podium. Silence chased her back to her seat before everyone took a collective breath.

The notes of "How Great Thou Art" filled the room, and the pastor dismissed them.

Standing in the foyer shaking hands and hearing condolences, she tried to ignore the cold anger emanating from her mother. Ruth, Carla, and Ginger, three of Esther's closest friends appeared next in line, and Maggie reached out to shake their hands. "I'm so happy you could make it. I know how much my aunt cared about you."

Ruth's nose was red and her eyes puffy. Her breath caught as she tried to answer. She swallowed and tried again. "I can't believe she's gone," she said. "We had lunch last week. How can this be happening?" She broke down, and Maggie put her arms around her, patting her back. Ruth lifted her head, and the other two led her off.

Greg stayed by Maggie's side through the last well-wisher and gently drew her away. "Come on, sweetheart. It's time to go to the reception."

Maggie's limbs hung heavy as she trudged toward the doors. "I feel like I've been up for days. I wish I could go straight home and forget facing all these people again."

Greg tucked her hand under his arm and led her outside into the bright sunshine. Most had already left, but a few people stood on the sidewalk talking. He quickened his steps as he led her onto the grass to avoid them, and she kept her gaze down, purposely not making eye contact. "It won't be too long," he whispered. "Robin's there already. She'll have fed everyone, and by the time you get there, it'll be half over."

Maggie tried to smile. "Yeah, the one thing that drove me crazy when I worked with her was how she organizes everybody. But it's what makes her great, you know?"

"Yeah. Robin shines in a crisis." He guided her through the almost empty parking lot to his car. "I don't see your mom or Allie. Did they leave already?"

"They went with George. It's funny how Mom still gets along with Allie's dad. She hates mine." Greg opened the door for her, and she waited for him to go around and get in before continuing. "Did you notice how she stood next to me receiving condolences? She barely tolerated Aunt Esther, she was always jealous."

Greg remained silent.

Maggie tucked her hair behind her ears. "It was to stop me from saying any more bad stuff about her. I shouldn't have said what I did in the eulogy. Dad feels guilty, and Mom wants to pretend we were the perfect family. But the truth is, I wouldn't have made it without my aunt. I don't know what I would have become if she hadn't been there, and I'm tired of pretending."

He reached over and patted her knee. "You spoke from the heart, honey, and it was the truth."

"Yeah, but remember what Aunt Esther used to say?" She imitated her voice. " 'Maggie, darling, you can tell the truth without sharing everything you know.' "

Greg chuckled, which made her smile. She stared out the side window, remembering her aunt's face when she'd said it. "I never told her how much she meant to me." Her voice dropped close to a whisper. She cleared her throat. "I hope she knew how I felt."

Greg stopped at a light and tapped her

hand. He waited for her to look at him. "I'm sure she knew. You guys were close. Anyone could see it. Besides, she surely knows now."

"She's in heaven, isn't she?" Maggie twisted a soggy tissue in her hands. "I mean really in heaven, not just what you say to people to make them feel better. If anyone deserves to go to heaven, it's her."

"Yes, I believe she's in heaven," he said. "But not because she was good, or because she deserved it. She believed in Christ, and that's what got her into heaven." The light changed to green, and Greg refocused on the road as he moved into the intersection. "He's also why she did the charity stuff. She loved God so much it spilled out all over the place. Your aunt was an exceptional person."

Maggie sniffled but stayed silent.

"You remind me of her," he said.

"What? How do you mean? I'm nothing like her. She was giving and selfless. I am selfish and inconsiderate." Maggie shifted in her seat. "I would love to be like her, but . . . I'm not."

"Yes, you are. You're going to be just like her. I can tell."

Maggie remained silent, but a battle raged inside. Should she speak up? He needed to understand now, before it was too late. If

73

he'd asked her to marry him thinking she was like Aunt Esther, then when he found out the truth, he would leave, just like her dad. She opened her mouth, but he was already outside, halfway around the car.

He opened her door. "This is as close as I could get. It looks like the whole county is here." He held his hand out to help her stand.

Cars bordered both sides of the tree-lined road, and as they walked around the block, there wasn't an open space along Esther's entire street. Maggie's knees shook as she stumbled up the steps and stopped on the porch. The door was open, and the clink of dishes and the low hum of people reminiscing drifted through the screen. She tightened her grip on Greg's elbow, took a deep breath, and walked through.

Inside, food was piled high on the dining table, and beyond the propped-open kitchen door, Robin bustled about, readying even more. Maria flitted around with a coffeepot, and Libby filled pitchers with punch and iced tea.

Maggie crossed to the food-laden table, stopping to receive condolences along the way. Her stomach quivered at the smell of food. After placing a few items on her plate to forestall any appetite questions, she

moved back into the living room.

Monica Tate approached on Edward Blake's arm. She appeared tiny next to his athletic frame.

"Maggie, what a beautiful speech you gave," Monica gushed. "You described your aunt so perfectly it made me cry."

Maggie gulped at the sudden lump in her throat. "Thank you, Mrs. Tate. I appreciate it. And, Edward, thank you for coming."

"Esther was a good friend." He gave her a quick hug and returned to Monica's side. "You know, she had a mean backhand. She and Monica played doubles with Jonathan and me. I used to dread it when I saw the ball go to her left side. One day, she nearly took my head off."

"It's because you're old, pops." Blake's son, Jonathan, joined them and bent to kiss his grandmother's cheek. Straightening, he winked. "Just kidding, Dad. She was good. She gave me a run for my money a few times."

Maggie laughed, and it felt good. "Wow, that's saying something, since you're the club pro."

"I should know better, right? But her strategy would be to start me running all over the court. I knew she was doing it, but I was helpless to stop her before I was hoofing it from one side to the other. Honestly, she was one of my best students. She had a gift for the sport."

As the conversation lulled, Libby joined them. "Talking about tennis, Jonathan, I was sorry to hear about your doubles partner. How did it happen?"

His smile faded. "It was an accident. Stephanie fell in her apartment and hit her head on the hearth."

"How awful. How are you holding up?"

"I'm OK." He glanced at her hardly touched plate. "Let me get you some punch." He lurched in the direction of the kitchen.

Libby placed her half-full glass on the nearest table. "I'm so sorry. I stuck my foot in it this time. It must be hard for him."

Mrs. Tate's gaze tracked her grandson's progress. "It's OK, Libby. He's a strong young man, and he'll be fine." She patted Edward's hand. "Edward was pretty tough when my daughter died, and Jonathan is the same. Did you know he and Stephanie were engaged?"

Red suffused Libby's face. "I knew they were doubles partners, but I had no idea they were so close. I feel horrible." She looked away, and tears sparkled in her mascara-laden lashes, threatening to spill over.

Maggie stood frozen, unable to think of anything to help her friend.

Edward leaned forward and patted Libby's shoulder. "No need to feel bad. You couldn't have known. They hadn't made the engagement public yet." He stepped back, his eyes mournful. "Jonathan was out of town, so he didn't find out for a couple days. Stephanie had told him once she didn't want a funeral, and since she didn't have any family, he took care of everything."

An awkward silence stretched between them, and Maggie wanted to say something to fill it. But again, nothing came.

"Maggie, I didn't know Esther kept a diary." Monica changed the subject. "Had she always done it?"

Maggie smiled her gratitude. "I remember her writing in diaries since I was a child, but I didn't realize how many there were. I found years of them in her bookcase."

"Have you had a chance to go through them yet?" Edward asked.

"No, I've just skimmed the surface. But I can't wait. It's almost like having her with me again. Plus, she led such an interesting life. I'm enjoying reading about it."

Maggie shoved some of the finger food

around on her plate. "By the way, I'm glad I got a chance to talk to you, Edward. I finished the designs for the first six show homes in the Woodland series. I'd like to get your feedback before I finish the rest."

With a promise to meet for lunch the next day, she moved on. Esther's best friends waited a few feet away. Carla gripped her hand. "I can't believe she's gone," she said. "We were together just last week. We all went to Lindy's for lunch, the day that woman died, wasn't it, Ginger? Wasn't it a Tuesday?" Her cheeks grew pink. "I couldn't help but overhear."

And you made it impossible not to, didn't you? Maggie shouldn't have such uncharitable thoughts. But the Tate family had been important members of the community for decades, and Carla was a notorious snoop.

Their voices faded to a whir, and Lindy's Tea Room swirled into focus.

"Maggie, darling, let's buy you a pair of shoes to go with your new coat, and then we'll show them off at Lindy's. How would that be?"

Maggie had felt so smart in her pretty blue coat and black patent leather shoes as she and her aunt sipped tea.

Greg touched her arm. "Is everything OK, sweetheart?"

Coming back to the present, she nodded. Across the room, George started toward them.

Carla shuffled to let him through.

"Maggie, I'm so sorry. Are you OK? Is there anything I can do?" George grasped her hand and then drew her into a side hug, careful not to spill her plate.

Of all the men her mother had dated, Maggie thought she'd been happiest with him. She wondered what happened. "Thanks. I'm fine."

"Can I talk to you for a minute?"

Maggie smiled, glad to be rescued from Aunt Esther's friends. "Sure. Would you ladies excuse us?"

Ruth nodded, and Carla gawked as they moved away.

Greg shook hands with George and reached for her plate. "I'll take this if you're done."

She relinquished it, and he left them alone.

"Is it OK if Allie stays with you?" George got right to the point. "I can get her a hotel room if it's inconvenient."

"Of course, she can stay with me. Don't even consider a hotel."

He smiled, and relief loosened the taut lines on his forehead. "Thanks. I talked to the police, and it seems they're more interested in this kid she's been hanging around with, Cameron Hayes, than they are in Allie. But she won't give him up. I tried to make her, but she insists she doesn't know where he is. Maybe she doesn't. I don't know." He sighed. "The thing is, I have to return to Iran. I'd like to take her with me, but she won't go, even if the police let her. She keeps reminding me she's eighteen and doesn't have to do what I say. It's very frustrating."

Maggie smiled. "I can imagine. I was like that at her age. They say it passes."

George laughed. "I shouldn't complain. She's been an exemplary daughter. It's just . . . we used to be so close." His eyes lost their sparkle. "I don't know what happened. I guess I travel too much." His face reddened. "Sorry, you don't want to hear that. Anyway, I know she'll change her mind if I don't push it. She'll do the right thing. She always does. In the meantime, she'll be safe with you." He gave her his card. "Call my assistant if you need anything, and she can get you whatever you need."

He started to say something else but shook his head and moved away. Maggie tucked his card into her purse as Greg stepped up beside her.

"Everything OK?"

She nodded. "Yeah. He just thanked me for keeping Allie and gave me his assistant's number if I need anything."

"He's not staying?"

"No, he has to get back to Iran. She'll be fine with me. I'm glad for the opportunity to get to know her again."

They traveled from group to group until the last few guests said good-bye and the room emptied.

"You look exhausted." Robin touched her hand. "Are you staying here tonight?"

"No, my car's at home, and I'll need it tomorrow. I have an appointment with Edward concerning the Star Lake designs."

"Wow, I forgot. You must be very excited." Wistfulness edged Robin's smile. "It almost makes me want to go back to work."

"If you ever want to be partners again, just let me know. We can work something out."

"Naw. I like being a stay-at-home mom, but sometimes I miss the creativeness of the old life, you know?"

Maggie didn't know, but she could imagine. In fact, she often wondered how Robin could go from a dead run to what seemed like a full stop. But when she considered it, running after a baby had to be just as busy. It wasn't something she thought much about, which was a good thing since she wasn't married yet.

The next morning, Maggie finished the remaining touches to her design boards and slipped them into her portfolio. She hoped Edward would like them. The opportunity was such a great one. Imagine having all the Blake properties to design. She would still be able to do the small remodel jobs she loved, but she'd have the security of steady work. And if he liked her designs, maybe he'd give her a free hand.

He never promised them all, she reminded herself, but the excitement wouldn't leave. She rehearsed her presentation as she backed out of her driveway. Should she sell herself as a designer or let the designs speak for themselves? She still had no idea what she was going to say, but she prayed it would go smoothly, and turned in the restaurant's direction.

He waited until he was sure she wasn't coming back and then inched past her house. These older neighborhoods were easy. As long as the windows hadn't been replaced, he could slide his knife in and catch the latch. Or he could jimmy the French doors in the back. He hoped to not have to break a window. No evidence could be left behind — she could never know he was here.

His vehicle hugged the curb at the end of the street, and he circled back on foot through the alley until he read her address on the garage behind her house. He crept through the back gate into the yard. A window stood open, a perfect invitation for him to enter. He reached for the small screwdriver he brought with him to remove the screen. Sharp barking drew him up short, his heart pounding.

Oh, yeah, she had a dog. A small one. The jerky in his pocket should do the trick. He fumbled for it. If not, he could shut it into another room. He was good with dogs, even if he'd never been allowed to have one. He slipped closer to the house and stopped. The canine might not deter him, but what he saw did — someone, a woman, walked past the window. He swore under his breath and backed away. Had she seen him?

"Honey, be quiet!" The voice drifted across the yard.

He held his breath and tiptoed to the fence, easing the gate open. He'd have to find another way.

6

Maggie arrived at the Chateau right on time. Beautiful chandeliers sprinkled warm light on fine china, and soft music whispered through the air, adding to the relaxed elegance. Edward drew out a chair for her at a round table in the corner where she could prop her portfolio against the wall. The crystal glasses shimmered when she sat, being careful to tuck the linen tablecloth under so she wouldn't yank it off when she rose to show him the designs.

A vision of herself, tablecloth tucked into her skirt, and an entire table full of food in Edward's lap made her giggle. This was not the time for mindless frivolity, but the laughter threatened to bubble to the surface. Better concentrate on the menu. The food was so fancy, she hardly recognized anything. A waiter walked to their table, and choosing a salad with chicken seemed like a safe bet. Edward ordered steak, and they engaged in small talk.

He slid his napkin out of the ring and unfolded it in his lap. "Have you heard anything from the police?"

"Not yet." Maggie tried to copy his casual manner, unfolding her napkin. "But the strongest theory seems to be burglary."

He took a sip from his water glass. "Are there other theories?"

She waited while the waiter placed her salad and Edward's steak in front of them and left. "I don't see how there could be," she said. "No one would want to hurt Aunt Esther. Burglary is the only reasonable explanation."

He nodded. "Did I hear your sister's boyfriend might be a suspect?"

Good grief, was there anything in this town he didn't know? Considering how powerful he was, probably not.

"So I hear, but I haven't met him. I do know Allie would never have hurt Aunt Esther. She loved her as much as I did."

Compassion softened his gaze as he changed the subject. "What made you decide to become an interior designer?"

Was this more small talk or part of the interview? "When I was younger, I constantly changed my room around, trying new colors and accessories. Aunt Esther let me decorate however I wanted, so I experimented."

Edward smiled and nodded but kept silent as though he wanted more.

Must be part of the interview. "I went to college for marketing, expecting to get a job in advertising, but I kept drawing out rooms instead of writing ad copy. I changed my degree to Interior Design, and I met Robin at school. We decided to start Sunshine Interiors together. When Robin chose to become a stay-at-home mom, Aunt Esther helped me buy her out." She laughed. "And that's my story. Anyway, what about you? Did you always want to be a builder?"

Edward had eaten most of his steak while she'd been talking, leaving a small hunk on his plate. "Not at first." He sliced off a piece. "I started working for a builder to pay my way through business college. I found I liked the work more than I liked sitting behind a desk, so I quit school." He popped the steak in his mouth and talked around it. "I built a house for myself at night, while working my other job during the day. I moved in as soon as I could to help with expenses, and when I finished, a realtor friend said he could sell it for a profit. He did, and I started looking for another place to build. The business took off from there." A faraway look glazed his eyes. "Someday Jonathan will inherit it, and his son after him." He blinked and forked in another piece. "That is if I can get him to give up this tennis nonsense."

Maggie smiled back and wondered if the slip in table manners was done on purpose to make her feel at ease. If so, it worked. Her visions of scattered tableware vanished. She glanced down, surprised to see her plate clean. "I can't believe I ate everything," she said. "I must have been hungry."

Edward laughed. "The portions here are tiny. Why don't fancy restaurants feed you enough? Do you want dessert?"

She declined.

He ordered cheesecake. After the waiter left, he continued, "What about Esther's house? I assume it's paid for."

Maggie nodded. "Uncle Ron left it to her free and clear, and she left it to me. It's in such great shape it shouldn't be hard to find a buyer." She sighed. "I haven't gotten that far yet."

He tapped his mouth with his napkin. "Understandable. But isn't it bigger than yours? Wouldn't you want to keep it and sell your place?"

The waiter showed up with his dessert and coffee, saving her from having to answer.

Using the distraction, she rose and slipped her design boards out of the portfolio. He could inspect her designs while he finished his dessert. Dragging out the chair between them, she propped the first one on it, allowing him plenty of time to see every detail.

Keeping one hand at her side, she forced herself to refrain from chewing her nails while she waited. Would he like it? When enough time had passed, she positioned another board in front. "The smaller homes are brighter and make more use of the space, while the larger ones have muted, elegant palettes. I've used the materials from the design center, so I put prices in for all the upgrades."

He studied each board.

Had she over decorated? Her palms felt slimy. She surreptitiously wiped each hand on her skirt, supporting the boards with the other.

At last, he broke the silence. "They look terrific."

She puffed out the breath she'd been holding.

"We're ready for you to start the first house right away." He reached into his briefcase and handed her a stapled set of papers. "Here's our construction schedule and a standard contract for your services. If it's acceptable, please sign and return it as soon as possible."

He waited for her to slide her designs back in her portfolio, and held out his hand. "I want to thank you for stepping in like this after our other designer bailed. I love what you've done in such a short time. We'll get along fine."

She thanked him and left the restaurant, practically skipping to her car. As she picked up her cell phone, it hit her again. The person she most wanted to call was Aunt Esther. She tossed the phone in her purse, wiped the fresh tears off her cheeks, and proceeded home.

Aching for the sound of her aunt's voice, she ran upstairs. If she couldn't be with her, at least she could read her thoughts, and imagine the sound of her aunt's voice as if she were in the room with her. Allie's door was closed, and hearing nothing inside, Maggie moved into her own bedroom and shut the door. The diary she'd been reading waited on the table beside her bed. She changed into shorts and lay down to read once again.

I'm amazed by how much the children want to learn. We teach them in their language first (I'm useless there), and then

I teach them English. We've gotten better at communicating with gestures and giggles. The children, though they have so little to laugh about, love to laugh.

One of the tiny girls, whose name I cannot for the life of me pronounce (I call her Kiki), has learned to sing "Jesus Loves Me" in English and wants to sing it every day. She's precious to God, I know. I don't know her family situation, but she comes in the morning with her younger brother and sister. She's a regular little mother, caring for them at the age of ten. I wonder if she has a mother at home.

The clock chimed and startled Maggie awake. She needed to leave for Greg's, and she wasn't ready. Yelling to Allie, she hurried into the bathroom. No time for primping, a quick brush of the teeth and a comb through the hair would have to do. She glanced at the sink and noticed her ring. She'd forgotten again. How long would it take to get used to wearing it? Slipping it on her finger, she rushed downstairs. Wonder of wonders, Allie was ready and waiting in white shorts and a blue-flowered, cotton blouse. Maggie snatched her keys from the dish and pulled the back door closed behind them.

Although the day remained in the high seventies, a cool breeze wafted the daisies next to the brick path. Her roses were in full bloom, their flowers bright pink against the wooden fence. She breathed in their fragrance and bent to pull a lone weed before preceding Allie into the garage.

Allie buckled into Maggie's old red sedan. "You need a new car, Mags. How many miles does this have on it anyway?"

Maggie backed out of the driveway and headed for the street. Hearing the old nickname made her smile. "Only a hundred thousand. It's still good."

"Good?" Allie snorted. "You'll be lucky if it doesn't break down on the highway. Besides, the paint job's seen better days."

"I know, but I like my car." She turned in the direction of Greg's. "Let's talk about you. Who's this boyfriend? I'm dying to know. What's his name?"

Allie shrugged. "Just a guy. I don't want to talk about him."

It didn't take long to reach Greg's place, and they were silent as the elevator rose to the twelfth floor and deposited them in front of the penthouse.

"Wow, how much does a cop make in this town?"

Maggie rang the bell. "He has family

91

money. His uncle left him land in Montana, and he sold it for a fortune."

"Whew, no wonder you like him."

The clop of Greg's cowboy boots on the other side of the door forestalled her comment, which was good, since what came to mind wasn't very Christian. The door swung open to reveal Greg in a barbecue apron, sporting a giant, grinning pig on the front. He greeted Allie and bent to kiss Maggie.

"The perfect man — sexy, yet domesticated. What are we having?" She playfully dodged the meat fork in his hand.

He grinned. "You know man's preoccupation with fire. Of course, I'm grilling steaks."

He led them through his leather-filled living room to a huge balcony on the roof of one of the lower units.

Pushing Snowball, the beautiful white Persian, better known as Stinky, off the chair, she made room for Allie near the railing.

The sun shimmered off rooftops, and Star Lake glistened in the distance, hemmed in by mountains. Even though they were at nine thousand feet, even higher peaks rose against the horizon.

"Hey, this is cool. Can we see your place from here?" Allie asked.

Maggie pointed it out as the doorbell rang. Mark, Robin, Libby, and Peter arrived together. She invited them out to the balcony.

Mark strode to the railing. "I never get tired of this view." He smiled at Allie. "Don't you love it up here? It's so relaxing."

Allie nodded and glanced away. She must still remember his questioning at the station.

"It's why I chose this apartment," Greg said. "The twelfth floor is high enough to see the lake without all the houses in the way."

"This huge roof patio didn't hurt." Peter spooned a large portion of potato salad onto his plate. "Did you buy the building specifically for this apartment?"

Greg stabbed a piece of meat and held it up. "It was a major selling point, but not all. Now who wants a small one?"

Robin lifted her plate to receive a steak that was anything but small. "Maggie, how will you want to decorate?"

Maggie looked at Greg. "Why, are you redecorating?"

Robin laughed. "I mean I like it and all, but it's a little masculine, don't you think?"

"Yeah, but Greg's a masculine kind of guy,

so it works. It reflects his personality."

"But it doesn't reflect yours," Greg interjected. "When we get married, you'll want to change everything before you move in, and I'm fine with it." A devilish look glinted in his eye. "In fact, I'm planning a long honeymoon, so maybe you can have the workers come in while we're gone."

"Is that how it works?" Libby set her plate in Greg's waiting hand. "She plans the wedding, and you plan the honeymoon?"

"It worked for us, didn't it?" Peter said.

Heat rose from Maggie's neck to her scalp. "When I move . . . what do you mean when I move in? Who says we'll be living here?"

"Your place is smaller, so I assumed you'd want to move in here. Mark, you'd better claim this one before it goes from medium-rare to torched."

"Everyone is trying to move me out of my house." The words escaped before she could stop them. "First, Edward says I should move into my aunt's, and now, you all," she swept her hand around the group, "assume I'll move in here. I like my house, thank you very much, and what about Honey? Doesn't she count?" She sucked in a breath.

"What? Of course, she counts." Greg stopped, the grill fork waving in the air.

"I don't see how if you think I'm going to move her from a yard to a high rise." Her voice elevated to a mosquito whine, and her friends shifted in their seats. She should stop, but the words tumbled out. "And isn't my house good enough for you?"

"I didn't say it wasn't good enough. I like your house. We can discuss this later. I didn't know it would be such a sore spot."

He was right. They had guests for heaven's sake. Everything inside her wanted to escape. Now. Somehow, she had to get through the rest of the evening without making an even bigger fool of herself.

"I'll get the lemonade," she mumbled, slipping into the coolness of the kitchen. She gazed at the high-end, black-and-white surfaces. Even though she felt comfortable enough, she couldn't see herself living here. She plucked several glasses from an upper cabinet and began pouring lemonade.

The muted voices became louder as Robin drew open the sliding door. "Everything OK?" She stepped in.

"Yes. No. I don't know. I'll have to get back with you."

"I'm sorry. I didn't mean to start something."

Maggie reached for a tray and loaded the glasses. "It's good to get it out in the open.

He would have said something eventually."

Robin patted her arm and picked up the heavy tray. "You'll figure it out," she said as she balanced it on her hip and slid sideways out onto the deck.

Maggie wasn't so sure. They'd never discussed where they would live. In fact, they hadn't discussed a lot of things. Did he want children right away? He loved kids; she knew that. But no way was she ready to be a mother. Maybe this was happening too fast. They'd only known each other a year, and she'd been living by herself a long time. Maybe she was too set in her ways to get married. She lifted the pitcher, plastered a smile on her face, and stalked outside.

The rest of the evening, laughing and talking with everyone, was less than the party she pretended. Greg tried to catch her eye, but she avoided him. The last thing she wanted was another scene, so she and Allie slipped out without saying good-bye.

"Why are you so mad?" Allie asked when they got in the car. "I'd love to move in there."

Maggie gripped the wheel and glanced in the rearview mirror. Lights from the car behind reflected off her ring, causing bursts of light to travel around the car. "It's complicated."

Her cell phone rang as she walked in the door, the display showing Greg's handsome face.

Allie gave her a quick wave and ran up the stairs, leaving Maggie alone. Her finger hovered over the *reject* button. Then she pushed *accept.* She should explain. She owed him that.

"I hoped you'd be home," he said. "I didn't want to call while you were driving. You left so fast, I didn't get a chance to talk to you."

She wound her fingers into the hem of her shirt, the ring digging into her palm. "I didn't know what to say."

"I do. I'm sorry. I shouldn't have assumed you'd move in here. I realize now it seems arrogant of me to start running your life. I don't want to, you know."

"I know. I overreacted." Why didn't the admission ease the knot in her stomach? "We just haven't discussed it yet."

"I don't care where we live. We can live at your place if you like, and I can rent this apartment out. You're right — Honey is more comfortable with a yard."

He waited for reassurance, but she didn't have any. "Listen, I'm pretty tired. Let's talk tomorrow, OK?"

He agreed, although she sensed his reluctance. Uncertainty plagued her as she hung up. He was a great guy, but the idea of constantly being with someone left her claustrophobic. If they were married, he'd be with her right now. Her house enveloped her with warmth and sanctuary. What should she do?

7

Maggie finished her breakfast and drained her orange juice as she wrote a quick note for Allie. Then she headed for Aunt Esther's. Her key slipped into the lock the way it had thousands of times before. Inside, she hesitated with the door open, muscles tense. The ticking of the living room clock echoed in the silence. How had she never noticed it was out of sync with the ticking in the dining room?

The impulse to call for Aunt Esther was so strong, she almost couldn't resist. Fighting her emotions, she drew the list out of her bag and cleared a large space in the living room. Consulting the sheet, she leaned a painting willed to her dad against the wall, and a small table in Allie's spot. Robin and baby Tony would be here soon. Then the place wouldn't seem so hollow.

The bell rang, and she jumped. Beyond the screen, Robin and ten-month-old Tony waited on the porch. His chubby arms reached out for her when Maggie opened the door. She scooped him from his mother, cooing and nuzzling his roly-poly neck. He giggled and squirmed, showing all four front teeth. "He looks so cute in those shorts!" Maggie said. "I wish they made clothes this cute for adults."

He kicked in her arms, and she put him down. He crawled to the ottoman and heaved himself up.

Robin set a couple plastic blocks in front of him.

Tony squealed and knocked them to the floor, falling on his padded behind in the process.

Maggie smiled. His laughter dispelled the creepy silence.

Robin glanced around. "Is Allie here?"

"She's at home in bed. It's amazing how long she can sleep. I don't remember sleeping in so late at her age, do you?"

"We probably did. We just don't remember. I know your dad left when you were nine, and you went to live with Esther when you were fifteen, where does Allie come in?"

"I was ten when Mom and George got married. Allie came along after that, but they got divorced after a couple years. Mom had joint custody, but she lost interest after a while. I used to beg her to let Allie stay the summers with us, but she said George wouldn't allow it. I always thought she was making an excuse, but maybe it was true. Maybe Mom's boyfriends made him nervous."

Robin placed more blocks on the ottoman, and Tony knocked them off. "Is that the last time you saw her?"

Maggie kept her gaze on Tony. "She visited me at Aunt Esther's. I saw her a week out of every summer until I went to college. We lost contact then, although she and Aunt Esther stayed close. Has Mark told you why the police suspect she was involved?"

Robin blinked at the quick change of subject. "Didn't Greg tell you?"

Tony threw his rattle across the floor, and Maggie bent to get it, hiding her face. "I haven't called him yet."

"OK, what gives? You're not still mad about last night? You know he didn't mean —"

"I know. But right now I want to hear about Allie, and I don't want to ask Greg." She put her hand up when Robin would have protested. "Please, just tell me what you know. We'll get into my love life later."

Robin held up both hands, palms out. "OK, OK. Mark said there were fingerprints in the kitchen from her boyfriend, Cameron Hayes. He's been arrested for some small time stuff, so his fingerprints were on file. Mark said that Cameron has a brother, Grady, that they'd like to bring in for questioning. Bad news. I hope she's not really involved with them. If Esther wouldn't answer the door, Allie might have lowered the ladder. Maggie, Allie's prints are on the knife block."

"Were they on the knife, too?"

"No, the knife was wiped clean."

"It doesn't make any sense, why wouldn't she just let him in? Why the ladder?"

Robin shrugged.

"And why would she have wiped the knife but not the block? Besides, she could have left those prints any time."

"Not with Maria in charge of the cleaning."

Maggie nodded and pinched her lip between two fingers. Maria was very thorough.

"And she was living in Esther's car. At least, for the couple days it took to catch her. They're assuming she stole it."

Maggie shook her head. "Theft won't stick. You know Aunt Esther would have loaned it to her."

"What does Allie have to say?"

"She clams up. She won't discuss the

boyfriend at all." Maggie played with Tony while Robin unloaded the portable crib from the car and dumped it in Esther's room. When she returned, she picked Tony up and carried him to the kitchen.

Maggie followed. "Allie must have used the knife block at some point while she was here. It doesn't mean she killed her. If they believe she's guilty, why haven't they made an arrest?"

Robin set Tony in a chair and opened a jar of baby food. "I don't think she's a murder suspect, but they assume she's protecting Cameron."

Maggie scooted her chair next to Tony, nervous he might fall. "I have to find out more about this guy. The other night was the first I'd heard of him, so either Aunt Esther didn't know anything, or she didn't approve. Do the police know where he is?"

Robin put a spoonful in Tony's mouth and made yummy noises. "You should ask Greg. Mark didn't tell me much, and besides it will give you a chance to call him."

"I don't want to call him." Maggie hesitated. "I'm going to break it off."

Robin glanced up. "What? Why?"

"Something doesn't feel right. I'm not cut out for marriage. In fact, even having Allie stay with me is a strain. I'm just not good at relationships." Hearing herself say it out loud validated the feelings she'd had the night before.

Tony squawked, and Robin stuck another spoonful into his mouth. "What makes you say that?"

"I feel claustrophobic. I don't want to move. I love my house. And I don't want anyone to move in with me either."

"Hmm."

"OK," Maggie folded her arms across her chest. "Let's have it."

Robin glanced up from Tony again. "I think you're making a mistake. Greg isn't your father, Maggie. He won't wait until you're comfortable and start needing him and then leave you. I know him. And so do you."

Maggie traced the pattern on the table-cloth. "I know he's not my father. I never said he was like my father."

Robin blocked Tony's reaching hand and plopped another bite in his mouth. He promptly spit it out, and she screwed the lid on the jar. "Please think about it. And pray about it a lot before you do anything rash, OK?"

Maggie ran a clean cloth under warm water and handed it to Robin. "I suppose I do push men away," she said. "It's never gotten as far as an engagement before, though."

Cooing, Robin wiped Tony's face and hands, cleaned up, and put everything back in the diaper bag.

Maggie picked him up, kissed his round cheek, and carried him up the stairs.

Robin slid the cover off the crib and started unfolding it. "Remember Donald? You guys dated the longest before Greg. Didn't he want something serious?"

"Yeah, but he wasn't right for me. I figured I'd know when the right one came along, and truthfully, I thought it was Greg. But if he's the one, why do I feel this way?" She perched on Aunt Esther's bed with Tony in her lap while Robin snapped the final piece in place. "How do you know if a person will be right for you for the rest of your life? What if you change? Or worse, what if he changes and doesn't want you anymore?"

Before Robin could answer, Maggie sprang to her feet, facing the bookcases. A large empty hole gaped right in the middle. The diaries were gone.

8

Maggie and Robin checked the entire house, but the diaries weren't anywhere. "I guess I have to talk to Greg now," she said. "And you can stop smirking at me." She plucked her phone out of her purse and left the room, punching in Greg's number. "By any chance did you guys come back after the funeral and take my aunt's diaries?" *Great, Maggie. Don't let the niceties of hello slow you down.*

"No, in fact, I'd like to borrow them if I could."

"Unfortunately, you can't. They're gone."

She pictured his face as he processed her statement.

"Gone? As in missing?"

"Yes, and I know they were all here after she died, because I flipped through them."

"When was the last time you saw them?" At least, he didn't ask if she was sure.

"Monday, the day before the funeral."

"Does anyone else have a key?"

"Maria comes in every other week to clean, so she has one. I don't know if my dad does or not. I know my mom doesn't. She asked to stay here for the funeral, but the lawyer wouldn't let her. If she'd had a key, she wouldn't have asked. He told me I could let her in if I wanted to, but her attitude of entitlement irritated him, so he said no. I had to laugh since I've had the same reaction." Embarrassed by rambling, she got to the point. "Anyway, I'll call everyone who may have a key and ask if they've seen them. Maybe Dad came in and borrowed them or something. I'll let you know."

She hung up from Greg and called Maria.

"Diaries? I don't have no diaries, Miss Maggie. I no touch the *señora's* diaries." Stress edged the lady's voice.

"It's OK," Maggie soothed. "But did you happen to see anyone go upstairs? Maybe someone could have been glancing through them?"

"No, but I was in the kitchen most of the time. I didn't see anyone go upstairs." She paused. "Those were her private thoughts, Miss Maggie. She wouldn't want anyone but you to read them."

Assured of Maria's sincerity, Maggie dialed her dad's number.

"A key? Yeah, I had one at some point, but I never use it. I don't even know where it is. Why, did you lose your key? I can have a locksmith out in no time if you —"

"No, Dad, but thanks. Aunt Esther's diaries are missing, and I wondered if you had borrowed them or if you saw anyone with them."

"I haven't seen them, but if someone can get in her house, maybe you'd better let me send over the locksmith. I don't want you in there alone until we're sure it's safe."

"It must have happened at the funeral reception. Did you see anyone go upstairs?"

"No, I didn't, sweetheart, but maybe one of her friends knows something."

She thanked him and hung up. She didn't want to call her mom but couldn't find a way around it.

"It's not enough your stupid lawyer doesn't trust me to stay there overnight, now you accuse me of stealing?" Her mother gave the expected response.

"Mom, I'm not accusing you of anything. I just wanted to know if you saw them during the reception."

"No, of course not. I didn't even go up there. I'll bet it was one of her snooty friends. They'd be interested, wouldn't they? Wanting to see what she wrote? I'd better not find my name published in her memoirs or anything. I mean it, Margaret, I'll sue."

Maggie hung up regretting the call. She and Robin ate lunch and then worked for a couple of hours while Tony slept. Subconsciously, she thought the diaries would show up. Unfortunately, they didn't. Driving home, she had to assume the worst. Someone had stolen them.

Back at home, she stared at the four volumes she'd taken. Why would someone want to steal another person's diaries? And how did they get them out without anyone noticing? There must have been twelve books. She opened the last one to the final pages and the lunch Ruth had mentioned.

"Lindy's was cheerful as always," it read. "And the food was terrific. I met Ruth outside the door, both of us having arrived at the same time. Carla was already there, and Ginger was late as usual. It amazes me how Ruth can come from Colorado Springs, and I can come from Pinon Heights, both over an hour and a half away, and we can arrive on time, but Ginger can't make it from Golden, thirty minutes away. Annoying, but we love her anyway."

Maggie smiled. Aunt Esther had been a stickler for punctuality.

She continued reading.

Dale McDonald waved at us from a corner table, and Janet Livingston was having lunch with her new beau. I'll have to tell Maggie I saw Bluebird on the street out front, but he flew off. The afternoon reminded me of when she and I used to go there when she was a little girl. We would get all dolled up and have lunch in the city. Christmas was especially fun when they had the moving figures in the May D & F window.

Warmth flowed up from Maggie's abdomen and knotted somewhere in her chest. Knowing the same memories she held dear were special to her aunt as well made her want to laugh and cry. But before she could do either, Allie bounded up the stairs.

"Are you ready for dinner yet? I'm starving."

Maggie set the diary down and looked at the clock. Six thirty. Having a teenager in the house sure was different. She'd have to eat more often. "How does pizza sound?"

Allie agreed, and Maggie called Nico's, the pizza place that delivered. When it showed up, she brought out paper plates, and they dug in. Wow, how much could a teenage girl eat anyway? Between the two of them, they put away a large pizza, and Maggie hadn't eaten much.

When they finished, Allie pranced into the living room, plopped on the sofa, and flipped on the TV. So much for helping with the dishes. Although, to be fair, they'd used paper plates, and Allie was a guest. Did she get away with this at home?

As Maggie finished wiping off the table, her phone rang. The display showed Greg's picture. Oops, she had forgotten to call him back.

"I take it no one you called today knew the diaries' location?"

She ambled to the nook and melted into her favorite cushy chair, putting her feet up. "No. In fact, a few people were angry or scared when I asked."

"Who was scared?" His voice sharpened.

"Maria. She thought I would accuse her of stealing." He was silent, so she continued, "I'd never suspect her — she's too honest. And she's been with my aunt for years."

"When was the last time she saw them?"

"Maria and I cleaned before the funeral reception, and they were there then." Maggie's feet hit the floor, and she leaned forward, ready to pounce. "But wait a minute. She didn't take them. I wouldn't have told you at all if I thought you would accuse my aunt's trusted friends."

"Whoa, who made accusations? I didn't say a word."

"It was what you didn't say. Like you were suspicious but didn't want to call attention to it."

"Suspicion is my job." A smile warmed Greg's voice. "But if it makes you feel any better, I don't believe Maria took them. She had no reason to, and she has an alibi for the day Esther was killed. You said someone was angry. Who was it?"

"My mom," she repeated the conversation and leaned back, putting her feet up again. "The only time the house was open since I mentioned them at the funeral was at the reception. I think they were taken then."

"That's pretty bold."

"I know. But it's better than someone coming and going as they please in her house." She drummed her fingers on the chair arm. "I think I'll get new locks put on anyway. There's still a lot to go through, and being alone there now gives me the willies."

"It's too bad they're gone. I'd like to know why someone would find your aunt's diaries interesting enough to steal. I doubt your mom's theory is correct."

"No." She frowned. "Aunt Esther wouldn't have written gossip. She didn't even speak it. I can't figure out why anyone would want the diaries so bad. They mean a lot to me, but no one else would get anything out of them. I'm glad I brought some of them home, so at least I have those."

"You have some of them?" Greg's response was abrupt. "Which ones?"

"I have the first one, two in the middle, and the last one."

"I'd like to have them, please — at least the last one."

"Why?"

"It's pretty coincidental — you mentioning the diaries in your eulogy and them going missing the next day. Someone could be worried she wrote something to implicate them."

"Of course, you can have it." She nodded. "But I'd like to copy it first. I'm enjoying them."

"I'm not sure that's a good idea."

"Why not?" An edge sharpened her voice.

"You might be in danger if someone knows you still have them."

"No one would know I kept a copy."

"The fact you read them might be enough.

And you'll be looking now, you won't be able to help yourself. I just want you to be careful."

She heard the concern in his voice at this last bit, and she smiled, her irritation leaving as quickly as it came. "I promise I won't tell anyone I have them, and I'll let you know if I find anything. I just want to read about her life, you know? I want to hear her voice again, even if she's talking to herself."

He hesitated. "I know I'll regret this," his voice was light. "But bring the last one by the station tomorrow, along with a list of people at the funeral, would you?"

She hung up, confused. If she wanted to break up, why did talking to him feel so good? She shook her head to clear it. Maybe she could ask some of her aunt's friends if they saw anything suspicious. First, she needed to copy the last diary. She entered her office and started the machine. The business phone rang, and choosing to ignore it, she put the first page on the glass. The answering machine blipped on.

"Maggie? Maggie, are you there?" A pause. "I guess not. This is Ginger. You know, your aunt's friend."

Maggie raced over and grabbed the handset off the base. "Ginger, wait. Don't hang up." She wrestled with the machine and sighed. "Sorry. How are you?"

A hiccup came over the line. "I'm OK, I guess, but I wanted to let you know Carla passed away."

"Carla Graham? What happened?" Maggie pictured Carla — Aunt Esther's age and in good health. At least, she looked good. "Was she sick?"

"No, it was a car accident. It happened yesterday, but I thought you should know." Ginger's voice cracked. "I can't believe I lost two friends in the same week. I know these things happen, but it doesn't seem fair they happened so close together, you know?"

Maggie moved back to her favorite chair and settled in. Words flooded out of Ginger about how close she'd been to both Carla and Esther. The wave ended, and Ginger gave an embarrassed chuckle. "You don't need to come to the funeral or anything, honey, but I thought you'd want to know. Maybe send a card or something."

"Yes, of course, thank you for telling me." Maggie wasn't quite sure why Ginger called her, since she barely knew Carla. Then she realized it was Aunt Esther she'd wanted to call. Just like Maggie, Ginger was missing Esther.

Maggie hung up and sat for a moment,

considering the coincidence of two friends dying in such unusual ways so close to each other. Although the car accident, she guessed, wasn't unusual in today's world. Speaking of Carla, didn't she read her name in Esther's last diary?

She snatched it off the glass and thumbed through it, searching for Carla's name. There it was, the lunch they'd had together. She reread the paragraph. Nothing there, except the part about Ginger being late. Unless . . . could it be possible something happened in the restaurant? But if something serious enough to kill over had happened, wouldn't they have called the police? She was being fanciful. The whole idea was ridiculous, but when she gave him the original, Maggie would draw Greg's attention to it anyway.

9

Greg waited at the station for Maggie. There'd been something in her voice last night. Something wrong. Not in the words she used, but her voice . . . distant, as if she couldn't wait to get off the phone. Ever since their disagreement over where they would live, he'd felt her drawing away. How could he get their closeness back?

He had tried to persuade her to come at noon and have lunch with him, but she'd declined. He straightened the piles on his desk. Should he have agreed to let her keep a copy of the last diary? Not like he had a real choice. He was surprised she'd told him first. But then her honesty was a character trait he loved most. She put it out there, and one could do with it what one would, but she wouldn't lie to anyone.

As if drawn by his thoughts, Maggie arrived to the usual turning of heads. She attracted appreciative glances, which became jealous as he rose to meet her. She had no idea how beautiful she was. Tall and slim in well-fitting jeans, her long brown hair swinging from a ponytail, she strode toward him.

"The list is inside." She thumbed through the pages. "I didn't see anything suspicious, but you might take a look at the lunch she had at Lindy's." She found the page and pointed.

Keeping her place, he flipped the book around and read the section above her finger. It didn't look promising. "Is something relevant to her death in here?"

"Only that two of the people at the lunch are now dead."

"What? Two? Who's the other one?"

"Carla Graham. She was killed in a car accident in Denver." She explained Ginger's call the night before. "I'm sure it's a coincidence, but it's weird." She smiled her heart-stopping smile, promised to see him later, and left.

Unable to stem his disappointment over her quick departure, he carried the diary to his desk and began to read, starting with the last week of Esther's life. A few new names showed up, but nothing to indicate a reason for murder. Although it was most likely coincidental, he couldn't ignore the deaths of two friends in the same month.

Who did he know in Denver?

He called Jackson Bristol, someone he'd met a few times, and got right to the point. "I'm interested in a fatal car accident involving Carla Graham. It happened a couple days ago in your area. Did you identify the person who caused the accident?"

"No, we didn't. It was a hit and run. What's your interest?"

"I'm searching for a connection to a murder investigation we have here in Pinon Creek. Our victim, Esther Campbell, was killed June fifth in what we assume was a burglary. But it appears Carla and Esther, along with two other women, had lunch together the week before it happened." He doodled on his pad. "One of the four, Ginger Phillips, called our victim's niece and told her, and she passed it on to me. I promised to check it out. A normal accident would be one thing, but a hit and run is suspicious."

"Does anything other than the lunch connect the two episodes?"

"No. It's probably not related, but would you keep me in the loop on Carla's investigation?"

After getting a promise from the detective, and agreeing to do the same, Greg opened the journal and examined it again. Another person joined them for the lunch, Ruth. He remembered her from the reception. He checked the list Maggie had given him. There she was, Ruth Baker. Greg would get her address and give her a call.

He wrote down the other names Esther mentioned, but without any other information, finding them might be hard. He pored over the diary from front to back, but found nothing incriminating. Certainly nothing worth stealing the diaries over. Maybe the killer didn't know and didn't want to take any chances. Or maybe the thief got what they came for, and it didn't have anything to do with Esther's murder, but with something else. Something they wanted to remain private. If so, it could be in any of the diaries, and he might never know. Could it have been Darla, Maggie's mom? If so, and it had nothing to do with the murder, maybe he didn't want to know.

That was awkward. Maggie twisted her hands on the steering wheel as she drove home. He'd obviously wanted to talk — why did she feel the need to escape? Was she ready to break it off? *Why can't the answer be clear, Lord? Why can't I figure this out?*

She drove into her driveway, remembering

something her aunt used to say. If you don't know what to do, then do nothing. Float like a snowflake, she would say. Was she floating, or was she stalling?

Allie stood in front of the open fridge, studying its contents as Maggie walked in the door.

"Hey, sleeping beauty, how was your night?"

Allie drew a comb through her hair, wet from her recent shower. "Good."

"Are you hungry? There should be eggs in there or cereal in the pantry."

"OK, thanks."

Was this what having teenagers around was like? How did you get them to talk? The phone rang.

Allie tensed.

"Maggie, it's Jonathan. I thought we might play some doubles. Isn't your sister a great tennis player?"

"Yes, she is, and I'm sure she'd love it." She covered the phone. "Jonathan wants to play tennis. Have you met him before?"

Allie let out the breath she'd been holding, and her body relaxed against the counter. "Yeah, he's good. I brought my stuff just in case. Are you playing, too?"

"Well, he says we're playing doubles, but I imagine it will be you two. I don't know who his partner is, but hopefully, they won't be too good. My psyche can't take it." She put the phone back to her ear. "On one condition, Jonathan. Your partner can't be good. I don't want to be the only one bumbling around."

He laughed. "It'll be fine. Charlie's close to the same skill level as you."

"Horrible then, I assume?"

"Come on. You're not bad. You have a lot of good moves."

Hmm. What moves was he planning to use on her sister? No wait. Didn't he just lose his fiancée? Maybe she was being too hard on him. After all, there weren't many tennis players in his league in Pinon Creek. He probably just wanted some competition.

At the club, Maggie climbed from her car and slid her sunglasses onto the top of her head.

Allie slammed her door, rattling the hinges.

Jonathan approached from the visitor's lot. A redhaired man with freckles walked next to him. Jonathan introduced him as Charlie, someone from work.

"Which work?" Maggie grinned. "The construction company or the tour?" She looked around. "Is that what you call professional tennis?"

Charlie laughed, and his eyes danced. "I'm afraid I handle bookcases much better than a tennis racket."

"He's our carpenter." Jonathan turned to him. "You'll be working with Maggie on the design of the built-ins for the Spruce and the Aspen."

As Maggie shook his outstretched hand, the roughened calluses told more of his work ethic than words ever could. "I may want them for the smaller models, too. It's funny how people expect a lot of storage in the bigger homes, but it's the smaller ones that need it. We'll talk."

His smile was genuine, and he clasped Allie's hand gently.

Maggie couldn't help herself. She liked him.

It soon became obvious the game was between Jonathan and Allie. After the first three games, Maggie and Charlie gave up and sat out, watching the other two do battle in a singles match. Taunts were volleyed along with the ball as the lead went back and forth between the players.

Charlie's gaze seldom left Allie. "Wow, your sister's good. I've never seen anyone outside of a pro work Jonathan over like that."

True. Allie was in her element. Her blonde

ponytail whipped around as she slammed the ball toward Jonathan once again. For the first time, Maggie saw him struggling to keep up, stretching to return her vicious serves. "I haven't seen her play in years. I had no idea she was this good." *Or that Jonathan wasn't as good as he talks.*

Charlie faced her, his smile gone. "I'm so sorry about your aunt." Compassion tinged his light gray eyes. "Do they have any leads?"

"They'd like to question a guy named Cameron Hayes. I understand he has a brother named Grady. Do you know them?"

He watched Allie again. "Isn't that her boyfriend or something?"

"Yeah, but I don't know how serious it is. She's only eighteen. I hope she doesn't tie herself down yet."

He nodded. "I don't know him, but Grady has a rough reputation."

"In what way?"

"He runs with a tough crowd. They've been known to operate outside the law."

"You mean stealing?"

"Maybe. I don't have any proof, but it wouldn't surprise me."

The match ended with a fierce shot by Jonathan to the side of the court. Allie stretched and tipped it, but it hit the net, giving the final game, and match, to Jonathan. They panted back to the bench where Maggie and Charlie waited. Allie's blue eyes sparkled in her flushed face.

Both Jonathan and Charlie couldn't keep their eyes off her. This might be a problem. Allie had matured into a beautiful young woman, and George wouldn't appreciate it if she returned with another romantic entanglement. Although come to think of it, maybe he would if it got her mind off Cameron.

After showering in the posh ladies locker room, they headed for the visitor's lot and wended their way past fancy foreign cars to Maggie's old sedan.

Allie flinched as they approached. "Hurry up, Mags. I don't want to be seen next to this heap."

"Hey, this heap gets good gas mileage, thank you very much, and she's reliable." She unlocked the doors.

Allie popped inside, sliding down in her seat.

A light blue truck squatted in a corner space. Maggie craned to see the driver as she passed. But he reached for something below the window, and she missed his face.

"Allie, what does Cameron drive?"

"An ugly blue pickup. Why?"

"A blue pickup drove behind us when we left the station the other night, and one's at the club just now. I noticed because it makes my car look good."

Allie craned her neck to see behind them. "Is he following us?"

Maggie glanced in her mirror but didn't see the truck. "I don't see him now. Probably my imagination. Has he been trying to call you?"

"I don't know. I have my phone off, so I don't have to talk to either him or my dad."

"What if the police want you to?"

Allie stared out the side window. "Rat him out, you mean? No. I'm not doing that. If they want to catch him, they can do it themselves. I'm not helping."

"If you care so much, why were you flirting with Jonathan?"

"Flirting? I wasn't flirting." Her oh-so-innocent tone so perfectly matched her wide, ingénue eyes.

Maggie scarcely kept from rolling hers. "Oh, come on. I know flirting when I see it. You don't need to feel guilty. It's not like you're married or anything."

Allie crossed her arms and pouted her mouth. "I don't feel guilty, because I wasn't flirting."

Maggie glanced in her mirror again.

"There it is, the same truck. He's back a ways, but still there. I'm sick of this. I'll find out why he keeps tailing us." She made a sharp right, raced down the street cornering again and again until she saw him up ahead. There he was, easing around the corner, trying not to get too close. Flooring it, she sped up, chasing him around the corner. She honked her horn, making Allie laugh. Waving her arm, she yelled out the window, "Pull over!"

He glanced back and gunned it, flying through a red light, nearly T-boning a dark blue SUV.

Maggie lifted a shaking foot off the gas and slowed the car to a stop. "I guess that wasn't such a good idea." She drew in a deep breath. "I might have caused an accident."

"I think it was hilarious." Allie leaned forward, trying to glimpse him between the moving cars in the intersection. "That'll teach him to spy on me."

A few more deep breaths dispelled the vision of twisted metal and broken bodies. Maggie shook her head to clear it. "I have to go to a jobsite and see how they're doing on one of the houses I'm designing. I shouldn't be too long. I can drop you off at home if you like. Maybe there's something on cable, or you can watch some movies."

Allie gave up her search and sat back. "Do you mind if I come along? It might be fun to look around."

Did she hear right? Allie interested in something other than tennis? "Are you sure? The houses aren't finished or anything." Maggie hoped she wasn't wanting to run into Jonathan.

Allie's face shone. "Yeah, it sounds like fun."

Maggie changed direction for the jobsite. "I hope this won't be too boring for you."

They'd already paved the development streets, but the area around the construction trailer remained gravel. "I need a revised schedule if the foreman's around." She shut off the engine and opened her door. "He's pretty busy, so we may not be able to find him."

They climbed the wooden steps into the small trailer. Two metal desks faced the entrance. Mike, the foreman, reclined at the larger one behind piles of paper. His feet rested on a cleared corner, and he pressed the phone to his ear. His feet thumped to the floor when Maggie entered, and he beckoned them to a couple of folding chairs in front of his desk. A dusty film covered most surfaces, including an empty smaller desk, which, if she remembered correctly, belonged to his assistant. A door hung ajar to a room in the back, she assumed Mike's office. He must like being out front. At a click, she returned her focus to him.

"Hey, Maggie, who's this?"

"My sister, Allie. She's visiting for a while. Allie, this is Mike Travis, the construction foreman."

"I didn't know you had a sister. And a pretty one, too." He smiled as he shook Allie's hand. "You two here to see the Spruce?"

"I came for an updated schedule, but I wouldn't mind seeing how far you guys have gotten."

"We started work in the master bath yesterday. You're going to love it. The colors look great." He reached into his drawer and handed her a stapled set of papers. "Do you want to see the other houses? If so, I need you to wear hardhats. There's still a lot of construction going on in some of the models."

She glanced at Allie. "Would you like to see them? They're not very exciting before the finish goes in."

Allie nodded, and Mike retrieved two hardhats from a metal file cabinet next to the door.

"I'll go with you." He grabbed his hat off the desk, dislodging a pile of paper, which slipped to the floor. He bent, scooped it into a heap, and dumped it on the smaller desk. "Laura's on vacation."

Maggie winked at Allie, who stifled a grin.

"Oh, how cute!" Allie paused by a three-foot stuffed dog, standing on two legs in the corner, a hammer duct taped to one furry paw.

"Meet Buster, our mascot." Mike opened the door for them, and Maggie wondered if she would always get this great service, or if it was due to her pretty young guest.

"So, did you say some of the tile is up?" She made her way down the steps and across to the first house. "How is it possible? I just gave Edward the specs a couple days ago. You guys must be working fast."

"Our tile man finished another job early, and since you used materials from the design center, we had some in stock. The glass accent tile is up in the shower, and he's starting on the field tiles."

The Spruce was the first house on the street. As they were about to enter, raised voices emanated from the house next door. A man strode out the front door with a clipboard in his hand. Jonathan Blake trailed him, screaming something she

130

couldn't catch.

Mike changed direction and spoke over his shoulder. "Go ahead, Maggie. I'll see you later. It was nice to meet you, Allie."

He broke into a trot but didn't reach the group before Jonathan dashed in front of the guy and knocked the clipboard out of his hand. It bounced on the cement porch.

"I don't care what your stupid report says!" Jonathan's screech carried once he was outside.

The man lurched back, his body stiffening.

Maggie couldn't see his face, but she could imagine his expression.

Mike stepped between them and made soothing gestures. He bent to retrieve the clipboard, dusted it off, and handed it back.

The man jerked it out of his hand, swiveled on his heel, and stomped to his truck. He slammed the door and raced off.

Maggie craned her neck to read the logo, but the angle was wrong.

Allie's eyes widened. "Wonder what made him so mad?"

Maggie shrugged, leading the way into the Spruce. "Who knows?" Maybe this was good. Allie would see Jonathan like this and realize he wasn't her type.

The smell of sawdust and fresh paint filled

Maggie's nostrils. This model was almost finished. She wandered into the kitchen, which had been designed before she was hired, and ran her hand over the gray solid surface island. A stone backsplash covered the wall between the counter and the upper cabinets. She had to hand it to the previous designer — the effect of the different materials provided an interesting contrast.

Allie disappeared upstairs, and after a brief glance around, Maggie followed. Country music drifted through the stairway, and tracking the sound, Maggie ended up in the master bath. Mike was right — the colors worked perfectly together. The aquamarine accent tiles produced a sense of serenity, which drew her to choose them in the first place.

She poked her head in and knocked on the doorframe so she wouldn't scare the rather large man standing in the tub, tiling. "Wow, things are coming along great in here."

He faced her, a trowel in one hand and a tile in the other.

She raised her hand in a quick wave. "I'm Maggie, the new designer. Just checking to see how the colors look. Don't let me interrupt you."

He nodded. "I'm Walter. Good to know ya."

She continued her tour. The other two bedrooms weren't exciting, and floor tiles and fixtures were the only finish in the main bath. She caught up to Allie outside.

"Let's pick out the house we would buy if we could have any one we wanted," Allie said, pointing to the biggest house in the series. "I like this one, and the lot is big. Let's go see it."

"It's actually two lots. The other house hasn't been started yet."

"What? You're kidding. I thought living in the mountains meant people understood the love of the land. This whole area is smaller than my backyard."

Maggie nodded. "I know. It's a slice of the city right here in the mountains." She flipped through the stack of papers in her hand. "We can go see it if we wear our hard-hats. It's the least finished of all the models."

Allie put her hat on, and it slid down past her eyes. She tipped it back, laughing. "This doesn't seem too safe. If I can't see where I'm going, I'll have a problem."

Maggie laughed and snatched her own too-large hat off to adjust the plastic inside. "I can never get them small enough, so you may have to hold it on. Here, have mine, and I'll try to fix yours."

"This is a little better," Allie said. "If I

hold it on, I can angle it back far enough to see."

They entered an obvious construction zone. Since the drywall wasn't up yet, she could scarcely tell which rooms were which. When they passed into what would become the living room, the space opened up to a double staircase.

Allie grinned like a child. "Wow, look, two sets of stairs in one. Why do they need those?" She began climbing up one side.

"Just for looks, honey. One will end in the living room and one in the family room. Be careful now. Those don't have any railings."

"Yeah, I can kind of see that, Mags."

Smiling, Maggie made her way into the kitchen. PVC piping stuck out of the floor, indicating where the island would be. It looked as if they'd made a mistake and put it in the middle of the room, but when the cabinets were in, it would all balance out.

Allie's footsteps tromped around upstairs, and her voice called dibs on the room she would choose if she lived here. Obviously, she would choose the master. Several thuds shook the ceiling.

What was she doing up there? Redecorating? The laugh died in Maggie's throat when someone screamed.

10

Loud thumps morphed into a huge crash.

Maggie raced into the living room.

Allie lay on the floor, not moving.

Before she could reach her, something slammed into Maggie, knocking her off her feet. Flat on her back, she gazed into the eyes of a man dressed in black with a ski mask over his face. She blinked, and he bolted out the door.

She raised herself to her feet, her hip and shoulder throbbing, and limped over to Allie. Scooping her phone out of her purse, she called for an ambulance and knelt clumsily next to her sister. "Allie, are you OK? Allie?" She didn't dare move her without knowing what could be broken.

Allie's eyelids fluttered open. She shifted and cried out.

"Don't move, honey. An ambulance is on its way."

Maggie stood guard over her sister until

the paramedics arrived. They splinted Allie's leg and positioned her onto a gurney and into the ambulance.

Several men, including Mike, had come running when they heard the sirens, and they stood around waiting to see if she was all right.

"What happened?" Mike asked. "Is Allie hurt?"

Maggie explained as she climbed into the ambulance.

"I'll meet you," he said and ran for his car.

She wanted to tell him he didn't have to, but the doors shut, and they were on their way. She'd given in to her panic and called Greg while they were getting Allie onto the gurney, and she was already regretting it. Once she broke it off, she wouldn't be able to call him every time she needed a strong shoulder. The thought was a funny one. Did it mean she'd made her decision?

Greg must have used his siren, because he was already at the hospital, along with Mark and Robin, when she arrived.

Mike screeched into the lot behind the ambulance, just in front of Jonathan and Edward Blake.

When Greg met her at the emergency door, she cocked a weak smile. "You're going to get tired of rescuing the damsel in distress."

He folded her in his arms, and it felt good. "Not if the damsel is you, I won't. Now tell me what happened. You said she fell down some stairs?"

"She was pushed." She described the man in the mask.

He took out his notebook and started scribbling. "He wore a ski mask in June? He would have had to bring it with him, which means he must have been planning something. Do you remember what he looked like? Was he tall or short? Could you see his arms or hands? What was his skin color? What he was wearing? I imagine you couldn't see his hair."

She closed her eyes and struggled to focus. Her mind wouldn't form the picture at first, but as she concentrated, it appeared. "I couldn't see his hair — the mask covered it. I'm not sure how tall he was, because I didn't see him clearly before he mowed me over. I was on the ground looking up when he ran out the door, but he seemed tall and thin. He wore a black t-shirt with black jeans. It had writing on the front, but I don't know what it said. His arms were tanned, but he's Caucasian."

"He hit you? Are you OK?"

"I'll have a few bruises in the morning, but nothing more serious. I'm worried about Allie. I don't know how far she fell. It could have been anywhere on the stairs because there was no railing."

Edward stepped forward. He, Mike, and Jonathan were waiting nearby and must have overheard. "Are you sure you're not injured? We've never had anything like this happen before." He moved aside to let Mike and Jonathan join the group. "Mike, did you see anyone?"

"No, but I was in the Linden looking at the furnace until I heard the sirens. I didn't notice anyone unusual at the jobsite today, but I was pretty busy." He turned to Greg. "You know when you said it must have been planned because of the ski mask? Not necessarily. We have a dog mascot in the construction trailer, with a black ski mask folded back on his head. I don't remember if the mask was there when we left or not. The guys are always messing with him, so I tend to ignore it unless I find it in my chair. Maggie, do you remember?"

She bit her lip. "We looked at the dog as we were leaving the trailer. I don't remember it having a mask, but if it was folded back, I might not have noticed."

Edward touched her shoulder. "I feel terrible. I hope your sister's OK. We occasionally have kids messing around or thieves looking for something to steal, but never any violence. What would someone want in an unfinished house in the middle of the day?"

No one seemed able to answer his question, and the conversation died.

Maggie left the group to fill out a police report brought in by another officer. She wrote everything she could remember about the attack but couldn't recall anything other than what she'd told Greg. It had happened so fast. She wondered what Allie would say. Did she see him coming at her or did he surprise her from behind? Would she have recognized him without the mask? Could it have been Cameron?

She finished her statement and signed it. An older woman in blue scrubs with Sharon on her nameplate pushed Allie out in a wheelchair. Her left leg stuck out straight, a cast covering it from mid-thigh to her ankle. Her left arm rested in a sling.

Maggie rushed over. "Allie, are you OK? Are you in pain?"

She grimaced. "Can you believe it? The doctor says I have to wear this stupid thing on my leg for six weeks. My muscles will be mush by then. It'll take months to get back in shape." She shifted in the chair, putting her good foot on the floor as if to rise.

Sharon placed a hand on her unhurt right shoulder to restrain her. "Just relax a minute, sweetie." Glancing at Maggie, she continued, "If you bring your car around, I'll help you get her in."

Maggie remembered her car was at the jobsite. She must have looked perplexed, because Mike was the first to step up.

"My car is right out front. I can take you. I have to go back to the jobsite anyway."

Maggie heaved a relieved sigh. "Thanks. That would be —"

"Don't worry about it," Greg interrupted. "I'll take them."

She stared at him, opened her mouth to argue, and then closed it. This was not the time.

Mike raised his eyebrows and stepped back. "Oh. OK, then." He sketched a half-hearted wave, and left.

What was that about? Maggie's stomach tightened. She followed Sharon through the motion sensor doors and waited in the shade under the overhang while Greg sprinted to retrieve his car. She smiled down at Allie. "So, what else did the doctor say?"

"He said I torqued my knee, fractured the tibia, and strained my arm. Oh, and I'll need these pills and some crutches." She handed over a prescription with the casual ease of someone expecting prompt service.

Maggie stood holding the slip of paper, wanting to mention she wasn't a personal assistant, but the tiny figure swallowed up by the large wheelchair made her pause. Allie was only eighteen, after all, and she was injured.

Tucking the prescription into her purse, she waited in silence until Greg eased his car to the curb. She held the wheelchair steady while Greg and Sharon transferred Allie into his back seat. Sharon wheeled the chair up the ramp, and Greg held the passenger door for Maggie. "We can settle Allie at your place first. Then I can take you to pick up your car."

The tightness in her stomach traveled up to her throat and threatened to choke her. But seeing she had no real choice, Maggie nodded. She didn't trust herself to speak during the ride to her house.

In her driveway, Greg helped Allie out of the car.

Maggie put an arm around her, and Allie leaned her weight on it and hopped a couple times.

Watching their slow progress, Greg bent and scooped Allie up in his arms. "It might be easier if we do it this way."

Allie laughed and smiled her flirty smile. "Wow, I'm not used to such manly behavior."

Maggie wanted to smack her. Instead, she dashed ahead to open the gate, swinging it wide. Was she this transparent at eighteen, in the company of a handsome older male? She hoped not. And this handsome male was off limits to Allie. Even if Maggie decided to end her engagement, Allie was much too young to chase after Greg. Once they were through the gate, Maggie secured the latch and jogged to the back door.

He moved into the living room and set Allie on the couch, helping her adjust the ottoman, oblivious to her flirting and Maggie's irritation.

In the kitchen, Maggie thumped the plastic mayonnaise container onto the counter, trying to organize her thoughts. She was mad at Greg, right? Not Allie. She was just a kid. Maggie made a tuna sandwich, listening while Greg questioned Allie.

"Tell me what happened."

"I got bored with the kitchen, so I went upstairs to look around. I checked the two smaller bedrooms. They were connected by a bathroom, you know, the kind with two doors?"

Maggie assumed Greg nodded, because Allie went on, "Then I went into the master. I came out to yell down at Maggie that I found the room I wanted, and someone pushed me. I was already on the stairs, about halfway down. I heard him behind me, but I couldn't avoid him. He came at me so fast and hard, there was nowhere to go. He slammed his body into me, and I fell down the stairs."

Poor kid, she must have been terrified. Maggie visualized the stairway, open on both sides, with no railing. A tide of emotion rose in her chest, and her hands started to shake. If she ever got a hold of the man who did this . . . She pulled a glass out of the cabinet and poured some iced tea, slopping some out on the counter.

"Did you know him, or can you describe him?"

"I didn't know him. He was tall and thin, with a black ski mask on."

"Did you see his eyes?"

There was a pause. "No, it happened too fast. I'm sorry."

"It's all right. Don't worry about it. We'll talk later, OK? Call me if you remember anything else."

Recognizing her cue, Maggie brought the sandwich and tea in and placed them and the remote on a side table within reach. "I'll be back after I pick up your prescription."

Allie nodded and focused on the remote.

"You have my cell number, right?"

"It's OK, Mags. I'm a big girl."

"So I've noticed," Maggie mumbled as she walked away. She erupted the minute she was alone in the car with Greg. "What are you doing?"

He stared straight ahead, starting the engine. "I'm taking you to your car."

"Why are you trying to control me?"

He swiveled in his seat, and his gaze found hers. "Control you? How does giving you a ride and making sure you're safe, control you?"

"First, you want me to give up my house, and now you decide who I can ride home with? It's control, mister. I've lived with it all my life, and I'm not having it anymore."

He shifted his attention to the rearview mirror and backed into the alley. "Whoa. I don't want you to move out of your house. I said I was sorry. We can live in your house, and I'll give up my place. It doesn't matter to me. And today, I was trying to keep you safe. Did it occur to you Mike could be a suspect? I couldn't let him take you anywhere."

Her thought process jolted to a stop. "Oh."

He continued to focus on the road, and a muscle in his jaw twitched.

Her anger dissipated. "I guess it does make sense for anyone who was at the job-site today to be a suspect, but I've known Mike for years. He wouldn't hurt me. Or Allie. In fact, he thought she was cute."

"I imagine a lot of murderers think young girls are cute. It doesn't stop them from killing one if she gets in the way."

"Do you suspect him of pushing her?"

He slowed as his tires hit the gravel of the construction site parking area, and he drifted to a stop next to her car. "He could have. He was in the area at the time. I've known him a long time, too, and I don't want him to be guilty. But I'm not willing to risk your safety on it."

Heat suffused her face as she unhooked her seatbelt and leaned forward to grab her purse from the floor. "I guess I shouldn't have jumped to conclusions. I overreacted. Again. I'm sorry."

No answer.

"I realize you were just trying to protect me." She climbed out of the car and turned to smile at him, but he stared straight ahead. If she said any more, it would just make it worse. Why did she keep reacting this way? She didn't used to. Lately, it seemed she

145

wanted to believe the worst. Maybe Robin was right. Maybe she was trying to push him away. But did she want to stop?

He sat and waited for her to get in her car, still not looking at her. Once her car started, he got out and took long strides toward the construction trailer, not looking back.

Maggie stared after him. It hadn't occurred to her that Mike, someone she'd known for years, could have pushed Allie.

Greg disappeared inside the trailer.

Maggie headed for the local pharmacy.

Who was on the jobsite at the time? Mike, of course, and Jonathan. The tile guy — what was his name . . . ? Walter. He could have left his work on the bathroom, pursued them across the street and into the house. Then he could have waited for an opportunity to push Allie off the second floor. But why? She pictured him tiling the bathroom. He wasn't the right build. He was too heavy.

Mike, however, was the right build, and so was Jonathan. Maybe even Charlie. Why would any of them want to hurt Allie? The long fall could have killed her if she'd landed wrong. Was it a warning? Did someone assume Allie knew something?

Maybe it was this guy she was dating,

Cameron. Last time she saw him, he was scurrying away, tires squealing as he escaped through a busy intersection. She thought he was running scared, but maybe not. Maybe he circled back, entered the house, and slipped upstairs while they were in the kitchen. If he killed Aunt Esther, he or his friends might feel Allie knew too much. Did she? Surely, if she knew who killed Aunt Esther, she would have said so. Maggie needed to know the truth. She and Allie would have a conversation the minute she got home — right after she stopped at the pharmacy and retrieved Allie's meds and some crutches.

Once inside the garage, Maggie shut off the engine and hesitated, her hand on the door handle. How should she broach the subject? "Alexis Taylor! What's the matter with you!" No, that approach had never worked with Maggie, she didn't imagine it would work with Allie either. She plucked the pain meds off the seat and popped the trunk to retrieve the crutches. The silly things were unwieldy, but once she positioned them sideways under one arm, she closed the garage door with the other hand and proceeded through the yard.

It appeared Allie hadn't moved. She still lounged on the couch with her legs up, the empty plate and glass on the side table. She looked so young and pitiful, Maggie almost didn't want to question her, but waiting might be a mistake. And she was tired of messing around. "I know the police questioned you already, but I need to know. Do you think Cameron pushed you?"

Allie's head jerked up. "No. He wouldn't. He would never hurt me."

"What about Aunt Esther? Would he hurt her?" Maggie sat on the ottoman by Allie's feet, careful not to touch them. The toenails were a shiny red. She stared straight into Allie's eyes. "I want to know exactly what happened. Not the story you told the police. Start from the beginning before you left home."

Allie dropped her gaze and fingered the bottom of her shorts. "I left home because Dad and Cameron were driving me crazy. Dad's never home. He travels all the time, and I end up alone with the housekeeper. He says I should go to college. Cameron wants me to run away with him. He says I could start my career with small tournaments, and then get into the bigger ones. They both pushed so hard I left home and went to Aunt Esther for advice."

"What did she tell you . . . to go to college?"

"No."

"No? She said to skip college?" She must have misunderstood. Aunt Esther was a major supporter of higher education.

Allie glanced up, tears shimmering in her eyes. "She said no one could tell me what to do because I already know what I want. She said I needed to take a little time away from both of them to hear the voice of God."

"And have you?"

"No." Her shoulders slumped. "I'm still not sure what to do. But getting away from both of them was a relief."

Maggie decided to make it more a conversation and less an interrogation, so she moved to the couch beside her sister. Allie leaned into the corner so she could still see Maggie's face. It seemed like a good sign. She forced lightness into her tone. "So tell me about Cameron. What's he like?"

"I don't know. He makes me feel . . . outrageous."

Maggie raised her eyebrows. "Outrageous?"

"Yeah, you know, wild, not the same boring me."

Hmm, interesting. "Do you feel boring?"

"Sometimes. I mean, look at my life. Nothing out of the ordinary happens. I go to school, or I did before summer, tennis

149

practice, home, dinner, and bed. Every night. I didn't start doing anything different until Cameron showed up."

Fearing what she would hear, but needing to know, Maggie continued, "So, what's different? Drinking?"

Allie looked away.

"Allie, have you been drinking? You're underage. How old is Cameron? Is he buying the alcohol?"

"We got fake IDs. I don't know where he got them, but they work."

Great. Now what should she do? If she acted too much like a mother, Allie wouldn't listen anyway. But it seemed as if she should do something.

Before she could voice her thoughts, Allie spoke again, "Cameron's OK. But sometimes he spends money, and I don't know where he gets it. He doesn't have a steady job."

"Have you asked him?"

"He comes up with different ways. Sometimes he does odd jobs for people. Or his brother gives it to him." Her gaze became fierce. "Grady's a thief, I don't want Cameron to spend money on me that he gets from him."

Not knowing what to say, Maggie waited.

"I think he's stealing with Grady." Allie's

voice barely rose above a whisper. "He wanted me to leave the back door unlocked and leave the house."

Now they were getting somewhere. "And did you?"

Allie shook her head.

Maggie's heart thudded and then nearly stopped. "Did he break in?"

"No. I would have heard him. I was there all morning."

"Wouldn't he have rung the bell when he knew you were home so you could let him in?"

Allie stared at her feet, still propped on the ottoman.

"He did, but I didn't answer. Aunt Esther answered, though, after she got home."

"You thought it was him when you left out the window, didn't you?"

Tears gathered in Allie's eyes. "I should have stayed. If I had, Aunt Esther would still be alive."

"Or you'd be dead, too. Don't imagine you could have stopped him just by being there. We need to call the police. Has Cameron been trying to reach you?"

"He did at first, but I turned my phone off. I don't want to talk to him right now."

Not knowing what else to do, Maggie called Greg. When he arrived, Maggie stayed in the kitchen.

Allie told Greg everything she'd told Maggie.

"Can you tell me where Cameron and Grady hang out?" Greg's voice was gentle.

"When they're not home, they're usually out with friends playing pool." She gave him the name of a few bars.

Maggie wiped the counter, wondering how many times Allie had been there with her fake ID.

"So did you hear the voice of the person at the door before you left Esther's?"

Maggie crept closer, rag in hand.

Allie paused. "Yeah, I guess I did."

Maggie stepped into the doorway. "So was it Cameron's?"

Greg frowned at her, and she stopped, silenced, but still watching.

Allie wound her hair around her finger. "No. At first, I thought it was Cameron, and I didn't want to deal with it. But it wasn't his voice. It was someone else. I thought it might be Grady."

"Do you know him?"

"Not well. I've met him a few times. But he makes me uncomfortable, and Cameron knows it. He doesn't put us together."

"Would you recognize the voice if you heard it again?"

"Maybe — I don't know. I might if he was yelling."

"So he was yelling at your aunt?"

"Not at first, but then they were both yelling when I threw the ladder out the window. I thought the noise they were making would cover the horrendous clatter it made." Tears filled her eyes again, and a hiccup escaped as she spoke. "I thought she was OK. I figured she would threaten to call the police, and they would leave. I wanted to be gone so they wouldn't come running up the stairs and find me."

"Were you afraid of them then?"

"Just Grady. I've never been afraid of Cameron. I can handle him. But he's different when he's with his brother, like he needs to be tough or something. I didn't want to go there. But Aunt Esther could have handled him. I never dreamed she wouldn't be safe. I wouldn't have left her if I thought she was in trouble."

Greg looked Allie straight in the eye. "Do you believe Grady killed her?" He kept his voice soft.

The tears flowed unchecked down Allie's face. "I don't know. I don't even know if they were there." She was sobbing now. "It wasn't Cameron's voice I heard. I swear."

Greg reassured her and left.

Allie's words rang in Maggie's ears as she rubbed spice on some chicken and placed it in the oven. Did Allie believe Grady killed Esther? Could Grady have pushed her? And how would they find him? The police had been trying since Aunt Esther's murder, but he hadn't shown up at home or at any of his known haunts. There hadn't been anyone in the truck with Cameron earlier, and she believed Allie didn't know where he was. Using her sister as bait wasn't an option, so how could they get him to come out of hiding? As she set the timer, her phone rang.

"Maggie, it's Monica Tate. I heard about poor Allie. Is she all right?"

"Yes, Mrs. Tate, she's doing well. Her leg was broken, but thankfully, the doctor thinks it'll mend quickly since she's young and in good shape."

"I'm so glad. Would you mind coming to the house tomorrow? I'd like to discuss the situation with you. Your aunt and I were good friends, and I'd like to talk to you about some things."

Things? What things? "Can you tell me now?"

Monica hesitated. "Let me organize my thoughts, and we can talk tomorrow. Will ten o'clock be acceptable?"

Maggie agreed and hung up. She couldn't

help herself; she was excited about seeing the inside of the Tate mansion. As a decorator, she would love to see the whole place, but it probably wouldn't happen. Snatching her mind back to the present, she wondered what Monica could know. And if she did know something, why hadn't she told the police?

11

Greg headed back to the jobsite. When he drove through the entrance, uniformed officers stood with some of the workers outside in the sun. No doubt David would be nice and comfortable inside, making his suspects come to him.

Sure enough, David had commandeered the office in the back. He sat in a padded chair behind a clean desk.

Walter Forrest, the tile guy, overflowed a metal chair in front of him.

As Greg entered, a whine warbled in Walter's voice. "I know you guys want to pin this on me. It makes it real easy for you. I'm the new guy in town, so you don't have to explain why you didn't realize someone you've known your whole life is a monster."

Greg set a chair off to the side where he could watch.

David rocked back in his perch. "What do you mean? Do you know who pushed her?

Is it someone who's lived here his whole life?"

"No. I mean . . . I don't know. They must have because there aren't many new people here. I'm your best candidate." Walter placed both hands on the desk. "Except for one small detail. I didn't do it. I was in the Spruce tiling the master bath. The girls can verify it. They saw me."

David scooted his chair closer. Even with the desk between them, it made Walter lean back. His chair groaned. "Yeah, but maybe you stopped tiling long enough to chase them to the Aspen and push Allie down the stairs. What's the matter, were you afraid she'd identify you as having been in the house?"

Confusion crinkled Walter's face. "What house, the Spruce? I already told you I was there."

David appeared to study his nails, but his focus never left the suspect's face. "The lady's house who got killed, you know, the one in the news all week."

Walter gripped the edge of the desk. "Hey, I didn't kill nobody. And I didn't push the poor girl down the stairs. I came to work, and I worked."

Now was the time to interject. Greg leaned in. "So, did you see anyone else around? Was there someone who might have been stalking the two women?"

"I was in the bathroom from the time I talked to them until I heard the sirens. If someone followed them, I didn't see him."

"Did you hear or see anything else suspicious?"

Walter relaxed his hands and crossed his legs, putting one ankle on his knee and fingering the hem of his jeans. "Nothing you'd want to hear."

David wrote something in his notes and yawned. "Spit it out, Forrest. You're starting to bore me. In fact, maybe an arrest would be just the thing to wake me up." He drummed his fingers on the desk. "Now what did you see?"

"I didn't see it, but word is the inspector came to look at the wiring in the Willow, and Jonathan flew off the handle and slapped the clipboard out of his hand." He lowered his foot to the floor with a thump and leaned forward. The chair shrieked in protest. "Let me tell you. You don't want to tick off an inspector. I heard Mike was mad, 'cause he was forced to do a lot of damage control."

David jotted another note. "And it has to do with this . . . how exactly?"

"I've seen it before. A guy's got a bad

temper, it always leads to problems. If he can't control it toward someone who can hurt him, what would he do with someone who can't?"

"So you think Jonathan pushed her?"

"It's possible, isn't it? Maybe he was still mad at the inspector, and he took it out on the girl. It makes as much sense as me doing it."

Greg kept his voice light as if he was taking Walter into his confidence. "You know, he's the right build. Who else is tall and thin around here?"

Walter relaxed and stared up at the ceiling. "Mike, the foreman, is about six two, and Charlie's maybe five eleven or so. A lot of thin guys work here. They're not dumpy old codgers like me." He laughed, and his smile faded. "If I keep sitting around talking to you two, I'll get canned, and I can't afford it." His gaze skittered toward the door. "You guys won't tell the boss what I said about his kid, will you? I need this job."

Greg reassured him, and he and David stood.

Walter pushed to his feet, and he and David moved out into the main area, David handing him a card. "If you hear of anything to help us, call one of these numbers. And tell Mike we're looking for him, would you?"

Walter nodded and lumbered out.

David smirked. "Walter couldn't have run anywhere, let alone down a bunch of steps."

"Yeah, I think he's telling the truth."

Mike entered the trailer, marched to the large desk, and sat in the rolling chair behind it. David sent Greg a pointed look, as if acknowledging a power move. He sauntered over and settled himself in one of the metal chairs before the cluttered desk. "So, who gets the office in the back?"

"It's Jonathan's." Mike relaxed. He fit Maggie's description: Caucasian with a tan, tall and thin. He was pretty well built, so pushing a young girl down a flight of stairs would have been easy for him. Of course, almost anybody could. Allie was a petite girl.

"It's too clean. Doesn't look like much work gets done in there."

Mike shrugged. "How can I help you?"

Greg folded himself into a chair next to David. "Tell us the sequence of events after you saw Maggie and Allie in the office."

Mike shoved some piles aside and placed a stack of papers on the floor, clearing the middle of his desk. "I was going to walk over with them to the Spruce to see how far Walter was on the bathroom. Before I could get there, I had to take care of something at the Willow."

"The inspector thing?" David asked.

Greg flashed David a quick glance and returned his gaze to Mike. "Maggie told me there was some trouble with the inspector."

Mike exhaled. "Yeah. Jonathan lost his temper when the inspector wouldn't approve the electrical in the Willow. It was a small thing we could have fixed right there, but the inspector insisted on marking it down. It made Jonathan mad because it will cost us time."

"Do all your houses have trouble with inspections?" David seemed to be going for the jugular, but if he wanted to put Mike on the defensive, he missed his mark.

Mike's face didn't change. "We normally sail right through them, but sometimes someone misses something." His voice remained even. "It's Jonathan's job to check before the inspector gets here, but he was out all morning and didn't get it done. The inspector was early, which probably threw him off."

David tilted his head. "So are you used to making excuses for him? Doesn't it irritate you that he's your boss?"

"He's not here much, and he leaves me alone to do my job."

Greg couldn't tell from Mike's face whether it bothered him or not. "So, what

161

happened after the inspector thing?"

"I assigned someone to fix the problem, and I went to check the furnace in the Linden. I was there until I heard the sirens."

"Where's the Linden in relation to where Maggie and Allie were?"

Mike selected a sheet of paper from a pile on his desk and placed it in the space he'd cleared between them. The schematic of the model homes displayed the name of each house, as well as some specs. He extracted a pen from his shirt pocket, bent, and put an *X* on the Aspen. "This is our biggest house. They were in there." He flipped it around so Greg and David could read the names.

Greg picked it up and studied it. "Can we keep this?"

"Sure."

Greg wrote Mike's name in the square marked Linden, and Maggie and Allie in the Aspen — diagonal from each other and down the street from the Spruce, where he wrote Walter. The Willow stood next door to the Spruce, where the girls were when they saw the inspector. The day's events started to come together.

Greg laid the diagram between them. "What we really want to know, Mike, is who could have been close to the Aspen when it happened? Did you see or hear anyone near it either before or after?"

"No. If I'd been in the main part of the house I might have, but I was in the basement. I didn't see anyone. I didn't even see the girls go in. I thought they were still in the Spruce." His desk phone rang, and Mike eyed it as if he wanted to answer. He didn't though.

Greg waited for it to stop before continuing. He glanced around the office and sighted the large stuffed dog. "So is this the famous mascot?"

"Yeah, his name is Buster, but there's usually a ski mask on his head. It has holes for his ears, and it's rolled back so his face shows."

"Have you been able to remember whether it was on the dog this morning?"

His expression grew pensive. "I've been trying to remember since we talked, but I just don't recall if it was on his head this morning. The last time I'm sure was last week. Sorry, I know it's not helpful."

"Why last week?" David exploded as if he couldn't hold it in.

"The guys are messing with him all the time. I came in and found him in my chair, the mask on backward covering his face. I find him all kinds of different ways. Sometimes he has it on like he's skiing, or he has a hardhat on. Once he was missing altogether, and we found him in the Aspen."

"Was there anyone with you in the Linden?"

Mike met David's stare. "You mean like an alibi?"

"Yeah." David tensed, ready to pounce.

Greg wondered if he would have to restrain him.

"I was in the basement alone."

"Hmm." David gave Mike a silent stare.

Greg had to hand it to him — he was good at intimidation.

Mike filled in the silence as most people do. "Someone might have seen me go down. There were plenty of guys around."

"What about on Saturday, the third? Where were you then?" David's crisp tone bordered civil.

Mike's mouth formed a tight line. He made a pretense of checking the calendar, but Greg didn't expect a helpful answer. Why would he help someone so bent on making him look guilty? "There's nothing on the schedule, so I would have been here working."

"Can anyone verify that?"

Mike's face remained calm. "Probably. I deal with people all day. You'll have to ask

164

around."

"I will."

The two men glared at each other, neither backing down.

After a minute, Mike turned to Greg. "Is there anything else I can answer for you guys? I need to get back to work."

Greg responded before David could. "One more thing. Can you tell us where the other guys were while you were in the basement? Whatever you remember will be fine."

Mike leaned back and closed his eyes, as if picturing everyone coming and going. He spoke with his eyes closed. "Jonathan disappeared after he made the inspector mad, probably came back here to cool off. Charlie was going to measure for the built-ins on the Aspen and the Spruce, but I didn't see him, so I don't know. Walter was in the Spruce working on the bathroom tile, and Kurt was supervising a framing crew in the Juniper." He opened his eyes and sat up. "They were framing the next three houses here, here, and here." He pointed to the drawing and wrote their names on the diagram. "I don't know if they were all where they were supposed to be. I don't watch them all day — I wouldn't get anything done."

Greg and David excused themselves and

went in search of Charlie and Jonathan.

One of the framers pointed them to the basement of the Spruce.

Greg motioned for David to tread quietly, hoping to hear what was being said. The smell of wood stain grew stronger the lower they went.

"I can't believe I have to be here at all." The whine must be Jonathan's. "It's not like I'm taking over or anything. I don't want to do this. I want to play tennis."

"Have you tried to explain?"

"He won't hear me. He says I'm not good enough. If I didn't have to work all the time, I could practice more, and I know I can make it as a serious professional. I figure if I can just hang in a few more months at the company, I'll be twenty-five, and I'll inherit from my mom. Then I won't have to work for the old windbag. I won't have to coach little old ladies either."

Apparently deciding they'd heard enough, David marched through the door. "Where were you guys earlier today?"

Charlie dipped his rag into the stain and rubbed it over the wood, deepening the color of what was obviously a bookcase. With all the windows open, the smell wasn't as bad here as in the closed stairwell.

Jonathan reclined against the concrete,

one leg bent, with his foot flat against the wall. He stayed there as if unconcerned about their questions. "We played tennis with Allie and Maggie this morning then came here."

Charlie said nothing, just kept rubbing.

"We know you were here. We heard about the incident with the inspector."

Jonathan shrugged.

David's face remained expressionless. "Where were you when Allie was pushed?"

"You think that was us? Why would we do that?"

"Did she beat you at tennis?"

"No, of course not."

Greg interjected, "We're asking everybody, trying to get a sense of where people were when it happened."

"Oh. After the inspector thing, I went back to the office."

David smirked. "The clean one in the rear of the construction trailer?"

"Yeah."

"What do you do? It looks like all the work is done out front."

Jonathan sneered. "I supervise."

Greg watched to see if Charlie would react, but he kept his head down, dipping his rag into the stain and drawing it across the wood.

"Can someone verify that?"

"I don't know. Mike wasn't there, and Laura's out this week."

Greg broke in before David could make another smart-aleck remark. "What about you, Charlie? Where were you?"

He stopped staining and straightened, rubbing his back. "I was at the hardware on Fourth Street, picking up stain. Maggie's plans specified this color, and I didn't have any."

"Let's talk about Saturday, the third. Where were you?"

Jonathan lowered his foot to the ground, but continued to lounge against the wall. "I was playing a tennis tournament at the club. You can ask. Everyone was there."

Charlie wiped his hands on a clean rag. "I was working."

"On a Saturday?" Disbelief rang in David's voice as his eyebrows shot up to his hair.

"Yeah. In the summer we work as much as we can."

"Do you know if Mike was here?"

Charlie leaned down and placed the lid on the can of stain, tapping it in place with the end of a five-in-one tool. "I saw him in the morning, and then again at two when I finished for the day."

David held out a card, signaling the interview's end. "Let me know if you think of anything."

Jonathan slipped it in his shirt pocket. "Sure thing."

They questioned a few more people, but no one had anything more to add. Kurt and the framing crew saw Mike enter the Linden, just as he'd said, but when David and Greg checked, they discovered it had a walkout basement.

As they walked out to their vehicles, David stopped. "If you're going soft on your friends, maybe I should ask the questions."

Greg stopped as well. "Who do you mean?"

"Mike. He could have left the house without using the front door."

"He would have been spotted. He'd have to cross the street right in front of the framers."

"He wasn't where he said he was the day Esther was killed."

"I don't know about that. Charlie didn't see him, but that doesn't mean he wasn't here."

"You just don't want him to be guilty."

"It's too soon to tell who's guilty, and there's no reason to alienate a witness. They'll provide more information if you

169

don't give them a reason to be afraid."

David snorted. "Oh, come on. He's hiding something, and I plan to get him to spill it."

"You can't bully information out of everyone, David. Some people don't respond to threats; they shut down. If they're guilty, they'll not tell you, and if they're innocent, they'll be afraid you'll twist their words, and they'll watch what they say." He started walking, heading for his truck. "I want everyone to feel free to tell me whatever they want to at first, and then we'll get tough if we have a reason."

David caught up and smiled like a carnivore. "Ah, let them assume they're safe and then snap the trap shut. Right?"

Greg exhaled. "Something like that."

12

Maggie arrived at the gate of the Tate mansion at nine thirty. After admiring the stunning stone and ironwork, she leaned out of her car window and pressed the buzzer.

A tinny voice emanated from the box. "May I help you?"

"Maggie Schreiber to see Mrs. Tate."

"Please follow the driveway," the voice said, and the gate swung back on oiled hinges. A blanket of green grass spread beyond like a moat protecting the castle.

She kept her window down as she drove in, breathing in the scent of rose bushes blooming along the driveway on either side. Not a weed in sight. As if a weed would dare poke its ugly head up into one of Larry's gardens. As she slid out of her car, Larry stood up from the bush he was trimming and threw up a hand. She waved back, wondering how long the elder gentleman would be able to handle an estate this large.

Although he had help, it must be a lot of work to keep the place up to Monica Tate's standards.

Maggie strolled along the flagstone walkway to the front door and rang the bell, not quite knowing what to expect. Being summoned to Monica Tate's was no small matter. Even though Aunt Esther and Monica had been good friends for years, Maggie had never been invited to her house.

Lucinda, Mrs. Tate's maid, opened the door with a smile. "Miss Maggie, Mrs. Tate is expecting you. May I show you to the salon?" Of course, Monica was expecting her. How many people declined a summons from Monica Tate? Though it had been couched like a request, everyone knew one didn't refuse her.

And Maggie hadn't wanted to. Did Monica know who pushed Allie? Maybe even who killed Aunt Esther? If so, why hadn't she told the police?

Realizing she hadn't answered Lucinda, Maggie nodded. She clicked into full-awareness mode, taking in as much of her surroundings as possible. She might never get another chance to see this place. She tipped her head back. A massive chandelier glittered above the grand, two-story entry. A round table, so large it wouldn't fit in her entire kitchen, supported a bouquet of fresh flowers in a sparkling crystal vase. The marble floor beneath her feet shone.

Lucinda allowed her a minute to ogle and then led her off to the right into the salon. Her uniform crackled as she moved. She was dressed in the standard pink all the staff wore, but she'd accessorized it with a scarf in a calming mix of blues and greens.

"Lucinda, what a beautiful scarf."

Lucinda led her past a curving staircase and into a soft green room with white furniture and dark hardwood floors. "Thank you, Miss Maggie. It's my favorite. Can I get you some iced tea or lemonade?"

After settling her with a glass of tea, Lucinda went in search of her employer.

Maggie barely waited for her to leave the room before popping up to explore. She'd heard about the treasures in this house; artwork and statuary collected over generations were rumored to be everywhere. If this room was a sample of the rest of the house, the gossip was true. She tiptoed over to a Monet on the far wall, the colors blending beautifully with the room. She wondered who had chosen it and who had decorated around it.

Monica seemed to glide into the room, startling her. Must be what good breeding does for one. It allows the ability to sneak up on people.

"Maggie, thank you for coming. Please have a seat. I knew I could count on you."

"Count on me for what, Mrs. Tate?"

"Monica. You must call me Monica."

Uh oh, this must be serious. Maggie moved to the sofa and perched on the edge. "Monica, then. How can I help you?"

Monica lowered herself into a side chair next to a table holding a genuine Tiffany lamp. "Actually, it's I who wants to help you."

Maggie tried to hide her surprise. "Help me? How?"

"It's this horrible killer. He must be stopped. We can't let him get away with Esther's murder, and I know she would want me to do something about her niece being hurt."

"Shouldn't we leave it to the police?" Maggie didn't see anywhere to put her glass, so she held on to it, resting it on her knee.

Monica reached into a drawer in the table next to her and retrieved a coaster. "Here you go, dear. Rest it on this." She waited until Maggie had her glass resting on the coaster, and then continued, "I know your fiancé is very smart, but he and his friends have so much to do. I figure we can do some of the legwork and give it to them to do the rough stuff. How does that sound?"

Her tone was more than friendly; as if they were co-conspirators. Maggie felt drawn in, even though she had no illusions about Monica Tate and her becoming best buds. She cleared her throat. "Do you have any idea who killed Aunt Esther or hurt Allie?"

"Who are the police considering?" Monica answered with a question.

Was this a ploy to get information? Maggie considered not telling her. But it wasn't a secret, and it might help to find Cameron and Grady if more people knew. "Right now, they're looking for Cameron Hayes and his brother, Grady."

Monica tapped the arm of her chair. "We don't want to cover the same ground . . ."

When Monica's voice drifted off, Maggie leaned forward. "Do you have someone else in mind?"

"I told your fiancé about this, but he didn't take me seriously. I want to look at her maid."

"Maria? You think Maria killed her? What makes you say that?"

"She's always been so forward, and I know Esther, bless her heart, was too good to notice. I wonder if there are other things

175

she missed."

"Like what?"

"Have you checked Esther's finances? Maybe she was stealing."

A lump formed in Maggie's throat. If Monica convinced her friends that Maria had been dishonest, she could damage her livelihood.

"My aunt never said anything, and I'm sure Maria would never steal from her."

Monica raised one eyebrow.

Maggie lowered her eyes and kept her voice steady. "I've gone over a few things with her lawyer, but I haven't had time to visit with her accountant yet."

Mrs. Tate — Maggie couldn't pretend she was anything but Mrs. Tate now — pursed her lips. "Hmm, her accountant would have noticed if either the maid or the gardener were stealing, wouldn't he?"

Now it was the gardener? This didn't sound good. Anyone without a pedigree would be targeted. Maggie picked an imaginary piece of lint off her white cotton skirt. "I believe they've both been cleared."

Mrs. Tate stood and paced, jiggling her wrist until her diamond watch fell into place. "What kind of work has she had done lately? Have there been any workers in the house?"

176

Time to end this line of questioning. "I don't know, but a visit to her accountant may be a good idea. I'll make an appointment."

Mrs. Tate nodded once as if this plan would solve everything, walked over, and put her hand out, signaling the meeting was over.

Good thing Maggie didn't have anything she wanted to discuss. She rose and shook the outstretched hand, making the appropriate comments, hoping her face didn't show her disgust over being sent to do a hatchet job on Monica Tate's supposed inferiors.

Lucinda appeared in the hallway. "I'll show you out, Miss Maggie."

Maggie forced herself to smile. Lucinda led her to the front door and turned. "Maria would never hurt Esther," she whispered. "She loved her." Her face was passive, but her snapping brown eyes glowed dark. "Mrs. Tate thinks staff must never be allowed to forget their place, but staff aren't the ones with secrets."

Maggie paused. "Can we meet somewhere and talk?"

"What about?" Lucinda opened the ornate door and held the screen.

Maggie kept her voice low and inched by. "Whatever secrets you know or have heard that might help me clear Maria and Joe."

Lucinda stepped out on the porch for a moment, still holding the screen. "I don't know anything, and if I did, I couldn't say. Mrs. Tate would dismiss me for even talking to you. I only wanted you to know Maria didn't kill Mrs. Campbell."

"I'd still like to talk to you."

She backed into the house, closed the screen, and spoke through it. "I can't. I don't want any trouble." She closed the heavy main door, and a decisive click confirmed the bolt slid home.

Why did she have the feeling Lucinda knew more than she was telling? Maggie walked down the path to her car. How could she get her to open up without sacrificing her job? Maggie knew Monica Tate. If one of her staff was let go, no one would hire them. In her circle, it was an unwritten rule you didn't poach another's employee, even after they weren't in their employ anymore. And the people capable of hiring Lucinda would be in Monica's circle. She shook her head as she got into her car. There would have to be another way to find the killer. She wouldn't do anything to jeopardize Lucinda's future . . . She couldn't.

Greg hung up the phone, smiling. In this

rare moment, most of the detectives were at the precinct. A sponge ball hit him in the side of the head, and he turned to see who threw it. Six desks were set up in a grid, two wide, in the middle of a large open space. Offices and interview rooms lined the back wall, and the squad room and kitchen were set off to one side.

Mark sat at the back corner of the grid, grinning. "A call from the girlfriend, huh?"

"Maybe it's none of your business." Greg leaned over and, in one motion, scooped the ball up, and hurled it back, missing by a mile.

"It's not hard to tell. Every time she calls, you hang up grinning like an idiot."

David piped up from behind. "Yeah, it's kind of degrading how you drool after her like a puppy."

"If you had a girl like her, wouldn't you do a little drooling?" Peter joked. "You're just jealous 'cause you don't have a hot chick like us."

David laughed. "Who says? Mine just aren't permanent. I can date as many hot chicks as I like."

Greg waved his hand. "OK, enough. Anyway, it was about the case. Apparently, Maggie went to see Monica Tate today."

"Wow, you're coming up in the world,

buddy," Mark said. "Your girlfriend is on visiting terms with the elite?"

"Yeah, but it was just to accuse Esther's maid and gardener again. Maggie was peeved."

David sat back in his chair and glowered. "I checked them out. They're both clean. They were at their other employers, and there are witnesses."

"Yeah, I know, but Mrs. Tate wants them to be guilty."

"I wonder why?" Mark said. "Does she have a reason?"

David snorted. "You mean other than she considers them second-rate?"

"She does, for sure." Greg swiveled around, facing David. "And Joe has a criminal record, which doesn't help matters."

"It was thirty years ago. He was in his twenties then, and he drove the getaway car for his friends. It's not like he physically hurt someone. He did his time, and he's been a model citizen since." David's voice had raised. He cleared his throat.

"Wow, what has you all worked up?" Mark asked.

David opened his drawer and chose a pen. "Nothing. It makes me mad when people won't let something die. How long does it take for him to be rid of some foolish thing he did in his past?"

"We agree," Greg interjected. "Do you know Joe well?"

David rolled the pen in his fingers, staring at it. "Yeah. He used to let me help him when I was a kid. He'd pay me to mow or trim. Wasn't much, but it helped put food on the table sometimes."

Greg nodded. He'd forgotten David had been brought up by a single mom, and it was hard for them. Maybe it was why he had such a rough edge with people he thought hadn't earned their way. Time to change the subject. "So, let's go over what we have." He rose, walked to the white board, and started writing. "We're assuming the same person who pushed Allie also killed Esther, right?"

David picked up the file from his desk and stood with him. He laid the file on a nearby table and flipped it open. "Yeah. It's possible they aren't connected but not probable."

Greg plucked a blue marker from the tray. "Our list of suspects for Esther's murder includes the boyfriend, Cameron Hayes, his brother, Grady Hayes, and their accomplices. For Allie's assault, several guys at the jobsite including Mike Travis, Charlie Parker, and Jonathan Blake fit Maggie's description." He jotted the names on the board. "Am I missing anyone?"

David pulled his notebook out. "I still need to check on a couple guys at the jobsite who were alone when Allie was pushed. I put them lower on the list because they didn't have a connection to Esther or Allie."

Greg labeled the column of names *Suspects.* Next to it, he started a new column with Esther and one for Allie. Above that, he wrote *Alibis.* "We can't find Cameron or Grady, which in itself is suspicious. Why disappear if you're innocent?" He left the spaces next to their names blank.

David consulted his notes. "Charlie was picking up some stain at the hardware store in Lafayette when Allie was pushed. We have the receipt. But he doesn't have an alibi for the time Esther died."

Greg made a checkmark in Allie's column next to his name. "What about Mike?"

"He claims he was at work during Esther's murder, but Charlie says he left."

Greg left both spaces blank. "We have more blanks than checkmarks."

David refocused on his notes. "Jonathan was playing tennis at the club when Esther was killed — some kind of grudge match, so there were quite a few spectators. But no one knows where he was when Allie was pushed."

Greg put a checkmark in Esther's column but left Allie's blank. "OK, those are the people we know about. This doesn't include the people in the burglary ring that we don't know about. Other than Cameron and Grady, we don't have any burglary suspects yet, but we will. Someone will make a mistake and get caught. Then we'll have a few more names to add to our board."

David closed his file. "Cameron and Grady Hayes seem to be our best choices at the moment. We need to concentrate on finding them. And we need to investigate Mike."

13

The business phone rang three times before
Maggie could reach it. She snatched it off
the base but not before Allie reached it first.
Assuming the call was for her, Maggie
stayed on the line.

"You know I didn't kill your aunt. And I
would never push you down the stairs or
whatever they said I did. How could you
think I would hurt you?" The screamer
who'd called Maggie the night of Esther's
death was now pleading with Allie.

"If you yell at me I'll hang up, and I won't
answer again."

Good for Allie.

"I'm sorry. I won't yell. But have I ever
hurt you?"

"No, but maybe it was your brother."

"It wasn't. I'm telling you, I don't know
who pushed you, but it wasn't me or Grady.
Meet me somewhere we can talk. Please? I
need to know you're OK and you trust me.

Just for coffee. And maybe those donuts you like."

Allie hesitated, and Maggie wanted to scream into the phone. No! Don't do it! But she waited to see what Allie would say.

"Come on," he wheedled. "You know you want to."

"I don't know," she sighed. "Maggie's here, and she won't want me to go."

She wasn't kidding. Maggie wanted to tell her there was no way she was going anywhere with that creep, but she held her tongue.

"So? Do you always do what you're told? What do you care what she wants?"

Again, it was all Maggie could do not to scream at the little twerp. But she wanted Allie to tell him herself.

"I'll think about it," Allie said.

"Are you coming or not?" He clipped the words out in a testy tone.

"I don't know! Stop badgering me. If you see me, then I decided to come. If not, then don't call me anymore."

"Oh, come on. You're not —"

Allie hung up.

Maggie hit End on the phone and nestled it back on the stand. She needed to talk to Allie. To make sure she didn't go anywhere with Cameron alone. She'd love to tell Greg

185

where to pick him up while he waited for Allie, but he never said where they would meet. Must be a place they'd been before . . . Somewhere with donuts. Not helpful, since the town boasted several donut shops.

She was partway downstairs when the back door clicked open. Allie was going to meet this kid. The jingle of keys galvanized Maggie into action. She grabbed her purse from the table and raced outside. Only Allie's slow walk with the crutches permitted Maggie to catch up. "Allie, wait."

"Sorry, Mags. I need to borrow your car."

"No, you can't."

Allie hobbled into the garage, Maggie trailing her. "Look at you. You can hardly walk. How will you drive? At least, let me take you."

Allie hesitated and then swerved to the passenger side. Maggie yanked open the driver door and hopped in, holding her hand out for the keys. "Where're we going?"

"The Hungry Nun's Donut Shop on Fourteenth and Main."

Maggie dug her cellphone out of her purse.

"What are you doing?"

"Just what you think I'm doing. I'm telling Greg where to pick up his suspect."

"Why? I never said you could tell the police." Allie took a swipe at Maggie, but with her left arm in a sling, she couldn't reach with her right.

Maggie leaned away as she punched the *call* button and backed out of the driveway. Greg answered on the first ring.

Allie lunged again, nearly making Maggie drop the phone. "You can't do this. He'll think I betrayed him."

"Stop it. Do you want us to get in a wreck?" Maggie explained to Greg where they were going and then threw her phone in her purse. "He betrayed you first."

Allie grabbed her own phone, but before she could hit any buttons, Maggie wrenched it out of her hand and threw it in the backseat. Allie tried to catch it and missed. "I told you he didn't push me. You're just an overbearing, controlling maniac who can't keep her nose out of other people's business!"

Maggie swallowed the sharp words she wanted to shout, forcing calm. "Cameron betrayed you when he let you take the heat for Aunt Esther's death. He knows they want to talk to him. He knows you could be in trouble because they can't find him. He could clear everything up if he has an alibi."

Allie yanked Maggie's phone out of her

purse. "What if he doesn't? Then they'll arrest him."

"And why is that different from them arresting you?"

Allie didn't say anything, just dropped Maggie's phone, and faced the window.

Silence radiated through the car for several blocks. As they approached, Maggie tried again, purposely keeping her voice soft. "I don't care if you're mad at me. I would rather have you mad than not know where you are and let Cameron finish you off." She swung into a space. "If he's innocent, why doesn't he surrender? The police are very good at finding the right guy."

She heard the rattle before she saw the truck jerk into the spot to the right of her vehicle.

A slender, sandy-haired young man swung out. Clean cut and handsome, not what she expected at all.

Allie rolled down the window and he leaned in to kiss her, but she turned her head. She had this pouty thing down to an art.

"You'd better not stay," she said. "Maggie called the cops."

He swore and took a couple steps toward his truck then stepped back. "Allie, please come with me. I can't stay here, and we

188

need to talk. Someone's been trailing you."

Allie reached for the door handle.

"No! You can't go with him!" Maggie panicked.

Considering her broken leg, Allie was out of the car faster than Maggie would have thought possible. She stood on one leg.

Cameron bent to pick her up, leaving her crutches in the car.

Maggie threw her door open and flew out, tugging at his arm as he hurried to the passenger side of his truck. "Leave her alone! Put her down!"

"Do you want to make me drop her?" He yelled. "Knock it off!"

He shoved Allie in, slammed the door, and ran to the driver's side before Maggie had a chance to think.

She yanked open the passenger door and jumped in.

Allie automatically slid to the middle of the bench seat to make room for her.

"What are you doing? Get out of my truck!" His desperate voice rose to a high-pitched shriek.

"She goes; I go. You'd better decide what you're doing. The police station isn't far. It won't take them long."

He swore again, threw the truck into reverse, and gunned it, screeching out of the lot. He flew down the street, around the corner, and slowed when he neared traffic. It was as if he were out for a Sunday drive.

Maggie checked the mirrors several times, hoping to see a police car, but it looked like he had eluded them. She glared at Cameron over Allie's head. "What did you mean before? Did you see someone following us while you were following us?"

Red started at the base of his neck and traveled up his face. "I was just trying to get Allie to talk to me."

"In this state, that's called stalking."

"I'm not the one you need to worry about. A black SUV keeps showing up. Maybe you should worry about him."

"Did you see who was in it?"

"No, the windows are tinted, and before you ask, I didn't get a look at the license number."

"How about make and model?"

He shook his head, appearing to concentrate on his driving.

Maggie focused, trying to remember if she'd seen any vehicles like that in the past week. "How convenient." She smirked. "Do you know how many black SUVs there are in the mountains?"

"Maggie, stop, OK?" Allie faced Cameron. "Tell us what you saw."

He drove onto a side road, and Maggie wondered where he was taking them. Maybe it hadn't been such a good idea to get in the truck. She thrust a hand in her purse, all the while looking for street signs. She couldn't feel her phone. Jerking the bag open, she stared inside. It wasn't there. It must have fallen on the floor of her car when Allie dropped it. She pictured Allie's phone where it landed on the rear seat. Great, she and Allie could be in here with a killer and no way to communicate.

"I haven't been watching you the whole time." Cameron calmed. "But I've driven by your house, trying to get up the nerve to knock. I've seen a black SUV several times. He saw me once and left but not before I saw him get out of his vehicle and go through your back gate. Something must have spooked him halfway through the yard though, because he stopped and left without knocking."

"He was in my backyard?" Maggie stopped at the squeak in her voice, took a breath, and tried again. "What did he look like?"

"I was pretty far down the street, so I didn't see his face. He had short, dark hair, and a decent build. I wouldn't have wanted to mess with him."

"How tall was he?"

"Hard to tell from a distance; taller than me though."

Maggie counted the guys she knew who fit the description. Mike was tall and well built. Could he have needed something from her and then noticed she wasn't home? But why go through the back? It could have been Greg. He parked in the alley and came in the gate. But he was a lot taller than Cameron, and he drove a pickup, not an SUV.

Cameron turned north on a quiet street and pulled over to the side.

A creek flowed east to west under the road ahead of them, and its tinkle was making her wish she'd visited the restroom first.

He put the truck in park, left the engine running, and reached for Allie's hand. "I didn't kill the old lady, and I didn't push you down the stairs. I know you don't like Grady, but you've got to believe me, I would never hurt you."

"What about Grady? Could he have pushed her?" Maggie perched on the edge of the seat to stare at Cameron, wanting to jerk their hands apart.

"Grady wouldn't do that."

She slid back and changed her focus. "Allie, what does Grady look like?"

"He has light, brownish-blond hair like Cameron, but he's shorter and heavier."

Cameron piped up. "What she's trying to say is he has a fat gut. Grady likes his beer."

If Grady was heavy, then it couldn't have been him in the model home. Maggie closed her eyes and pictured the guy again. She wasn't sure how tall he was, but he was lean.

Cameron interrupted her thoughts. "I want to talk to Allie."

"So talk."

"Alone." His face was set, and he stared straight ahead.

"I'm not getting out of this truck." To emphasize her point, Maggie yanked the seatbelt down and snapped it in place.

"Then we'll get out." Allie pointed toward a group of trees on the right side of the road, a short distance from the truck. "We'll stand right by those trees over there. He can't take me anywhere without his truck, Mags. I'll be fine."

Maggie nodded. "But stay where I can see you." She was way overreacting, but one look at Allie's cast firmed her resolve. As they got out on the driver's side, she wondered how Greg would react when he found her empty car at the donut shop. She knew what he would do: he'd worry.

Cameron walked with an arm around Allie, steadying her as she hobbled around the front of the truck toward the trees.

Maggie rolled down her window and stuck her head out. "And make it fast. I don't want to be here all day." She didn't mention the police were looking for them. Instead, she gazed around the quiet neighborhood, enjoying the breeze and listening to every word they said. Obviously, they didn't realize how their voices carried out here in the stillness.

The street was clear, but looking in the side mirror, Maggie counted three different black or dark gray vehicles fitting Cameron's description, driving west on the street behind them. Maybe he was making it up about the SUV. It'd be a good ruse, hard to disprove. As she watched, a green truck rounded the corner behind them, hesitated for a second, then leaped forward, as if the driver stomped on the gas.

The engine roared behind her. An explosion rang in her ears, and she slammed sideways into the door. The truck backed away, then jerked left around Cameron's vehicle and backfired. Another bang filled the air and then another as it rocketed back into the lane. Then it dawned on her. The sounds weren't backfires. They were gunshots.

■ ■ ■

Greg circled the Hungry Nun again. No sign of Maggie. He and David had checked every table in the place, and no one had seen her enter the donut shop. He returned to her car and tried the door. Locked. He peered in the driver's side window while David did the same on the passenger side, but neither saw anything to indicate a problem. So where was she?

"Her purse is gone," David said.

"Yeah, she was together enough to take it with her." Greg cupped his hands around his eyes. "Is that her phone? No, it must be Allie's. Maggie's doesn't have rhinestones."

"What about the other one?"

"Where?" Greg hurried to the passenger side, and David scooched over to give him room.

He put his finger on the glass. "There. On the floor between the seats."

There was something there. "It's hard to tell, let me call again." He dialed her cell number. Sure enough, the area under the seat lit up and faint music drifted from the car's interior. He disconnected. "Great. It explains why she hasn't answered my calls."

A young boy rode his bike over. A bag

with a nun eating a donut dangled from his handlebars. "You guys looking for the smokin' hot chick from this car?"

"Yeah, do you know where she went?"

He shifted off the seat and leaned the bike so he could stand. "Some dude picked her up and put her in his truck."

Oh, no. The scenario was worse than Greg had thought. "Picked her up? Physically?"

"Yeah. Well, she had a cast on, and it made it hard for her to walk, I guess."

Ah, he was talking about Allie. "What about the woman with her? The driver."

"Oh, yeah, she was hot, too. She tried to make him stop, but before I could get off my bike to help, she got in the truck with them."

"Did it look forced?"

"No, the blonde wanted to go, and the older one didn't want her to. So she got in with them. Then they hauled out of the parking lot and down the street."

David unclipped his phone from his belt. "What kind of truck was it?"

"It was kind of a cool old truck. A light blue pickup. Looked like a custom paint job, but it had seen better days for sure."

"Did you get the license number?"

He grimaced. "No, sorry."

"What's your name?"

While David took the kid's information, Greg called the station, putting a BOLO on the blue truck. When David finished questioning the kid, they got in their vehicle, Greg on the driver's side. "I want to cruise the neighborhood in case we spot them."

David snapped his seatbelt. "He's had plenty of time to get away. He wouldn't hang around."

"I know, but I don't know what else to do. Where would he take them? I mean it was in broad daylight, for Pete's sake."

14

"Get down!" Maggie screamed as she struggled with the seatbelt, regretting her earlier show of authority.

Cameron threw Allie to the ground and shielded her with his body. The truck roared off, and another crack burst out as it flew down the street.

Maggie jerked at the seatbelt, ripping her nails on the stiff fabric. She could see Allie's hand sticking out from beneath Cameron, and red bloomed on his white T-shirt. Was it Cameron's blood or Allie's? She dragged her eyes away to focus on the seatbelt latch and stabbed at it again and again. Finally, it clicked loose. She tore the belt off and stumbled out of the truck. "Allie!" she screamed, running toward them. "Are you OK?"

Allie struggled to get out from under Cameron. "Get off. You're crushing me." Her voice was muffled.

He rolled off her and lay in the grass. Maggie scanned Allie for injuries, but there didn't seem to be any new ones. She grabbed her under the arms and heaved her to her feet. Blowing out a sigh, she focused on Cameron. His forehead was sweating, and he gripped his upper arm — the source of the blood.

"He's been shot, Maggie. He's been shot!" Allie's voice escalated to a screech. "Now do you believe he didn't kill Aunt Esther?"

Maggie didn't say anything as she knelt beside him on the grass. "Let go and let me see." As gently as she could, she eased his hand away from his arm. Through the blood, she inspected the hole in his right shoulder.

"We need to get you to a hospital, and we need to do it fast, in case they come back. Allie, help me get his shirt off."

Together they helped him sit up.

Maggie half-pulled, half-ripped the T-shirt from his body. Another hole tore open the back where the bullet exited. "Here." She folded the material and placed it over his shoulder until both ends fell in front of the injuries. "Press on the front."

He brought his left hand up to hold it in place, and she pressed against the one on the back. He sucked in his breath.

Glancing around, hoping to see some neighbors, Maggie helped him stand. "Can you walk?"

"Yeah, I'm OK."

He faltered, and she tightened her grip, trying to help him balance while keeping pressure on the wound.

Allie hopped along after them.

The two houses on the street looked blank. If they didn't come out after hearing gunshots, they either weren't home or were too scared. Either way, she doubted they'd be a source of help.

She loaded Cameron first, and then Allie, before running to the driver's side. A large dent appeared near the front end, but clear of the door. A hissing emanated from the tire. The need to leave swamped her emotions. She tried to block out the image of a green truck coming back around the corner. They would be sitting ducks, with both Cameron and Allie unable to run.

Maggie climbed in and steered the truck onto the road in the direction of the hospital.

Allie maneuvered the shirt under Cameron's arm so he could lean against it in the back and she could press against the wound in the front.

Maggie marveled at the calmness of her

actions. A groan escaped Cameron's lips, causing her to push harder on the accelerator. The truck listed hard to the left and limped forward. Thank goodness the hospital was a block away. She steered into the emergency lot, and with the pedal down as far as she dared, the truck shuddered to the front doors.

As soon as she stopped, three people dashed from the entrance. She delivered Cameron into their hands and asked them to call the police. She realized she could have called the police with Cameron's phone on the way over, but in her haste to get away before the shooter came back she didn't think. With a gunshot wound, they'd call the police anyway, but she wanted Greg. She flipped his card out of her wallet and gave it to the desk clerk. The doctor from the day before was on duty again. Allie said her leg was throbbing, so Maggie asked him to check on her as well.

"I'm OK, Maggie. I don't need them to check on me."

Maggie's eyes met the doctor's over Allie's head. "Can you just make sure the bone hasn't shifted? I don't know if it's possible, but I don't want to take any chances."

The doctor smiled at Allie. "That's a very good idea, young lady. You don't want your leg to heal funny, do you? You don't want to go through all this and then have to rebreak it if it isn't healing straight?"

Maggie didn't know whether the doctor would break the leg or not, but it scared Allie enough to allow an X-ray through the cast. All was well, which made her feel better since she didn't relish calling George's secretary again.

Allie could call her dad tonight and explain.

Minutes later, Greg and David sprinted through the doors. There was no one she wanted to see more, and apparently, Greg felt the same way. He folded her into a hug. "Are you and Allie OK? What happened?"

She explained and described the truck.

Greg scribbled in his notebook. "Did you see the guy?"

Maggie shook her head.

"Who was the intended target?"

She blinked. "I assumed it was Cameron, but now, I'm not so sure."

"When Allie comes out, wait for me, and I'll take you back to your car. I'll arrange for an officer to guard your house until we make an arrest."

He waited, stubborn chin braced for an argument, but truth be told, Maggie was relieved. How in the world could she hope to keep Allie safe?

When she nodded, Greg strode through the automatic doors and down the hall, his phone already at his ear.

Soon Allie appeared in a wheelchair, handled by a young orderly named Bill. Her face was white, as though all the strength had seeped out of her.

Maggie popped up. "Honey, are you OK? We're waiting here for Greg. He shouldn't be long."

Bill wheeled her next to Maggie's chair and bent forward. "OK, miss, let me know when you're ready, and I'll help you out."

They sat in silence for about twenty minutes before the motion sensor doors slid open, and Greg appeared with a uniformed officer. "Maggie, you remember Bert?"

Maggie smiled. "Good to see you, Officer Daniels. This is my sister, Allie."

They smiled at each other, but even though he was a handsome man, no flirtation lurked in her smile. She must be tired.

"Bert and his partner will pick up your car, and he'll meet us at your place."

Relief washed over Maggie as she handed Daniels her keys. She wanted to get home and stay there, the quicker the better. Greg scooped Allie up in his arms, but this time Maggie didn't mind. She had no idea how she would have gotten her home otherwise.

It seemed much later than three o'clock when they arrived at her house. She and Allie waited in the truck while Greg checked inside. He then carried Allie inside, lowered her to the couch, and took their statements while he waited for Officer Daniels.

Allie swallowed her pills, and Maggie helped her upstairs for a nap. She stalled as long as she could, but eventually had no choice but to return to the living room.

And Greg.

"She's already asleep," she said when she entered. "She didn't move once her head hit the pillow."

Greg rose and moved toward her. It was so comfortable nestled in his arms, resting her head on his shoulder, feeling the tension leave her body.

"Are you sure you're all right?"

She tucked her face into his neck and breathed in his aftershave. "I'm fine," she mumbled. "He wasn't after me."

"Thanks be to God." He held her for a moment then inclined back to gaze into her face. "I'm feeling there's something wrong. With us."

Before she could answer, her doorbell rang.

"We're not done with this subject." He

drew away to answer the door, and a chill shivered over her, as though someone yanked a blanket off her. She would have to face him with the truth, but not now.

Daniels introduced Officer Anderson, and Greg left to take him back to the station.

Daniels went through the house, checking the windows and locking all outside doors. "Don't you worry, Ms. Schreiber. I'll be right outside." He gave her his cell number. "Just call if you need anything. And bolt this door after me."

She waited until he stepped out on the porch, bolted the door, and then watched him through the window until he got into his car. Having no idea what to do, she still felt she should do something. The longing to talk to Aunt Esther was stronger than ever.

Deep down, she knew Aunt Esther wouldn't have known what to do either, but talking with her would have been comforting. The diaries called to her. Maybe she could get answers to other questions, like what were Aunt Esther's thoughts on a dad walking out on his daughter?

She climbed the stairs to her room. Aunt Esther loved her brother, but she must have had some opinions. And maybe she knew the real reason he left. He would never tell Maggie, and when she begged to live with him, he'd declined. He said he couldn't provide a good home for her and suggested she go to Aunt Esther's. She was grateful, since it might not have occurred to her as an option if he hadn't suggested it, and the move had been the best thing for her in the end. She flipped to the summer he left and started reading. A few pages in, she found what she was looking for.

Danny left. I wondered how long it would take before he got tired of the infidelities. I know it's not right to judge, but none of this can be beneficial for little Maggie. This last affair was too much. The test he had taken when she was a baby confirmed it wasn't the first, and then Darla begged him to come back after he caught her again. I think she's searching for something to fill the emptiness. I've tried to explain to her there is One answer, but she won't hear it. Jesus is the only One able to fill the hole in her heart, but maybe she's been hurt by the church in some way. It's almost painful to see her turn her back on the only thing that will truly help her. Nevertheless, Maggie will need some extra attention. I wish I could do more. Her mother won't let her stay with me. She got almost violent when I suggested it.

A test? What test? Maggie's mind whirled. Could it have been a paternity test? Did it mean Danny wasn't her real father? If so, it could explain why he wouldn't let her live with him when she was so desperate. Her face was wet, but her mouth was dry. No wonder she didn't look like him. Her mother had always preferred blonds; Allie's dad was blond, too. Bile rose in her throat. Why didn't he tell her? Why did he let her believe he was her father? No wonder he didn't want her. She must have been a constant reminder of a painful past.

Another thought occurred to her. It also meant she was not related to Aunt Esther. She squeezed her eyes shut and let the waves of pain wash over her. She needed to talk to Dad. Or should she call him Danny?

15

Greg checked his phone. A text from David said he hadn't had a chance to question Cameron before surgery. Not surprising. Once David posted a guard, he was coming in. After what Maggie said about Cameron shielding Allie with his body, Greg doubted the young man would have pushed her down the stairs yesterday — at least, not on purpose.

A call crackled over the radio. A dark green truck with a broken headlight and damage to the right front had been located, and they were bringing in the suspects.

Greg sped back to the station. He wanted in on this.

He studied the young man through the one-way glass. Hunched over the table, his cuffed hands in his lap, the kid rocked back and forth. Once in a while, he whipped his head back, sending the longish, sandy-colored hair out of his face, to have it slide

back when he hunched again. The paper-
work said Cody Hansen. Even without
knowing there was no rap sheet, Greg could
tell he hadn't been in trouble before. This
could be the break they needed.

Greg breezed into the room as if he were
very busy, tossed a clipboard on the table,
and sat across from the suspect.

Cody stopped rocking, his eyes trailing
Greg's every movement.

"So, Mr. Hansen . . . Cody. Can I call you
Cody?"

The young man nodded.

"Let's get you out of those cuffs, shall we?
I'm sure they aren't very comfortable." He
lifted the key.

Cody held out his wrists. Once the cuffs
were off, Cody pushed the hair out of his
face, rubbed his wrists, and lowered his
hands back to his lap.

Greg took the voice recorder out of his
pocket and placed it on the table between
them.

Cody's gaze shifted to the device.

"First, the easy questions. Please tell me
your full name."

"Cody Andrew Hansen."

Greg flipped through some papers. "It appears they've read you your rights, and you

signed them. Did you understand what they mean?"

He nodded.

"Can you answer, please, for the recording?"

"Oh. Yes, I understand."

Greg asked him his address and where he was born, gauging his responses without seeming to pay much attention. "It looks as though you've never been arrested before, right?"

Cody relaxed his shoulders and gave another nod. "Yes. I mean, no . . . I have never been arrested."

Greg fixed his gaze on the young man, as if pinning him to the chair. "Attempted murder isn't a great way to start, Cody."

His eyes got huge, and he scooted back in his chair as though trying to put as much distance between them as possible. "Attempted murder?" His voice squeaked. "I didn't try to kill nobody."

"You were in the truck, though, weren't you?"

Cody looked like a rabbit faced by a coyote, unsure which way to run.

Greg toyed with his pen. "We know you were in the truck, Cody. People saw you. And I'm sure we'll find your fingerprints."

He squeezed his eyes shut and started

rocking again, but said nothing.

"So, why did you shoot Cameron Hayes?"

Cody froze. "I didn't! I didn't shoot nobody!"

"Well, somebody did, because Cameron's in the hospital with a gunshot wound."

"It wasn't me!"

"You know we can tell if you've fired a gun recently. There'll be residue on your hands."

Cody lifted his hands and held them out, palms up. "Go ahead and check."

"So were you driving?"

His hands faltered in the air for a second then fell to his lap along with his gaze.

Greg waited. He could almost see the thoughts whizzing around in the kid's head. He kept his voice even. Frightening him might shut him down. "Burglary is a whole lot different from murder, you know."

Cody's head jerked up. "I thought you said he was OK."

"He is right now, but if he dies, it's murder." Greg flipped through a few pages, holding the top ones in one hand. "How old are you again?"

"Eighteen."

Greg let the pages fall and studied the young man in front of him. "Oh, too bad. You're an adult, and the rest of your life in prison is a long time. What about Esther Campbell?"

Confusion scrunched Cody's face. "Who?"

"You know, the lady you guys killed a week or so ago when she walked in on your burglary."

Cody jarred the table as he jumped to his feet. "It wasn't us! We didn't take anything from her! We weren't even there!"

Greg remained seated, every muscle tensed, but he kept his voice calm. "OK, settle down and tell me about Cameron. What happened today?"

Cody's eyes pleaded with him. "You have to believe me, man. I didn't know he was going to do it."

Greg was silent.

Cody sat back down. "It's Bobby's truck, but Grady was driving. I was sitting in the backseat. We were watching Cam because he's been acting real strange. Grady was afraid he was gonna tell his girlfriend about us, so we were tailing him. It was a lark, you know?"

"Go on." Greg flipped the pen between his fingers as if he didn't care.

"Bobby was just playing, waving his gun around, but when we saw Cam with the girl, he went crazy. He started shooting out the window. Grady hit the gas cause Cam's his little brother, and he yanked hard on the wheel. We slammed into Cam's truck, and while Bobby was off balance, Grady flew out of there." Cody stared off to the side as if replaying the whole thing in his head. "We got a couple blocks away. Then Grady stopped the truck and started to beat on him, but Bobby pointed the gun at him and made him get out. Then he made me drive. We got pulled over after that."

Greg wrote a few notes, giving the kid time to settle. Then he glanced up again. "I need to ask you where you were the morning of Saturday, the third."

He didn't even stop to think. "I always work on Saturday, so I would have been at work."

"And where do you work?"

Cody leaned back in his chair. "I'm a cook at Flips."

Greg smiled. "Do you like it there?"

He stretched his legs. "I like it OK. The hours are kind of hard."

"What are your hours?"

"I start at five in the morning, and I get off at one thirty or so."

"You know the lady we were talking about, Esther Campbell?"

Cody brought his legs in under him and

tensed. "Yeah?"

"She was killed on the third. Do you know where Bobby and Grady were? Do you know if one of them killed her?"

He crossed his arms. "I don't know, man. I wasn't there."

"You do know they rob people, though." It wasn't a question.

"I don't know nothin' about that."

Greg asked him a few more questions but didn't get any helpful information. He finished up his notes, left Cody writing out a statement, and went to see how David was doing with Bobby.

David had his back to the glass, and it appeared he wasn't getting anywhere. Unlike Cody, this was probably not Bobby's first arrest. Greg hadn't seen his rap sheet, but Bobby sprawled in his seat, a bored look on his face.

The tense lines of David's body showed his frustration as he blasted him with questions, getting no response. After a few more tries, he stalked out of the room.

Greg joined him at his desk. "So, were you able to get anything?"

David sat in his chair and leaned back, looking up at him. "No, nothing. What about you?"

Greg swiveled to face David's desk and

explained what he'd gotten from Cody. "I believe the kid's telling the truth. I don't know if he was involved with the other robberies, but I don't think he was there when Esther was killed. It would have freaked him out, and I would have seen it on his face. He was scared enough with Cameron, even though he's still alive. Plus, he's not a very good liar."

"What about Bobby?"

"Cody says he wasn't there, and he doesn't know. He wouldn't make a guess. I want to see what the search team finds in their houses before I question him any further, but my gut says he's been hanging with them for a lark. He might be guilty of burglary, but not murder."

David skimmed Cody's file. "Did you notice the build on Bobby?" he asked without looking up.

"Yeah, he could be the one who pushed Allie. And he fits the description Cameron gave Maggie of the guy he saw crossing her yard."

David finished reading Greg's notes and slid the file back. "If it was Bobby, wouldn't Cameron have recognized him?"

"Yeah, he would. If he was telling Maggie the truth."

16

The morning sun blinded Maggie when she twitched the curtain aside to peer out her living room window. Relief washed over her — Officer Daniels was gone, and no one had taken his place. Last night Greg said they had some promising leads. He must feel pretty confident if he removed her guard. She glanced up the stairs. Allie was still in bed. She wouldn't feel like going to church. It didn't seem possible it had been over a week already. The empty space in the pew where Aunt Esther sat would haunt her, and she had told Greg not to pick her up. Instead, she'd ask Dad some questions. If he was her dad, that is.

Danny answered the door, his scrunched forehead showing his concern over her impromptu visit. "Your call was somewhat cryptic." He gave her a hug. "Come in and tell me what this is about."

She poured a cup of coffee from the half-full pot and sat with him at the kitchen table, tucking one foot underneath her. "I've been reading Esther's diaries."

He raised his eyebrows. "I thought they were stolen."

"Not all of them. Why didn't you tell me you're not my real dad?"

His head snapped back, and his eyes grew wide. "What? Where did you get that idea?"

"It's OK. You can tell me. I need to know. Are you my father?" An old children's book where the baby bird was looking for its mother flashed to mind. She felt like a baby bird now, lost and confused.

"Of course, I'm your dad. What did you read?"

"I read about a test. Was it a paternity test? Did you find out when I was born that you're not my real father?"

Danny hesitated, wrapping his hands around his cup. "Is there any way you'll leave this alone?"

"No, I need to know."

"Have you asked your mother?"

"No!" She hadn't meant to shout the word. She lowered her voice. "I'm asking you. Why don't you want to answer me? I guess you don't have to. I already know. You're not my real dad."

He hesitated.

217

Would he tell her the truth?

"I–I'm your dad," he stammered, "but I'm not your biological father."

Even though she was expecting to hear it, the answer stabbed through her like a knife twisting in her gut. "What do you mean?"

"It means I love you."

Maggie stared into the blackness inside her cup. "I should have known. When you wouldn't let me live with you, I should have known." Tears blurred her eyes.

"How could you know?" His words came faster now, as if the dam burst, and he couldn't stop them. "I didn't let you live with me because I'm not strong enough. I've felt guilty every day since. I didn't try harder. Your mother said she'd prevent me from seeing you." He took a breath. "Even though I couldn't see you very much, I was still able to find out how you were doing through Esther. If Darla cut me out of your life, I feared she'd cut Esther out, too, and then I'd never know how you were."

His fingers tightened and twisted on his cup. She could well imagine her mother using her to get whatever she wanted from him. "But this isn't about your mother," he continued. "It's about me." He sipped his coffee. "I should have fought for you. I knew you weren't happy, but I had no legal rights." He lifted a sad gaze to her face. "I was afraid of losing you, so I backed off. When I could see she was ruining you with her boyfriends, I forced her to let you live with Esther. I threatened to have her declared unfit."

It didn't seem enough of a threat. She'd come this far. She wanted the whole unvarnished truth. If her mother didn't want her, why wouldn't she let her go? "What else did it take?" she asked. "It's not like she cared." The whisper scraped her throat.

Danny — she supposed she should think of him as Danny now — reached out and covered her hand with his. "Yes, she did," he said softly. "She didn't want to lose you."

More like she didn't want to give up control. "OK, but what else did it take?"

He drew his hand back and continued to play with his cup. "I threatened to tell her current boyfriend about all the affairs she'd had during our marriage. She wanted to marry him. She had this vision of a happy family, but she had no idea how to do it. If I'd legally challenged her, everything would come out, and it might have been harder for her to get you back."

"Isn't unfit a hard thing to prove? How would you have done it?"

He let go of the cup, sat back, and

219

laughed. "I didn't have a clue. But I was so angry, she believed I'd do anything to get you away from her, and she was right." Red rimmed his eyes when he gazed at her. "I've wanted to apologize for so long, but I didn't know how without making you hate me more than you already do." The words gushed out. "I'm sorry I didn't fight for you when you were little. I should have made her give you up. I knew she wasn't the right mother for you. But I wasn't strong enough, and she knew it. I failed you, and I'm sorry." His tear splashed on the tabletop. "I hope you can forgive me."

17

Maggie hurried out to her car. Listening to her bitterness all this time and not telling her the truth must have been hard for Danny. Even though discovering they weren't related hurt, knowing he would have taken her if he could felt better. And he did the next best thing by forcing her mother to let her live with his sister. Maggie wondered again about the diaries. Had her mother stolen them to keep her from finding out? It would explain her response. Maggie snickered. Mom's reputation might suffer.

She called Allie, and upon hearing she planned to stay on the couch watching movies, Maggie turned toward Aunt Esther's. Some time alone might help her figure out her feelings. She climbed the stairs to her old room and sorted into piles what to keep, what to give to the thrift store, and what to throw away. The mindless activity allowed her thoughts to drift. She had to deal with her feelings about Greg. She couldn't keep calling whenever something went wrong in her life — not if she intended to break up with him. And she was pretty sure she wanted to break up.

She retrieved some boxes from the basement, assembled one, and taped the bottom. Was what Robin said true? Did she push all men away? Greg was a good guy. No doubt about it. He would make a terrific husband. But what if she wasn't cut out for marriage? What made her think she could make it work with the odds so stacked against her?

Her mother's four previous marriages hadn't worked, and the current one was on the rocks. Husband number five hadn't even showed up for the funeral.

Maggie finished loading the box, taped it up, and wrote *bedroom* on the top.

Mom never seemed to understand why her relationships didn't work. The new boyfriend was going to solve all her problems — sometimes before she got rid of the old one. Another guy willing to rescue her. She was never alone long. What would happen when the line of men ran out?

Maggie shook her head. The pressure to have a companion was too much trouble. She didn't want to need anyone so much.

She'd better get some distance from Greg before it was too late.

Having made her decision to break up, she worked through the morning, moving from her room to the spare room, and then into Aunt Esther's. This one proved the hardest. Everything looked as if she would pop in at any moment. Wait . . . not Aunt Esther . . . just Esther. She had to remember it. She wiped a tear from her cheek and rubbed the soreness out of her lower back. Her watch said three o'clock. No wonder she was hungry. After a quick call to Allie, Maggie found a can of tuna and some crackers in the pantry.

Crunching on the saltines, she checked her cell phone. Two missed calls — both from Greg — but he'd left a message on the second one. She'd known it was him the last time her phone rang. But she didn't pick up, because she didn't know what to say. She still didn't. Hiding from him wouldn't help, so she plucked up her courage and dialed his number.

"Maggie, I'm glad you called," he said. "I think we have your aunt's killer."

Her stomach lurched when he said 'your aunt,' but she didn't correct him. "Was it Cameron?" She almost hoped he would say no because despite the screaming phone call, she didn't want to believe he was guilty.

"We don't have that nailed down yet, but so far there's no evidence he was there. We're not sure about his brother."

She replayed the scene in her mind when Cameron threw himself in front of her sister. "It's just, well, Cameron doesn't seem like the type to kill someone . . . you know, with a knife . . . so cold blooded."

"I know what you mean. We've talked to him in the hospital, but he won't give up Grady. I think they were all part of a burglary ring. They stole cash, electronics, passports, jewelry, and expensive art. Which means at least one of them is more sophisticated than I am, since I don't know anything about art." He laughed, and the sound made her smile.

"So was it the guy you told me about? The one who shot at Allie?"

"Yeah. His name is Robert Maken. We've searched his house and found stolen items from other burglaries. We believe he and Grady tried to get Allie to let them in, and when she wouldn't, they talked Esther into it, maybe telling her they were Allie's friends. She may have caught him trying to pocket something, and he killed her. He has a violent streak for sure."

"Did he push Allie?"

"He's the right build, tall and thin. We may have you come to the station and get your impressions. The ski mask wasn't recovered, but he could have thrown it away."

"So is Allie safe now?"

"According to this kid — Cody — Cameron was the target of the shooting, not Allie. Bobby's denying everything, and if what Cody says is true, then I doubt he was trying to kill Cameron, just scare him. He might be able to talk his way out of attempted murder, but the murder charge rattled him. Maybe if he didn't kill Esther, he'll rat out the one who did. It's quite an operation."

They talked more, but she didn't tell him about visiting her fath . . . Danny. Instead, she brought up what she had been trying to say for the whole conversation. "I'm not sure I'm up to a relationship," she blurted.

"With Allie? Does she want you to take up where your aunt left off?"

"No, sorry. I meant marriage. I can't go through with it."

Greg waited for her to explain, and when she didn't, the silence stretched into awkward.

"Is it the house thing? I didn't mean anything by it."

Maggie put her hand up to smooth her hair back. Her head was beginning to ache. "I know. I'm just not cut out for marriage. It hasn't worked out so well for my family."

He hesitated again. "Do you want to break up?" His voice was soft.

"Yeah. I guess I need some time."

"OK." Another pause. "I know you don't care what I think right now, but you'd be great at marriage." He hurried on before she could protest. "Don't look at your mom's and dad's mistakes. You're a completely different person. Look at your aunt. She and Ron were happy."

He was right. Aunt Esther's and Ron's relationship was good. But he didn't know she wasn't related to them. And she wasn't in the mood to tell him. Aloud she said, "True, but she was an amazing person."

"So are you," he said. He was giving her an opportunity to speak, but she didn't. "I'll respect your wishes and give you some time. Call me if you want to talk, OK?" Strain tightened his voice. "Otherwise, I'll leave you alone."

She agreed.

"I love you," he whispered and hung up.

She staggered upstairs, crawled into Esther's bed, and cried. The linens still smelled like her, which made Maggie cry all the harder. What if it was her fault Cameron got shot? It sounded as if they shot him because they saw him talking to Allie. And they were able to get to him because she'd kicked them out of the truck. Right into danger. She shouldn't have let him talk to Allie at all. Face it. She wasn't good at relationships. Not with Greg, not with Allie, not with anyone.

Maggie stopped by the store on the way home, and picked up some ice cream. Didn't all teenage girls love ice cream? Besides, it was supposed to be comfort food for breakups. Turtle pecan had worked for her before. Stepping out of her car, she pushed down the voice telling her this time was different.

Allie loved having ice cream for dessert.

As Maggie cleaned up the dishes, alone again, her landline rang. She hurried to her office to answer.

"Maggie, is that you?"

The voice seemed familiar. "Yes, who is this, please?"

"It's Ginger, Esther's friend. I called a couple days ago?" Her voice sounded shaky.

"Yes, of course. Are you OK?"

She cleared her throat. "I'm sorry to bother you, but I'm not OK. I'm scared, and I didn't know who to call."

"What's the matter?" Maggie frowned and dropped into her office chair. "Why are you scared?"

"I think someone's after me. First Esther, then Carla, and now me."

"Carla? Is this about the accident?"

"Maybe. If it was an accident. Today someone tried to run me off the road. They had a big car, you know, like one of those truck-cars?"

"You mean an SUV?"

"Yes. And he came up next to me and kept edging over until I nearly ran over the edge. I was at the grocery. You know the intersection by the river? There's quite a drop-off there. I might have been killed!"

She tried to picture the intersection, but she wasn't familiar with Golden. "What happened then?"

"Another group of cars came along, and he sped off. If it weren't for them, I'd be dead. And I keep hearing someone outside my house. He's out there. I know it."

Maggie's heartbeat skipped. "Have you called the police?"

"No, they won't believe me. Every time I've called in the past, they don't do anything."

"Ah." Understanding dawned. She probably called every time she heard a noise, and the police had her number memorized. But she was upset, and after losing two friends, it would be natural for her to be afraid.

"Give me the number of your local police station, and I'll call. We'll see if we can get someone to patrol the area until I can get there. Keep your doors and windows locked, and I'll come and get you. You can stay with me for a few days until we sort this out. How does that sound?"

"It sounds great. Your aunt was right about you. You are special."

Maggie hung up the phone and called the number Ginger gave her. After considerable explanation, and Maggie threatening to go to the news station if anything should happen, the officer promised a few drive-bys. Maggie promised in return to have her stop in to file a report. After calling Ginger to give her the news, she explained to Allie and left the house.

Golden was west of Denver, but still an hour and a half drive from Pinon Creek. She'd be lucky if she got back by eleven. Her plans for an early night were not happening.

Even with a huge head start, and as scared as she was, Ginger wasn't ready. Maggie chuckled, remembering the entry in Esther's diary. When she was packed, Maggie helped load her suitcases in the back.

How long was she planning to stay, anyway? Judging by the number of bags, she must plan to move in. Maggie stopped by the station on her way out of town for Ginger to fill out a statement, and then set off for home.

Her watch read one o'clock when she drove into her garage, and by the time she settled Ginger in the last of her guest rooms, it was after three. She fell into bed and tried to sleep, but her mind wouldn't rest. Was Ginger right? Had someone tried to kill her? Maggie rolled over again.

Obviously, the woman scared easily, and with the trauma of losing two of her friends, her imagination was taking over. After a few days, she'd be ready to go home, and maybe Greg could talk the police in her area into doing some more drive-bys. But what if she wasn't imagining it? Two old ladies were dead, after all, but they were unrelated incidents. Weren't they?

Grady watched from his hiding place in the house down the street. He often laughed at how easy hiding from the police was. At least, if you were smart. Cameron had wanted to watch his girlfriend, and they couldn't go home anyway, so this was the best solution. He snickered at the poor realtor who thought he was interested in buying this place. Grady had looked so busy on his phone, the guy never knew he was filming him. Afterward, it took a couple tries, but Grady got the code. Then it was so easy. Just take the key from the lockbox and unlock the door.

It'd worked out fine until Bobby went crazy and started shooting at Cam. What did he think Grady was going to do, just sit there and let him shoot his little brother? Now Bobby was in jail, and Cam was in the hospital. He wasn't even sure if he was all right. Grady had called from a payphone but was put through to a police officer. So Cam was being guarded. Did that mean they were protecting him or were they going to arrest him? Surely, they didn't have any evidence.

Yanking his sleeping bag out of the closet, he prepared for bed. Not having enough light was a hassle, but it was nice and dry, and better than going home and getting caught. A light went on at Maggie's. Good grief, it was one o'clock in the morning. He picked up the binoculars.

Maggie and an old lady were hauling a ton of bags into the house. He didn't know why he was watching anymore, except he didn't have anything else to do. Cam's girl was pretty and all, but the sister, Maggie, was gorgeous. He wouldn't mind watching her all the time.

He set down the binoculars and lay on top of his sleeping bag. It was way too hot to climb in. After Cam got out of the hospital, they'd ditch this town. With Bobby in jail, it wasn't safe to stay. Cam would have to give up Allie. Grady would insist on it.

19

Ginger was already awake when Maggie got up the next morning, and a wonderful smell greeted her at the top of the stairs. Bacon. She entered the kitchen and smiled at Ginger, who wore an apron and handled a spatula, flipping pancakes on the griddle, while bacon fried in the skillet. The mouth-watering aroma even brought Allie out of her room.

"Pull up a chair, hon. It's all ready. I need to earn my keep, you know."

"You don't have to do any such thing," Maggie laughed. "But I'll enjoy your cooking just the same."

She and Allie sat down to a delicious breakfast, and when she left, Allie was doing the dishes. Maggie wasn't quite sure how it happened, but Allie was suddenly at the sink, and Maggie was ushered out the door to her first appointment. Ginger must have some magic with teens Maggie didn't know about.

Her day went well, if very fast, and she returned to the smell of dinner cooking. Wonder of wonders, Allie was setting the table. How did Ginger do it? Maggie helped with the napkins, and they sat down to eat. "This smells heavenly." Maggie inhaled the steamy scent of meat and potatoes. "I could get used to this."

"Well, darling, don't get too used to it." Ginger spooned some beef stew into a bowl and passed it over. "I've been thinking about it, and I should go home. I'm sure I was imagining things. It was a bad driver who nearly ran me off the road."

Maggie stabbed a potato with her fork. "What changed your mind?"

"Nothing really, but the more I think about it, the less sense it makes. I got spooked about Carla, and so when some crazy driver scared me, I let my imagination get carried away. Allie told me they have the guy who killed Esther, so Carla's death must have been an accident. Either way, hiding out here isn't doing me any good. I called the nice policeman we saw before, and he said he would have someone drive by my house several times for a few nights to make sure I'm OK. I won't go anywhere alone for a while just to be certain."

"Are you sure?" Maggie asked.

"Yes. There's no reason for someone to kill a couple of old ladies like us. No one would have wanted to hurt Esther either; she was just in the wrong place at the wrong time."

I wish I could believe that. "Maybe you should wait a bit longer. You know you can stay as long as you like."

Ginger patted her hand. "I know, and I thank you, but I'll feel better at home."

Maggie nodded. She'd ask Greg to phone the Golden policeman and make sure they were checking on her. Oh, but wait, she couldn't. He was respecting her request for space, and it wouldn't be fair if she bugged him every time she needed something but wouldn't let him call her. She'd get Mark to do it instead.

Having settled it in her mind, she finished dinner, and the three of them did the dishes. Then they sat in front of the TV.

The scenes passed in front of Maggie's eyes, but she didn't take them in. Her thoughts were on Greg. How long would it be before she could eat dinner alone without missing him? She used to do it all the time before, and she was never lonely. Well, maybe sometimes, but not like this. It had only been a day, for heaven's sake. Sometimes she'd gone a week without seeing him if they were both busy, and she'd never had a problem with it. But this felt different. This was an ache. The movie ended, but Maggie couldn't have said what it was about. She gave up and went upstairs early with Ginger, leaving Allie clicking through the stations.

As she readied for bed, her eyes drifted to the diaries. Wonder what Aunt . . . Esther thought about her own marriage. Was she nervous? Did she know all along that Ron was the one? She slipped under the covers and opened the year of Esther's wedding, flipping through the pages, searching for answers. She found what she was looking for.

Ron proposed last week, and I told him I would have to consider it. I hate making him wait for an answer to such an important question, but I hope he knows it's no reflection of my love for him, but rather of my careful nature. I do love him, but how will it affect Maggie? I know she loves Ron, but will she feel replaced if I bring him into our household? After the many men Darla brought home, Maggie needs stability more than anything. I can't disrupt her now.

Maggie lowered the book and closed her eyes. If it was possible to love Aunt Esther more, she did now. Her heart ached for the woman who was willing to put Maggie's happiness above her own. She flipped back to check the date. It was several months before her wedding. Something must have happened since she married him when Maggie was seventeen and they all lived together for a year before Maggie went to college. What changed her mind? She flipped a few pages and began to read again.

Ron is insistent, and Maggie with him. The truth is . . . I'm afraid. I've lived alone, with the exception of dear Maggie, for the better part of twenty-seven years. Ron deserves better. I'm not sure a woman of forty-five can adapt to marriage the way a younger woman would. I feel the gate closing, and I'm fenced in. I must decline his invitation. I know it will hurt him, but I'm not ready.

She read on. Aunt Esther did, indeed, tell Ron she couldn't marry him. Insecurities about her decision filled the next pages. A sentence caught her eye.

"I haven't seen Ron in three months. I keep trying to get over it, but I can't. I'm miserable without him."

She closed the book, embarrassed to read the intimate details of Aunt Esther's emotions. The experience opened a new world for her. The Aunt Esther she knew was strong and sure and kind. As a child, the stability Aunt Esther provided in her volatile, sometimes shaky, world comforted her. Aunt Esther was wise not to share those feelings then, but as Maggie drifted off to sleep, she let the knowledge they weren't that different comfort her. And no matter what, she was Maggie's Aunt Esther.

Grady watched the last light go out at Maggie's house before pulling out his sleeping bag. *Good night, beautiful.*

He started to drift off when the motion detector light flashed on in Maggie's backyard. A dark figure slipped through the gate, bent to pick something off the ground, and threw it. The light went out. What was up with that? He sat up and reached for the binoculars. What was this guy up to? He carried something at his side, almost as if he wanted to hide it. Grady focused on his hands and zoomed in. A gas can. He was going to light up Maggie's house! What could he do? If he called the police, he'd get caught for sure. But Cam wouldn't forgive him if something happened to Allie. Could he stop him? He zoomed back out until the guy was in full focus. He was big, that's for sure, and built pretty solid.

Frozen, Grady watched him creep to the house, splashing gasoline over everything. A dog started barking. The man emptied the can, lit a match, and ran. The fire caught fast and spread to the siding. He slithered away, fading into the darkness.

20

Something on the outside of Maggie's consciousness irritated her. What was it? As her dream slipped away, she woke to Honey alternately barking and tugging at her pajamas. "Honey, what's the matter with you? It's still the middle of the night. Are you so desperate to go out, you're jerking me out of bed?"

What smelled . . . was it smoke? She jumped out of bed and ran to the hallway. Smoke drifted up from the kitchen. "Ginger! Allie!" she yelled. "Wake up. There's a fire!"

Her heart pounded as she raced back to her room, grabbed the robe off the back of the door, and swept her phone off the charger on her nightstand. She struggled into her robe as she dialed 9-1-1, trying to hurry into Allie's room at the same time.

Allie jolted awake, and Maggie sprinted to the next room.

Ginger was fast asleep.

"Ginger! Wake up!" No answer.

The smoke reached the detector in the kitchen.

Maggie shouted her address into the phone in order to be heard over the alarms shrieking throughout the house.

Allie shook Ginger's shoulder, but received no response. Could she be suffering from smoke inhalation already? It wasn't smoky in here yet.

Maggie dumped the phone into her pocket and helped Allie shake harder, pulling the listless arm toward her. Panic built in her stomach like a volcano. How on earth was she going to get the heavy woman downstairs?

Allie switched to the other side of Ginger's bed, pushing her hard toward Maggie.

Ginger rolled over. If they kept it up, she would fall out of bed. At least, she might wake up. Before they got that far, she started to stir.

Maggie tugged again. "Wake up, Ginger. There's a fire!"

"A fire?" Ginger mumbled. "No, it's just breakfast. I'll have it ready in a minute." She opened her eyes and dropped her feet to the floor.

Allie shuffled to Maggie's side of the bed and hauled on her other arm. "Hurry. We have to go now!"

Ginger's eyes focused on Maggie's face. "What's the hurry?" She sniffed the smoke, fast becoming noticeable, and her sleepy eyes widened. "Maggie, the house is on fire!"

Maggie and Allie yanked on her arms and jerked her to her feet.

"Yes, we have to hurry!" Maggie tried to steady her.

Ginger, wide awake now, lurched forward.

Maggie scooped up her little dog, and all of them made their way to the stairs. Two steps down, Maggie stopped.

A line of flames snaked across the wood floor which separated them from the front door, and licked up the French doors in the kitchen.

Ginger bumped into her back.

"It's burning down there. We have to find another way." Maggie reversed direction. "A window. We can go out my bedroom window and climb out onto the porch roof." Pushing Ginger back to her bedroom, she wondered if she could get her through the narrow opening. She'd have to try. How she would get her off the roof, however, was another matter. The firemen should be here by then. They could figure it out. She pushed her blanket chest underneath the window. Allie climbed on top of it and then crawled out, her cast making her exit less than graceful. She scrambled to her feet.

Maggie handed Honey out to her.

"OK, Ginger, you're next. I'll help you up." She reached for her hand.

Ginger swayed back, her eyes huge with terror. "I can't."

"Yes, you can. It's perfectly safe." Maggie maneuvered behind her and started pushing, but Ginger wouldn't budge.

"Here, I'll go first." She climbed on the chest and out the window. Bracing both feet, she leaned her body back through the opening and held both hands out.

Ginger started forward and clambered on the chest, grabbing one of Maggie's outstretched hands. Her other hand shook as she put it on the windowsill. Sweat beaded her forehead. She froze. "No, I can't do this. I'm afraid of heights. I can't climb out there." She wrenched her hand out of Maggie's grasp and stepped down.

Maggie stood there, her arms stretched out, not believing her ears.

Allie leaned forward. "You have to, Ginger. The fire is coming," she said. "Just don't look down. You'll be all right. Then a cute fireman can save us. Sounds good, doesn't it?"

It sounded good to Maggie, but Ginger backed farther into the room, her body shaking violently. "I can't. You go and get help. I'll stay here."

Horror coursed through Maggie as the large woman turned away from the window and lumbered toward the guest room. "Ginger, no! It's too smoky. You won't be able to breathe!"

Ginger kept going. The smoke was stronger now, and she started coughing.

Ignoring Allie's cries, Maggie took a few breaths of precious air and climbed into the burning house.

21

Unable to sleep, Greg stared into the darkness. What could he do to convince Maggie they were right for each other? He had no doubts God had put them together. But if she didn't agree, what could he do? Her parents had made such a mess of things. First, her father left when she was young, and then he didn't stay involved. Maybe if he'd helped raise her, it would have been better. Truth be told, Greg couldn't have lived with Maggie's mother either. And speaking of Darla, he wasn't sure how he could be civil to her if she kept insulting Maggie.

A low growl caused him to glance at up Snowflake, who stared out the window flicking her tail. "What's up with you, Stinky?" Another rumble came from her throat. He climbed out of bed to see what had her so riveted.

A glow rose to the east several blocks

away. A fire? It looked as if it was near Maggie's place. He dragged his cell phone off the charger and dialed 9-1-1, giving them an approximate location, still staring out the window trying to pinpoint it. It probably wasn't as close to her house as it appeared. His breath caught in his throat. But what if it was, and she was asleep? He hung up and dialed her number. No answer.

He threw his clothes on and jumped into his truck, dialing her number again. Down at street level, he couldn't see the red glow anymore, and it was too dark to see smoke, so he headed for her house and dialed again.

22

Smoke curled through the hallway from Maggie's bedroom now, and as she climbed back inside, she wondered what on earth she was doing. How would she get Ginger and herself back out?

Ginger huddled on the floor by the bed, shaking and crying.

"Come on. We have to leave. We can't stay here," Maggie said, peering down the hall.

"Stay on the floor. They always say to stay on the floor," Ginger whimpered.

"Well, we need to go now. The firemen will be here soon, and we need to meet them outside."

Ginger stopped shaking. "OK." She hauled herself to her feet.

Maggie grabbed a blanket off the bed and ran to the bathroom. Ginger waited in the doorway as she threw it into the tub and turned on the shower. She yanked it back out, not as soaked as she would have liked, but no time to do more. She threw it around herself and Ginger, and they headed for the stairs.

Her kitchen curtains were ablaze now, the flames spreading farther into the living room. She veered toward her office and headed to the side window, the one without a planter box on the outside. The wall wasn't burning, but heat radiated from it. Ginger would go through this one, either voluntarily or she would get shoved out.

Both women were coughing now, and Maggie used the blanket edges to cover as much of her nose and mouth as possible. They reached the windows, and lights flashed on a yellow truck outside with firemen swarming toward the door.

She touched the window latch. But it scorched her hand, so she put the blanket around it and tried again. It wouldn't budge with the blanket, so she put her hand on it again and lifted with all her strength.

It flipped up, and she cranked the window open as wide as it would go. She called to the firemen, and the swarm flowed in her direction. Pushing Ginger forward, strong hands reached to pull her out.

Then everything went black.

23

Greg threw the phone across the seat in frustration and sped to Maggie's, both hands gripping the wheel. If the fire wasn't at her house, it was close. He swung onto her street, and his heart jumped into his throat as he approached the long yellow truck in front of her house. If possible, his heart pounded even harder when an ambulance buzzed past him, pulling away from the curb. *They always send one. Don't panic. If the lights aren't on, there's no one inside.* He sighed in relief as the dark ambulance passed him. Then, before it reached the corner, the strobes flashed on.

He frantically spun the wheel. Flipping on his lights, he pushed the accelerator to the floor, and his truck leaped forward. Traffic was nonexistent as he raced through town. He veered into the hospital emergency entrance and parked while ER personnel unloaded two stretchers. He wasn't close enough to see who they were, but then an EMT helped Allie down from the ambulance. She seemed OK, although she was breathing from a portable oxygen tank.

They took all three women inside, and Greg called Mark. Obviously, Bobby wasn't their killer. Whoever it was wasn't stopping, and Allie would need protection. Mark arrived with Robin, and Greg hung out with them in the waiting room until the doctor exited with Allie.

She looked unsure where she should go until Robin spoke up.

"Hi, Allie. Are you OK?"

She gave her a shy smile and nodded.

The doctor glanced down at her. "Is this your family?"

"No," she said. "I came in with my sister, so she must still be here somewhere."

Robin spoke up. "Speaking of Allie's sister, doctor, can you tell us how Maggie Schreiber and Ginger Phillips are doing?"

"We'll keep both of them a day or two. We're checking Ms. Schreiber for damage to her airway or lungs, but she looks pretty good. Ms. Phillips is older, so we're watching her heart as well as her lungs. But I think she'll be fine. You were all very lucky."

Robin put her arm around Allie. "Allie, we'd like to take you home with us until

Maggie gets out. Is that OK with you?"

After getting another nod, the doctor left. Allie was still in her pajamas and robe, and she reeked of smoke. Robin returned to her chair, and Greg noticed the paper sacks she had sitting there.

"We have some clothes for you to put on until we can take you shopping," she said as she picked up one of the sacks. "I don't know if these will fit, but hopefully, they won't be too big. I borrowed them from my niece. She gave me a couple different sizes, and since I wasn't sure which to bring, I brought both. Do you want to try them on?"

Robin took Allie and the clothes to the restroom to change.

Greg arched a brow at Mark. "How did Robin know, and when did you guys have the time to do this?"

Mark smiled. "That's my Robin for you, always three steps ahead. She thought about it when we were waiting and called Melissa. She brought them over while you were talking to the doctor."

Greg took the time to speak with the doctor and, knowing Maggie would be worried, called around to find Maggie's dog. After confirming one of the policemen had taken the dog to the station, Greg arranged to have Honey taken to his penthouse.

After a long while, Allie returned, cleaned up and dressed. Robin was right — one of the sizes fit her pretty well.

Allie seemed awed by Maggie's heroism, telling everyone who'd listen about her going back into the house to save Ginger. Then she smiled and laughed with Robin about the cute fireman who carried her down the ladder. She must be feeling OK, if she was ready to flirt again.

"We're taking Allie home with us to let her rest," Robin said. "Please call the minute you talk to Maggie. And tell her I'll call later, will you?"

He agreed and they left. The hospital staff allowed him to wait with Maggie in ICU. Her bed was elevated, and an oxygen mask covered her face. Her eyes were closed, so he found a chair, placed it as quietly as he could next to her bed, and lowered himself into it. He sat back and listened to the rhythm of her breathing. Her right hand was wrapped, and it and the left lay outside the blankets. He fought the impulse to tuck them underneath, afraid he would wake her, or worse, hurt her.

He waited next to the bed until she stirred and opened her eyes. At first, she focused on the fluorescent lights. Not wanting to scare her, he kept quiet. She must have felt the mask covering her face, because she reached up to yank it off. Her bandaged hand wouldn't grab the offending article, and she pawed at it, trying to sit up. Before he was able to stop her, it dislodged from her face, but her fingers tangled in the strap. She started to panic and shake her hand, but she froze when the pain must have hit.

"Wait, honey. You'll hurt yourself." Greg maneuvered the mask off her face and disentangled her hand from the strap. "Don't get up. They're moving you to a room in a minute."

She lay back down and smiled at him, the one that made his face smile back before his brain had a choice. Her eyes traveled to the oxygen mask in his hand, and she looked at her hands, discovering the bandages. She frowned in confusion. "What happened?" she croaked. Her whole body jerked as she remembered, and she tried to throw her legs over the side of the bed. "Allie and Honey are on the roof! I have to get them!" Her hoarse voice whispered into the room, and her bandaged hand went to her throat.

"They're all right." He kept his voice as calm as he could. "Allie's in seventh heaven because a cute fireman — her words, not mine — carried her down the ladder."

She stilled, and he continued, "They brought her here and checked her out, and she's fine. She's going to stay with Robin and Mark for a few days. A friend of mine carried Honey down and took her to my place. She's terrorizing Snowball as we speak. Ginger is staying here overnight, but they only kept her because of her age."

Maggie eased back to her half-sitting position. She melted into the pillow and cleared her throat. "Why do you never call Snowball Stinky except when you're home?" This time her voice was stronger.

"I don't know. I guess it's not as much fun if she isn't around to get mad."

Maggie grinned. "She does seem to know what you're saying. Every time you say it, she swishes her tail and turns her back on you."

"I know. It's a riot." He sat with her, not knowing what to do or say. After all, she'd said she wanted space. He should go, but she wasn't pushing him away, and he couldn't stand the thought of leaving her.

The doctor breezed in and smiled down at her. "Hey, hero, how are you feeling?"

"My head and hand hurt, and my throat is kind of sore," she said. "Otherwise, I'm OK."

"Your headache and sore throat are from

the chemicals in the smoke. I understand you put a blanket over your heads, and both of you breathed through it." He sat in the chair on the other side of the bed. "Good thinking. Your lungs don't seem to have sustained serious damage, but I want to keep you overnight. We're moving you to a room, and you'll be on oxygen for a little while today. But we can give you the nasal prongs since you seem to be doing pretty well without the mask."

"What about her hand, doctor?" Greg asked.

"You have some minor burns. We've wrapped it in a nonstick bandage to keep you more comfortable, but you probably won't have to have it on for very long."

After he left, Greg waited with Maggie until a nurse pushed a wheelchair up to the bed. "Hi, Maggie," he said. "I'm Ken. It's time to move you to a room. He glanced at Greg. "Um . . ."

Greg held out his hand. "Greg Williams."

"Well, Mr. Williams, you can come along if you'd like."

They moved into the elevator and up to a room on the third floor. Ken wheeled her past an empty bed, to the one next to the window.

Greg stepped out of the room so Maggie

could get into her bed without worrying about her hospital gown gaping.

"You can come back in now." Maggie was in the bed with the covers up under her arms.

Ken introduced them to a nurse named Rita, who helped her with the oxygen, wrote on her chart, and left them alone.

Maggie's eyes were beginning to droop.

"What did he mean by hero?"

"You don't remember?"

"Remember what?"

"You were safe outside on the roof, but you went back into a burning house to save Ginger. Allie's telling everyone about it. Trust me, that's not normal. It's heroic."

She squirmed. "I'm not heroic. Ginger was supposed to be safe with me, but she wasn't. No one is safe with me."

"You're not to blame. Do you think it was deliberately set?"

"Honey was barking at something outside, and I told her to be quiet." Maggie picked at her blanket. "She's the real hero. She kept barking and pulling at me until I woke up. I shudder to imagine what would've happened if she hadn't. The smoke alarm went off, but she gave us a head start."

"I'll give her some extra treats when I get home."

She shoved the pillow under her neck and spoke softly as if she were already dreaming. "This is so confusing. First, Allie gets hurt, then Cameron, and now Ginger. What's going on?" She reached out for him with her good hand. "You have to promise me you'll protect them. These people don't care who they hurt." She drifted off to sleep.

Greg left the hospital as the sun peeked over the horizon. Having had very little sleep and then sitting inactive for the last few hours, his body wanted to go home and crash. But there was no time. First, he had to know what happened. He drove to Maggie's house. The fire investigator was still on site, the brightness of his lights competing for supremacy with the rising sun.

"Alan, what can you tell me?"

"It was set in this area by the kitchen. My guess is he wanted to stay in the back, to avoid detection. Does the owner have a dog?"

"Yes, she said Honey was barking, and she told her to be quiet."

"If the dog was barking, he may have been in a hurry to finish. He probably assumed the flames would spread, so he didn't put any accelerant on the side."

"What kind of accelerant was used? It smells like gas."

"You're right. I'll have it tested, but I believe it was simple gasoline. He threw it everywhere. He's lucky he didn't burn himself up in the process."

"So this person wasn't an experienced arsonist?"

"I think it was a first timer, yes. Number one, if it was gasoline, it's pretty volatile. Like I said, it's a wonder he got out without setting himself on fire. I assume you checked the hospital to see if anyone came in with burns other than your victims?"

"I was just there, and so far no one has come in. They'll know to call us if someone does."

24

Mmm, it smelled like roast beef for lunch. Maggie's first thoughts had been about Greg. Had it been a dream? What made her think about him before she was fully awake? The memory of the last few days closed around her. The feeling was not of warmth, but of suffocation.

Her house had been violated, and maybe destroyed. Greg assured her it could be fixed, but would it ever feel the same? Now both of her sanctuaries were ruined. The ache in her spirit since Aunt Esther's death intensified.

She wiggled the fingers of her left hand. The ring, when she remembered it, weighed heavy on her hand — foreign almost. But now her finger felt naked. Was the additional anguish due to her house, or was there more? She shook her head and realized she shouldn't have. Pain shot through her temple, knocked around inside her head like a pinball, and settled somewhere at the base of her skull. Easing her head down on the pillow, she closed her eyes and waited for it to stop thumping.

Soft footsteps caused her to open her eyes. Lucinda stood in the doorway with a bouquet of daisies.

Maggie almost didn't recognize her without the uniform. "Don't go," Maggie said. "I'm awake." She pushed herself up on one elbow, trying to get her pillow in the right place. Not so easy with one hand out of service.

"Let me help you, Miss Maggie." Lucinda set the flowers on her side table and found the button to raise the bed. When it was at a comfortable height, she fixed the pillows.

"You don't have to call me Miss Maggie, just call me Maggie." Before Lucinda could object, she went on, "I'm so glad you came to see me. I need a smiling face like yours to help me feel better."

Her smile grew brighter. "Miss . . . I mean Maggie . . . I just wanted to say, you were right."

She wasn't sure what the young girl was talking about, and concentrating on it made her pounding head hurt even more. "I was right? What was I right about?"

"There was something I was afraid to tell

you the other day when you were at Mrs. Tate's house." Various emotions crossed Lucinda's face.

Maggie shifted. "Sit down and tell me everything. I promise I won't do anything you don't want me to."

Lucinda sat in the chair by her bed and straightened her spine. "There was something I wanted to tell you. I don't know if it will help, but someone should look at Mr. Blake. Young Mr. Blake."

"Jonathan? Why?"

Lucinda glanced around the room and then leaned forward. "Something happened a couple weeks ago." Her voice dropped to an urgent whisper. "I work at Mrs. Tate's, but I clean for Mr. Edward Blake once a week. I heard him yelling at young Mr. Blake. He said, 'The mess you made is serious this time. I have half a mind to let you deal with it yourself.' They shipped him off somewhere the same day."

"Do you know what the mess was?"

She smoothed the sheet and tucked it around Maggie. "No. I was afraid they would catch me listening, so I hurried outside and made a lot of noise coming back in. Mr. Blake heard me and closed the door."

What mess would Edward have to clean

up for his son? "Do you remember what day it was?"

Lucinda hesitated. "I usually clean for him on Tuesdays, and it was at least a couple weeks ago . . . no wait, it must have been three weeks ago." She fingered the scarf at her throat. "There is something else you need to know. Young Mr. Blake has a nasty temper."

Remembering what she'd seen at the housing development, Maggie nodded, which started the pounding again. "I've seen some evidence of anger issues." She put her good hand to her head.

Maybe having Lucinda draw her gaze to her throat made Maggie realize she'd never seen her without a scarf. "You know," Maggie said, "I've noticed the pretty scarves you wear. No one else wears much jewelry or accessories with their uniforms. Is there a reason?"

Lucinda nodded and pulled the scarf down. "I wear them to cover this." A scar in the shape of a large comma marred the left side of her neck. "It was made by Mr. Jonathan. He was angry at his grandmother and threw a glass at the wall. It hit near me and broke. A piece flew over and cut my neck."

"Did you press charges?"

Lucinda blinked as if the question had

never occurred to her. "No. They said it was an accident and took me to a doctor to have it sewn up. Mrs. Tate keeps me around to remind Jonathan to mind his temper. It doesn't bother him though. It was like he forgot the next day."

Maggie shifted on her pillows, seeking a more comfortable spot. "When did this happen?"

"It's been several years now. He was sixteen at the time."

"Has anyone said anything about it since then?"

Lucinda fussed with the scarf, sliding the knot to the right side of her neck, covering the scar with the wider part. "No. Mrs. Tate gave me several scarves and told me to wear them with my uniform. I've worn them ever since."

Maggie watched her face as she asked the next question. "Did you ever see him get intentionally violent — I mean where he meant to harm someone?"

Lucinda shook her head. "He never seems to hurt anyone intentionally. He's so used to getting his way, when he doesn't, he can be sarcastic and nasty. I've never seen him hit anyone."

Voices drifted in from the hall, and Lucinda slid to the edge of her seat. "I need to go, Miss Maggie. I don't want Mrs. Tate to find out I was here." Panic whitened her face as she shot up.

"I don't want you to get into trouble. Thank you for telling me. Can I tell Greg?"

She was already at the door, peering into the hall. "Yes, but please tell him not to say where he got the information, OK?"

Before Maggie could answer, Lucinda was gone. Maggie eased back on her pillows. How did Jonathan's temper fit in? As far as she knew, he wasn't mad at Aunt Esther. In fact, he had nothing but good things to say about her. And what could she have done to upset him anyway? Unless it was golf or tennis, they didn't have a reason to see each other. Allie told her Jonathan was a poor loser. But he didn't lose often, and she doubted very much her aunt was able to beat him. Besides, it seemed as if his temper tantrums were spontaneous, so it wasn't as though he'd plan to hurt her.

A woman entered with her lunch and arranged it on the tray table.

Maggie raised her bed up farther, suddenly hungry. The roast beef wasn't restaurant quality, but it wasn't bad either. She took a third bite.

Jonathan and Edward entered carrying a huge bouquet of salmon and yellow roses.

She hoped they hadn't passed Lucinda on the way up.

"Edward, Jonathan, how nice of you to drop by. And what beautiful flowers." She leaned over, trying to clear some space on the tiny nightstand, struggling with one hand.

"No, don't move. I'll clear a space." Jonathan stepped forward and rearranged the other flowers, making room for the large arrangement Edward carried.

After placing the roses, Edward clasped her good hand, gave it a gentle squeeze, and released it. "It looks like we're interrupting lunch, so we won't stay long. Are you all right? What happened? I heard you had a fire."

"Yes, my house was burned last night."

Edward's eyes softened. "What an awful experience. Was everyone OK?"

She glanced at Jonathan, trying to gauge his reaction. "Yes, my dog woke me up. She'll get plenty of treats when I get out of here."

Jonathan looked around for another chair, and he and his father sat. She missed seeing his expression.

He asked, "What happened? Do you know how it started?"

"An investigator came by and asked me

266

some questions. He said it was set. Gasoline was all over the place." She scooped a bite of mashed potato and let it slide down her throat. "I can't figure out why someone would want to burn my house. This is getting ridiculous. What did I ever do to deserve this?"

"We're just glad you and Allie are OK." Jonathan frowned. "The two of you alone, trying to get out of the house . . . I can't imagine it."

He looked distressed, but was he acting or was he genuinely upset? She wasn't good at judging people. She just couldn't tell.

"Where will you stay now?" Edward went right for the practical. "I assume it will take some time to fix everything."

"I'll probably go to Aunt Esther's, but to tell you the truth, all this is starting to give me the creeps. I'm almost afraid to leave the hospital."

Edward poured a cup of water from the pitcher on her tray and handed it to her. "I'm sorry this is happening to you. What is this town coming to? It used to be safe here. It's that burglary ring. Our town hasn't felt the same since the robberies started. I can't figure out why they would want to set fire to your house though. It makes no sense."

"I'd like to get my hands on the guy who

did it, is all I've got to say," Jonathan said. He turned his head.

A memory flitted through her mind. But she wasn't sure what.

"You guys could have been killed. We need a neighborhood watch or something."

Maggie finished her last bite and nestled her head into the pillow. "Maybe it would be a good idea, a full-town neighborhood watch."

Edward touched his son's arm and rose. "You're tired," he said. "We can talk later." They headed for the door, and Edward stopped, rotating on his heels. "Oh, I wanted you to know there's no rush on the designs for the development. You've given us plenty for a head start. Take as much time as you need."

Maggie thanked them, and they left. She pushed the tray table away, lowered the bed, and eased her pounding head into the pillow's softness.

25

Morning sun filtered through the blinds. Unlike yesterday, Maggie felt energized. It was time to leave the hospital and get back to her life.

Nurse Rita peeked around the curtain someone must have pulled across last night. "Hey, are you awake? The doctor released you, so after you sign some papers, you can go home."

Maggie called Robin, and she arrived after breakfast, handing over a paper sack. "Here, I thought you might want to go home in something other than the hospital gown."

Inside, she found an outfit, some under things, and flip-flops — all in her size. "Thanks. I guess our shopping trips were more beneficial than I thought."

Robin laughed. "It was easier with you than it was with Ginger and Allie. Although with Allie, I could borrow something from Melissa. Ginger was a total guess."

Maggie took the sack and started for the bathroom then swiveled. Tears brimmed in her eyes and threatened to spill over. "I don't know how to thank you, Robin. You've thought of everything and have been such a great friend."

Robin grinned at her. "You should withhold thanks until you try them on. I might have brought you clown clothes and planned to post your picture on the Internet."

Maggie laughed and continued into the bathroom to change. "If you did, you know I'll find a way to get even."

The jeans and t-shirt she pulled out weren't clown-like and fit like her own. Until Robin showed up, Maggie hadn't realized she had nothing to wear — she probably had nothing at all. From what she'd heard, between the smoke and the water, most victims ended up replacing pretty much everything. She opened the door while she brushed her teeth, speaking around the toothpaste. "Are we taking Ginger with us then?" She leaned forward and spit in the sink.

Robin appeared at the door. "No. She's made other plans."

Even though she hated herself for it, Maggie was relieved. She didn't want an audience when she checked on her house. But

Ginger still needed protection until they could figure out what was going on. "She didn't go home, did she?"

"She felt her being in your house may have caused you and Allie to be in danger, so she decided it was safer for everyone if she left. She's going to her sister's in Kansas. Greg got her a reservation and said he'd help get her on the plane. Her sister's husband is picking her up at the airport in Wichita."

Maggie could see the questions in Robin's eyes and knew she'd have to talk about her breakup with Greg, but she was thankful Robin didn't ask her about it.

Rita pushed in a wheelchair. "Time to go. Are you ready?"

Maggie picked up the most cheery of the flowers from the nightstand and held them out to Robin. "Do you want a bouquet for your house? I'm donating the rest of these to the hospital. Someone might as well enjoy them."

Robin took the bouquet, and together they headed out to her car. After buckling in, Robin paused. "Where do you want to go? As if I don't already know." She put the car in gear and waited. "I assume you want to stop by your place before we go to lunch and you tell me all about it? My treat."

Maggie shifted in her seat and gazed out the window. "The house, please. And tell you all about what?"

"Whatever made you decide Greg isn't right for you." Robin's voice softened. Kindness, not the judgment Maggie had been expecting, glowed in her friend's eyes. She should have known. Robin was tough on her sometimes, but her genuine concern made up for it.

Robin steered out of the parking lot.

It was the perfect time to ask the question burning in Maggie's brain since she woke up. "So before we get there, maybe you should prepare me. How's my house? Greg swears it can be fixed, but I'm afraid he might have said it to make me feel better." She gave Robin a half smile. "I know you'll tell me the truth. Have you seen it? Can it be fixed?"

Robin drifted to a stop at the light. "Absolutely. I haven't had time to get over there yet, but Mark tells me it isn't too bad. And even if it is, we'll do whatever it takes." The light changed, and she moved into the intersection. "It started in the back, so it's worse there. I imagine you'll need to rebuild the kitchen and dining room. The rest, I don't know. We can get some professional advice on the structure."

"The structure? Do you think it affected the whole structure?" Visions of the place flattened ran through Maggie's mind. Maybe today wasn't the day for this. But how ridiculous — when would be a good time to see one's sanctuary destroyed?

Robin eased to the curb in front of the house. "Instead of speculating, let's go see."

Maggie purposely stared at the other side of the street. Once Robin shut off the engine, Maggie held her breath and forced herself to take it all in. The front looked almost normal. She let out her breath in a whoosh. Smoke blackened the area near the front door, but the rest of the walls appeared untouched. Hope surged. Maybe it would be OK. "This isn't so bad," she whispered, getting out of the car and staring up at it from the curb.

"Yeah. At least, you won't have to rebuild the whole thing." Robin joined her on the sidewalk and grabbed her good hand. "OK, let's go see the back."

The warmth of Robin's hand steadied her. She couldn't imagine doing this alone. Maggie gave her hand a little squeeze, silently thanking her for the support when they walked through her gate. Blackened siding existed in some spots, but was totally missing in others. A tarp covered the hole, which had been her back door, and half the kitchen. The black parts on the wall licked clear up to the second floor.

She couldn't speak, could barely breathe. Her hand in Robin's shook. It didn't look like her house. It looked like a disaster. She swallowed hard and stiffened her spine. Renovation was a project, just another job. She could do this.

She dropped Robin's hand, realizing she was crushing it, but Robin hadn't complained. She stepped forward and, with her thumb and index finger, drew the tarp aside. Stepping through what used to be a wall was like stepping into someone else's house. Nothing was as it should be.

The kitchen would need complete renovation. Blackened cupboards dangled along the side wall — they'd burned completely where the window used to be. Avoiding debris, she and Robin picked their way past, through a corner of the dining room and into the living room. It was better in here, only the side with the front door was burned. Water had ruined the furniture, however. She couldn't recognize her chair and ottoman, the one Esther helped her choose. Instead, a burned, soggy blob hunkered in the bay window where it used to be. She didn't say anything, just stared at the blob for a few minutes and turned away.

Robin followed her from the house, letting the tarp fall closed as though sealing something from her past.

Neither said anything on the way to the Pine Table, a restaurant not far from Maggie's house. A new young hostess sat them in a window booth, took their drink orders, and placed lunch menus in front of them.

Maggie gazed at the parking lot. How would she keep Allie safe? Where could she send her?

Robin lifted her menu. "What are your thoughts? Are you OK?"

"I don't know. I guess so." Maggie turned from the window. "But I don't know what to do about Allie."

"Can she go home? They've arrested the people responsible for the burglary and Esther's murder, haven't they?"

Maggie stared at the lunch items but didn't take anything in. The server came to take their order, and she had no idea what she'd just read. Not being hungry, she ordered the soup of the day. When the waitress left, Maggie replied, "They've figured out most of the thieves, but of course, Grady's still loose, and he knows where she lives. Maybe sending her home isn't a good idea. And if they caught the murderer, why did someone burn my house?" She unwrapped her silverware and spread the paper napkin in her lap. "It's got to be Grady. He's still out there, and for some reason, he wants Allie out of the picture. Where can I send her?" She played with the saltshaker. "She sure isn't safe with me."

"Can't she go with George?"

"He's out of the country, and we haven't been able to reach him."

"Is that normal?"

"Allie says it is. She says he goes for months at a time, and she can't always contact him. He calls every so often, but not regularly. He doesn't even know about the fall down the stairs."

The soup came — clam chowder, one of her favorites.

Robin held her hamburger in both hands, ready to take a bite. "What about Greg's place in Montana? Didn't he keep a small house when he sold the rest?"

A heavy band loosened from around Maggie's chest. "The idea hadn't occurred to me, but it's perfect." The more she thought about it the lighter she felt. "Robin, you're brilliant. Grady can't possibly know about it. She'll be safe there."

Robin wiped the burger juice off her chin.

"You're just now figuring out how smart I am? Now you'll just have to call and ask Greg. Maybe he can go with you." She wiggled her eyebrows. "For protection, of course."

"Ugh. You and your matchmaking. Greg and I are done." There, she said it out loud. Did it sound as false to Robin as it did to her? "Who can I send with her to protect her? Greg won't want to go. He'll want to stay here and try to find Grady."

Robin closed her open mouth. "I'm sure the police will assign someone to stay with her. But won't you be going, too?"

"No, I don't want to." Maggie blew on her spoonful of soup. "I want to stay here and figure this out. My life won't be the same until this guy is caught and put away, and I want to get it back. What's left of it anyway." She put the spoon in her mouth. One word described the creamy flavor . . . yum.

"I'll let you and Greg fight it out," Robin said. Then the smile slid off her face. "And speaking of Greg, what has he done to make you say it's over?"

"It's not him; it's me. The time isn't right, and I'm not ready." She glanced up and glimpsed the patient disbelief Robin wiped from her face.

"Maybe it's all the stress of what's been going on." Robin focused on her burger. "You shouldn't make life-altering decisions during this kind of stress. Give it some time. You'll feel better in a few weeks."

Maggie took a sip of her iced tea. "I don't imagine I'll change my mind. I'm not who he thinks I am, and I don't want to be around when he finds out."

"What do you mean?"

"He has this idea I'll be like Aunt Esther. The problem is, I'm not. I'm not even related to her. She isn't really my aunt."

The words had their desired effect. Robin stopped chewing and stared, her face almost comical in its open-mouthed surprise. "What are you talking about?"

"I read something in her diary about a test when I was born. It made me wonder if it was a paternity test, so I went to Da . . . Danny's house and asked."

Robin laid her burger on her plate and wiped her fingers on her napkin. "What did he say?"

"He told me he's my dad, but not my biological father." Maggie spooned in another mouthful and gave Robin some time to process.

Robin frowned. "What did he mean?"

"He meant he loves me, and he wants to

be part of my life, but he's known for a long time I'm not biologically his. My mother had an affair, and I was the result."

"Oh, no, Maggie." She sat back, ignoring her burger. "Does he know who your father is?"

Maggie couldn't help the giggle that escaped without her permission. Maybe she was becoming hysterical. "I didn't even ask. I was too anxious to learn the truth about him and my mom."

Robin's eyes grew soft. "So how are you doing?"

Maggie stopped chewing, wondering the same thing. "You know, I thought I'd be devastated, but I'm not. It explains why he couldn't take me with him, which bothered me way more than not being physically related to him. I feel better, if that makes any sense. He loved me enough to stick around, even though it must have wounded him terribly to learn the truth."

The server stopped by to pick up their dishes, and Maggie was surprised to see she'd eaten the whole bowl. "It hurts more that I'm not related to Aunt Esther, but she loved me enough to take me in and to leave me everything." Tears filled her eyes and threatened to spill over. She sniffed and

blinked them away. "It blows me away sometimes."

Robin finished her burger and motioned
for Maggie to help herself to the fries. "So
how does this affect you and Greg?"

"He thinks I'll be like Aunt Esther, and I
thought her genes might show up in me. I
know it sounds dumb, but I thought if I was
related to her, eventually I would want to
do the things she did. But it turns out there
isn't any good in my blood. The goodness
in Aunt Esther will never show up in me.
I've tried to convince Greg I'm not like her,
but he believes otherwise. It's not fair for
me to mislead him."

Robin looked her in the eyes. "You know
you don't inherit goodness, don't you?"

Maggie tilted her head and smiled. "You
mean the nature versus nurture thing? Since
I was nurtured by her and it hasn't shown
up, I'd hoped nature would prevail. But I
guess it already did." She forced a laugh.

"Wait a minute." Robin sat back in the
booth. "She wasn't perfect, you know. She
was a wonderful person, and we all loved
her. But she was just a person like the rest
of us. She wouldn't like you putting her up
on a pedestal like this. She'd be the first to
yell at you. But since she's not here, I'm going to."

Maggie tried to interrupt, but Robin continued. "Stop feeling sorry for yourself."

What? Feeling sorry for myself? How could she talk like that?

Before she could voice her disagreement, Robin went on. "It doesn't matter whether Esther was your biological aunt or not. She loved you, and you know it. The fact she wasn't related by blood confirms even more how special you are. She didn't have to take you in — she wanted to. And it wasn't because she was a saint. She loved you because you're easy to love."

She took a breath, but her rant wasn't finished. "And you can't inherit goodness. You have to do it yourself. It isn't going to fall on you. You have to go after it." Her hand hit the table, startling Maggie, and maybe even surprising herself with the sudden sound. "If you want to do good things, do them. Find out what kinds of things you can do and go do them, but don't let the fact you weren't blood related to the person you loved most in this world stop you from being who you were meant to be." She leaned forward to emphasize her last point. "Esther would feel she failed you."

26

Maggie and Robin walked to Robin's car in silence — a perfect backdrop for Maggie's chaotic thoughts. Did people see her as a victim who spent her time feeling sorry for herself? She shook her head. She wanted to be tough, not timid. *Better start acting like it then, girl.* When they got in the car, she faced Robin. "Take me to the Star Lake Inn, would you?"

"What? Aren't you staying with Mark and me tonight?"

"No, although I appreciate the offer, I need some alone time to think things through. I don't want to go to Aunt Esther's yet, because I don't want anyone to find me."

Robin started the car and rotated in her seat. "Maggie, is it what I said? You know I have a big mouth. It gets me in trouble all the time. I didn't mean it about feeling sorry for yourself. You don't, even when you have every right to with everything happening to you lately." Her gaze pleaded with her. "Please don't let this come between us. Let me take you home with me. You can go to the guest room, and I'll make sure no one bothers you."

Maggie smiled at her friend. "It isn't what you said. At least, not only what you said." She patted Robin's hand on the gearshift. "You were probably right, but I need to work through this and decide what to do. And don't worry, it won't come between us."

Robin didn't want to take her there, but after a long look, she must have realized she couldn't change her mind, so she drove to the hotel. Grabbing her purse, Robin got out of the car.

It occurred to Maggie she had no purse. Which meant no money and no credit cards. She stopped on the sidewalk. "Oh, wait. I don't have my purse."

Robin smiled. "I know, but I have mine."

"You've already done so much. I can go to the bank. . . ."

"We can take care of it later. I don't know if your purse was burned or not, but I know Greg took some of your things to his place. Where do you keep your purse at home?"

"Upstairs in my bedroom, so it might be

OK. This feels weird, depending on you like this. I promise I'll pay you back."

"I'm not worried about it." Robin opened the back door and removed another sack. "Here, these are the clothes I brought you for now. We can go shopping when you're ready. It's only a few outfits, but it should last you a week or so."

Tears welled up in Maggie's eyes. "How do you know all these things?"

Robin smiled. "I just thought about what I would need. I didn't know about makeup, but there's a brush and some mascara in there."

They entered the hotel, and Robin booked her a room for the night. "At least call Greg and let him know you're here." She held tight to the key.

Maggie was noncommittal, but Robin gave up the key and left. Part of Maggie wanted very badly to talk to Greg, and part of her wanted some distance. Why was she not allowed to make a clean break? Why did there have to be all this communication? All she wanted was to be left alone. Didn't she?

Alone in her room, she fell into bed, fully clothed and exhausted. She wished she had Aunt Esther's diaries, but who knew if her copies were salvageable? At least, one of them was safe at the station. At the end of this, she would get it back and still be able to hear Aunt Esther's voice. Would Allie like a copy? Would it mean as much to her? If so, she deserved to have it.

Maggie bolted up in bed. Allie! She hadn't done anything to keep her safe. Some big sister she was. She was so concerned about getting her alone time, she forgot about Allie's safety. Good thing she'd dropped her phone into her pocket during the fire. It was the one thing she was able to keep. Greg had brought her a charger in the hospital. She scrambled to her feet and texted, asking him to take Allie away and keep her safe. Knowing he would, and was probably way ahead of her, she waited for a response. Once she got one, she closed her eyes and drifted to sleep.

Greg received the text from Maggie while waiting at Denver International Airport with Ginger. Using his badge, he'd been able to go through security with her, and sitting in the gate area, he texted back. "Where are you? Are you OK?" No answer. He'd already decided to find a place for Allie, and Montana was a perfect solution. Most people didn't know he had it. She should be safe there. He'd even made some calls and arranged for one of the female officers to drive her. The two would leave first thing in the morning. Until then Mark would continue to guard her. He texted the information to Maggie and waited.

Her response was thank you. Nothing else. Was this how it would be? Was she hiding from him until she could get up the courage to give his ring back? If it survived the fire. Maybe he should make it easy on her and stop trying. Everything in him fought against it. He couldn't give up. They were too good together. He couldn't sit and do nothing, so he called David at the station. "Any news on the whereabouts of Grady Hayes?"

"Not yet. The officers canvassed your girlfriend's neighborhood, and they found a neighbor who was up at the time but didn't hear or see a vehicle. So either the guy had a quiet car, or he parked somewhere else."

Greg swallowed down his frustration. He wanted to scream. How could someone carry in a gas can, pour it all over a house, set fire to it, and leave without anyone noticing? "Any leads at all?"

"I still have two houses left to check. One family was on vacation, according to the neighbors, and one is vacant. There's a For Sale sign in the yard."

Greg's spirits rose a few degrees.

"And before you ask," David said. "We're working on getting consent from both owners to make a search."

"Let me know when you do, and I'll meet you there. I need to do something. This sitting around is driving me crazy."

David laughed. "I get you, partner. Will do."

Eventually Ginger's flight was called, and she boarded.

Greg checked his phone for the thousandth time. No call from David yet. Frustrated, he glanced at his watch. He wanted to be with the teams to investigate those houses. He stood, willing everyone to hurry onto the jet way. The plane door closed, and he sprang away from the window, plucking the phone off his belt. His long strides made short work of the motorized walkways, and he skirted little kids and elderly people while calling David's number. No answer. Could they be searching already? Which one would they explore first? Waiting for the train was agony, but once he boarded, it whisked him to the terminal, and then he jogged to his truck.

About a half hour into the drive back to Pinon Creek, Greg's phone rang. The station number showed up on his truck's navigation screen. He hit the *answer* button on his steering wheel.

"Williams."

"We've got permission for both houses, and we're meeting the owner's niece at the vacation one now." David's voice. "The other one is a lockbox, and the owner gave us the code. Can you join us?"

"Text me the addresses, and I'll get there as soon as I can." Ending the call, he pushed his foot down hard on the accelerator. The truck ate up the last few miles, and he headed straight to Maggie's neighborhood. David's car wasn't on her street, so he went over one street to the address he'd been given.

David was walking back to his car.

Greg pulled up next to him and rolled down the window. "Anything?"

"No sign of anyone staying here, but we're leaving a man inside for a while in case Grady's a neat freak."

Disappointment tugged at him. "Have you already searched the other house?"

"No, we're going there now."

David opened the passenger door and climbed in. "The next one is on her street."

Adrenaline replaced the disappointment. This could be nothing. It probably was nothing. But somehow, he couldn't shake the feeling of expectancy.

He parked down the block from Maggie's house and waited for the two officers who had gone down the back alley to get in place. When they were ready, David and Greg walked up the driveway, took the key out of the lockbox, and opened the front door.

27

Maggie dreamed about Lucinda. She and Maggie were playing tennis with Jonathan and Edward while Allie and Greg watched. A bluebird flew in and perched on the net. Maggie kept trying to get them to stop so they wouldn't hurt the bird, but no one seemed to notice. She woke up. Her headache was better, and most of the scratchiness in her throat melted away with a glass of water.

What made her dream such a strange dream? She laughed when she thought about the silliness of Lucinda and her against Jonathan and Edward. And what was the bluebird about anyway? Then she remembered her aunt's diary. Didn't she say something about seeing a bluebird at Lindy's? A picture of the dream flashed through her mind. Jonathan twisting his head — wait! She didn't say *a* bluebird; she said Bluebird. She and Maggie used to laugh about Jonathan being birdlike in his movements.

Esther used to say he was light on his feet, and when he jerked his head, it was like a bluebird in her garden. Esther must have seen Jonathan at the luncheon, but he didn't see her.

And Lucinda said Edward was angry about some "mess" Jonathan had made three weeks ago. The luncheon was at least a couple weeks before that.

Could it have been the same event? How could Esther have threatened Jonathan? If she knew something damaging, she wouldn't have said, unless it had been criminal. If it had been, she would have told the police. And what else would be serious enough to get her killed, except something illegal?

Did it have to do with the burglaries in the area? How did they fit in? She bit her lip. Maybe they didn't. Maybe the killer used the burglaries to mask a calculated murder. The thought writhed in her brain and skittered down to her stomach. She needed to talk to Greg. No, wait. He was with Ginger. Plus, she couldn't keep calling him. She'd call Mark.

He answered on the second ring. "Maggie, is everything OK?"

"Yes, I'm fine. Are you at the station?"

"No, I'm home keeping an eye on Allie. Is there something at the station you need?"

Maggie paced in the small room. She didn't want Mark to leave Allie for what might be nothing. "I just wanted to ask when I can get my aunt's diary back."

"We didn't find anything, so I don't see any reason you can't have it back whenever you want. You might want to check with Greg though. He's the one examining it."

"Nice try. You're as bad as your wife."

He chuckled. "Must be contagious. I can call him if you want."

"Never mind, I don't need it right this minute. I'll check with him tomorrow." After she hung up, Maggie called the station. She'd feel better if she passed the information along. Then it would be out of her hands.

"Lister."

"Officer Lister, this is Maggie Schreiber. My aunt's diary is there at the station probably on Greg Williams' desk, and I need a favor. Can you have someone look and see what day she and her friends had lunch? It's mentioned near the last of the diary."

"Sure, but can you tell me why?"

"Aunt Esther may have seen something that day. And I think Jonathan was there."

"If it was the day of the lunch, we investigated when we heard about Carla. It was the same day his fiancée, Stephanie Franklin, died. Jonathan was at his cousin's place in Wyoming. Are you saying he wasn't where he said he was?"

Maggie tucked her hair behind her ear and chewed on her thumbnail. Should she start something? The Blakes were pretty powerful in Pinon Creek, to say nothing of Monica Tate. A false accusation against Jonathan would be the end of her career. And did she think Jonathan was guilty of murder?

"Ms. Schreiber? Are you there?"

She shook her head. It didn't matter how powerful they were, if he was guilty, he had to be punished. "Yes, I'm here. There was something in Aunt Esther's last diary about 'bluebird' being there. At the time I didn't notice it, but then a friend overheard Edward tell Jonathan he should have to clean up his own messes, and she said they shipped him off the same day." Maggie swallowed hard. "Bluebird was the nickname Esther had for Jonathan. I think she saw him."

"What else did your source say?"

"She said it was a Tuesday, about three weeks ago. It would be about the right time, and she said Jonathan has a bad temper.

I've seen firsthand what he's like when he gets mad."

"OK, Ms. Schreiber, we'll look into it. But we verified Jonathan's alibi for the day of Esther's murder. It's unshakeable. He was playing tennis in a very public tournament. I'll send this along though."

She stopped him before he could hang up. "Wait, Officer Lister, it's probably my overactive imagination. Please be careful how you deliver this information, OK? My source trusted me, and Monica Tate can be difficult if you cross her. I don't want to make any trouble for my source."

Officer Lister agreed, and Maggie hung up feeling better. At least, she'd passed on the information — if there was something to it, Mark and Greg would figure it out. Either way, she could trust them to protect Lucinda.

Saying Greg's name brought a strange feeling to the pit of her stomach. Maybe she was hungry. It was already six o'clock. She could order room service. Boy, she would owe Robin a lot when this was over.

Dinner came, and the hamburger she ordered was good, but she began to wish she had Ginger with her. Even her nonstop chatter would have been better than the hollow echo of her thoughts. She flipped on

294

the TV and watched a silly sitcom while she ate. It wasn't too late. She could still call Robin to pick her up.

What was the matter with her? Being alone never bothered her before. She'd finish dinner, watch some television, and go to bed early. Things would look better in the morning. Things always looked better in the morning.

28

Greg followed David inside the house, both
with their guns drawn. A faint scent of
cigarette smoke mixed with the more powerful, new-paint smell. It appeared everything
had been moved out, and the house remod-
eled for a quick sale. Greg wondered if the
flipper had been smoking in here, or if it
could have come from the elusive Grady.

The living room was empty, and David's
footsteps echoed across the hardwood floor
as he headed for the kitchen. Greg chose
the second floor and took the stairs two at a
time. The bedrooms were empty, new carpet
softening his footsteps. He inspected every
cabinet and closet, hoping to find evidence
of an unlawful resident. He could hear David doing the same downstairs.

A door in the middle of the hallway
revealed a narrow set of wooden stairs leading to an attic. He tried to quiet his footsteps
as he ascended, but the treads creaked. The

stairway opened up to an unfinished space. Plywood flooring spread beneath drywall-less wall studs with pink insulation puffing out between.

A sleeping bag was nestled near the window, along with a kerosene lantern and some binoculars.

Greg skirted the bag and looked out the window, knowing what he would find. Sure enough, a clear shot of Maggie's two-story rose over the ranch-style house next door. He returned to the second level and called down to David.

A few minutes later, David popped above the floor line. "Jackpot!" he said as he strolled to the makeshift bed. "It has all the comforts of home, right? Even some snacks." A bag of small candy bars lay open on the floor next to the lamp. "He's lucky he didn't set this house on fire, too, with the wrappers so close to the kerosene." He nudged the bag with his foot. "Are you thinking what I'm thinking?"

"Yep." Greg grinned. "Stakeout."

David hooked his thumbs into his belt loops. "Since you're so excited about it, you ought to sit in this hot attic while I take the back in my air-conditioned car."

"Not so fast." Greg plucked a quarter from his pocket and flipped it. "Call it."

"Tails," David chose as it hit Greg's palm, and he flipped it onto the back of his other hand. He glanced down. Tails. Greg groaned and lifted a hopeful brow. "Two out of three?"

David laughed. "No way, loser."

Greg left to tell the officers in the alley what they'd found while David called it in. When Greg returned, David had a rueful grin on his face. "It looks like we both lose. Boss says he wants double on this one because of the severity of the crime. He wants us inside, and the two guys in the alley to stay there."

Greg grinned. "I'd gloat, but it's too hot up here. Let's wait downstairs."

David had his whiny face on. "It isn't much cooler down there. I don't see why Donovan decided there had to be so many of us. It's not like it's a gang or anything. You should be able to handle one guy on your own."

Shrugging, Greg started down the steps. Not arguing was the best way to deal with David when he didn't get his way.

David slammed out the back door to inform the other officers.

Greg imagined they'd get an earful of his grievances. He dropped the key into the lockbox, and when David returned, they settled in to wait.

At dusk, the call came in. "Subject entering the alley on foot," the voice said. "He should be heading your way in the next ten minutes."

At this time of day, between light and dark, shadows lurk everywhere and even with a light making out features was difficult.

Greg grabbed the gun out of his holster, and he and David stood, poised and ready on either side of the door, waiting until Greg wondered if Grady was out there or a neighbor had gone out for a walk.

At last, they heard a footstep.

Greg tensed as the lockbox banged against the door.

A key clicked the lock, and the door swung open. Grady strolled in, stuffing the key in his pocket.

Good way to keep people from surprising him. He should have done it when he was gone as well.

"Police!" Greg shouted. "Let me see your hands."

Grady faced Greg while putting his hands up then bent his knees, ready to spring.

David strode out from behind the door. "Don't do it, Grady." He cocked his weapon and tapped Grady's back. "You got nowhere to go, man."

Grady straightened and held his hands in the air. "OK, OK. Don't shoot me."

Greg held his gun steady. "Put your hands behind your back."

David holstered his gun and cuffed him. "Grady Hayes, you are under arrest."

"What for? I have permission to be here. I didn't break in. I had the combination." Grady allowed himself to be led away by Greg, who gripped his upper arm.

David radioed the officers in the alley, and the three of them waited on the sidewalk for the car to come around.

"It's quite a list. You've been pretty busy, Mr. Hayes. You're wanted for arson, burglary, assault and battery, and the murder of Mrs. Esther Campbell. To say nothing of unlawful entry."

"What? I didn't do any of those things."

The car pulled up, and David spoke to Greg over Grady's head. "How many times have we heard that one?"

Greg laughed as he helped Grady into the backseat. "More than I can count. But it's good to know criminals are consistent."

At the station, Grady clammed up. After receiving his Miranda warning, he chose to be silent and to have an attorney present. A lawyer finally showed up after midnight, conferred with his client, and allowed the questioning to begin.

Greg and David sat in the interview room with Grady and his lawyer, Lyle Goodman.

"Mr. Hayes," Greg began. "I'm Detective Greg Williams, and this is Detective David Green. Do you know why you're here?"

"My client went to a house which was for sale, with the intention of buying it, when he was yanked in here and unjustly accused of things he did not do," Goodman answered.

David exhaled. "Save it for the courtroom, Counselor."

Greg leaned back and crossed his legs. "So, you were just looking at the house; you weren't camped out there?"

"No, of course not," Grady replied. "I like the area, and my brother and I wanted to buy a house here. We don't want to live in a place with a police department like this though." Grady tossed his head.

Greg wanted to laugh but he managed to keep a straight face. "How'd you get the lockbox code?"

"I called the real estate office, and they gave it to me."

"They didn't send anyone to go in with you? You aren't a licensed real estate agent, are you, Mr. Hayes?"

"No, and I thought it was kinda weird. But the lady on the phone gave it to me, so I thought it was OK to go in."

"Did you think it was OK to live there like a squatter?" David interjected.

Greg couldn't keep it in any more — he chuckled.

Grady glared at him and shook his head. "I wasn't living there."

"Your fingerprints were upstairs, Mr. Hayes," Greg replied. "Why don't you tell us how they got there when we arrested you before you could get past the living room." He waited for Grady's rehearsed speech. Might as well get his whole story instead of this game they were playing.

Grady sat forward with his elbows on the table. "I called last week, and they gave me the code. So I went and saw the place. They say you're supposed to see the neighborhood at all times of day, so I went back to see it in the evening."

"You weren't sleeping there and stalking one of the neighbors?"

"Stalking!" Goodman began to earn his fee. "Now wait a minute here. No one said anything about stalking. You'd better produce some evidence."

"Mr. Goodman, there was a sleeping bag in the attic with binoculars which had your client's fingerprints on them."

"I saw them when I went in the first time, so I picked them up to take a look. The view's nice, but that's all. I don't know who they belong to."

"Well, I can tell you who they belong to," Greg said. "They were stolen from Mr. and Mrs. Castro when their house was burglarized last month."

"My client doesn't know anything about any burglaries," Goodman snapped. "Obviously, someone else had to have put the binoculars there."

"Obviously." Greg changed the subject. "Tell me, Grady, why did you set fire to Ms. Schreiber's house?"

Goodman placed a hand on Grady's arm. "My client doesn't know what you're talking about. Was there a fire?"

Greg stared hard at the man in front of him, wanting to shake the truth out of him. "The house Mr. Hayes was casing through the stolen binoculars belonged to Ms. Schreiber. Her house was doused with gasoline and set ablaze. You might want to know we found gasoline on the clothes in your truck."

"I ran out of gas and had to take a can to the gas station. I dripped some gasoline on my clothes, and that's the truth."

Goodman held up his hand.

Grady quietened.

"You don't have enough to charge him, detectives," Goodman smirked.

"We know you were part of a burglary ring operating in Pinon Creek for the last few months. Someone identified you." Greg leaned forward. "But the worst part is, we believe in the course of a burglary, one of the homeowners wouldn't cooperate, and you killed her."

Grady jumped to his feet. "No way! You're not pinning it on me. I didn't have anything to do with it!"

Goodman grabbed his arm. "Don't let them get to you, son. Just calm down."

Grady flung himself down in the chair, nearly tipping it over. "OK, but I didn't kill anybody."

"We know you wanted to burglarize Ms. Campbell's home," David spoke up, "because your brother asked his girlfriend to leave the door open. When she didn't, Cameron rang the doorbell and the two of you went in and argued with Ms. Campbell. When she threatened to call the police, you killed her."

"No, we didn't! We never went in the house."

Goodman made calming gestures with his

hands, but his client was shaking, and his eyes were wild.

Greg stuck his hand up, palm out, and spoke in a conciliatory tone. "OK, calm down and tell me where you were Saturday, the third. Maybe we can take murder off the table."

Grady got control and sat back, lifting his gaze to the ceiling.

Greg couldn't tell if he was trying to remember where he was, or trying to come up with a plausible alibi.

Grady leaned over and whispered to his attorney. Goodman addressed the two detectives. "My client respectfully requests to continue this tomorrow. It's very late, and he's exhausted."

David snorted. "Respectfully, huh? You probably need time to concoct an alibi. Fine by us. Maybe a night in lock up will help you figure it out."

29

Maggie woke the next morning confused about her surroundings. It all came back — the fire, the hospital, and the trip to the hotel. She lay there picturing her house. The dread she expected didn't materialize. The kitchen and part of the dining room would need to be rebuilt. The drywall in the rest of the house might have to be replaced, unless the professionals Greg called could salvage it. The whole house would need to be repainted, and she was picturing the colors she'd use. If she looked at this as a project, it would be all right.

She called Robin and jumped out of bed, ready to start her day, almost as if a switch had been thrown in her psyche last night. Her house wasn't what made her feel safe, because even though it looked pretty destroyed, it could be fixed. The people in her life made the difference. Aunt Esther, whether she was related to Maggie or not, had been important to her. And Allie. How protective she felt now surprised her. She didn't want her to go back to her dad and then never see her again.

And, of course, Greg. Not seeing him . . . not talking to him . . . was making her feel isolated. Why had she tried to weather Aunt Esther's death alone? Had she thought shutting Greg out would somehow make her stronger?

The way she used to want solitude wasn't the same anymore. She'd proved it to herself last night. Maybe they could meet for lunch. A smile teased at the corners of her lips. First, she had to see if her purse was intact so she could pay Robin back. Then she'd go through her house and decide what could be salvaged.

She pulled a green tank top out of the sack and put a white shirt on over it. Robin hadn't packed any shorts, so she slipped on the jeans she wore yesterday. Robin called from the lobby, and Maggie crammed her belongings into the sack and headed downstairs. "I have to check out because I added dinner to my room last night. I'll run by the bank as soon as I can and pay you back. I hope my purse is still there. I guess leaving it wasn't a very good idea since the place is open. What was I thinking?"

When she stopped to take a breath, she noticed Robin had two bags on her arm, one of which was hers. It smelled horrible. But it was there, and it was whole. "When did you get my purse?"

Robin laughed. "I went back to your place after I dropped you off yesterday. I found it right where you said, and it looks like it hasn't been touched. I checked to see if your credit cards were there." She waited while Maggie rummaged through it. "At least, there are some cards in there," she continued. "I don't know if any are missing. There's some cash, too."

Maggie dug out her wallet and went through it. All her credit cards were accounted for, and her cash hadn't been touched. She sighed with relief. "Thanks, Robin. I can't believe I didn't think about this yesterday. Or even the day before, when I was in the hospital. I simply forgot about it." She walked to the desk and gave the clerk her card. "Put all the charges on this one, please." She smiled at Robin. "Now I just owe you for the clothes."

Robin waited until they were in the car and halfway to Maggie's before bringing the subject up again. "You don't owe me anything," she said. "It's what friends do."

Maggie opened her mouth to protest, but

before she could get it out, Robin continued, "I don't want to hear another word
about it." The way she set her mouth, Maggie knew arguing would not change her
mind. She'd have to find another way to
show her appreciation.

They pulled into the alley behind her
house, and into her short driveway. Robin
shut off the engine. "Here we are. Are you
ready?"

Maggie nodded. "Who has Tony? Do you
have time to go through the house with me?
I'd like your input on some design ideas."

Robin laughed as she got out of the car.
"Redesigning already? That's a good sign.
Libby has Tony, so I can spend some time
here, and then maybe we can go to lunch."

Maggie reached to unlatch the back gate.
"Um, I might have plans today, Robin, but
I'd love to take you guys to dinner when
Mark gets off."

She could feel Robin's gaze as she went
through the gate, but Maggie didn't look
back. Robin would want to ask who Maggie's plans were with but wouldn't want to
intrude.

"Ah, yeah," Robin said. "Dinner would be
great. We don't get out as much as we used
to. It would be a treat."

The sight of the house brought Maggie to

a full stop.

Robin joined her. "Does it look worse than you remember?"

Maggie started walking again. "No, in fact, it's not as bad as it was in my head last night."

The tarp was clipped back, and fans blew air from the open windows in front out the hole in the back. "Wow, what's going on? Did you get this started?"

"No, Greg did."

Maggie maneuvered around the fans and into the house followed closely by Robin. She couldn't believe he was still looking out for her even after she broke up with him. She headed straight for the stairs, skirting a generator in the middle of the room. Careful to avoid some cords, she paused halfway up the steps. "Was it bad yesterday when you went up to get my purse?"

"No, but I didn't get much chance to look. There's some damage to the back bedroom above the kitchen, but when I peeked into the other rooms, it looked like they just had smoke and water damage."

They had reached the upper floor. The soft furnishings were gone. The carpet had been ripped up, and all the mattresses and box springs were gone, leaving bed frames leaning up against the wall of one of the bedrooms. As Robin had said, only Allie's room had any structural damage. Danger tape crisscrossed the door below a Keep-Out note.

She moved into the other rooms. The walls had been cleaned and all the windows thrown open, with fans drawing air through from the front of the house to the back, just like downstairs. She crossed to the front windows and peered into a dumpster, which must have been put there yesterday. The soggy mess inside couldn't be identified from up here.

"Man, these people are fast! When did they do all this?"

Robin spoke from across the room. "A crew of five people were here yesterday. They'd already cleared all the furniture out and were vacuuming soot off the walls and the floors when I arrived. They must have set up the fans right after. I wonder if they've been here yet today or if they ran them all night."

Maggie went back downstairs and checked her office in the front of the house next to the living room. It didn't have any fire damage and sustained very little water damage. Her wood desk remained intact, and the built-ins storing her file cabinets appeared untouched. She'd go through them at some point to see if anything had gotten wet. In the meantime, she headed out to the kitchen where Robin was waiting.

"I'm considering gray and white for my color palette, with punches of the pretty blue so popular now." She glanced at Robin. "What do you think?"

"I think it would be beautiful. Are you going to put another chair and ottoman in this bay nook? I always loved it."

Maggie pictured a new overstuffed chair and a tall reading lamp. "Yeah, it'll be good to give buyers ideas for a space they might not have thought of themselves. Plus, I can keep the same palette in here since it's connected, and it'll be easier to stage."

Robin had been wandering around, no doubt picturing what Maggie was saying. She came to an abrupt stop. "Buyers? And did you say easier to stage?" She twirled on her toes, her mouth still partly open. "Do you mean you're not rebuilding to live here?"

Maggie shook her head. "I came to the decision last night."

Robin's brown eyes turned gentle. "Why? Don't you feel safe here anymore?"

"No, I've been safe here for seven years, and once the people responsible are caught, I would've felt safe again. I realized that last night too."

Robin cocked her head. "So are you moving into Esther's house?"

Maggie grinned, having fun dragging it out. "Greg and I will have to find a new house."

Robin hesitated until it sank in and then threw herself at Maggie, giving her a huge hug. "Are you guys back together? Have you talked to him?"

"No, but I'm hoping I can take him to lunch."

Robin beamed. "What are you waiting for, girl? Call him right now!"

Maggie's smile faltered. "He hasn't changed his mind, has he? I know I hurt him. He may decide I'm not worth the effort."

Robin gave her a sidelong glance. "Not in this lifetime. Call him and put the poor guy out of his misery."

"OK, but you can't tell him. I want to tell him myself." She pulled her phone out of her purse. "Oh, and you can't tell Mark either."

The disappointment on Robin's face was almost comical. "I can't even tell Mark?"

"Nope. He won't be able to keep a straight face, and Greg will find out. Promise me."

"OK, spoilsport, I won't say a word. But

hurry, you know how hard it'll be for me to keep this quiet."

"I'll call him now and see if he wants to meet for lunch." She moved toward the stairs. "I'd better get the ring. I'm so glad my bedroom didn't catch. I don't think the diamond would burn, but I have no idea if it would be hot enough to hurt the gold." She ran up the stairs. The diamond was in a small stone box on her nightstand, right where she'd left it. It slipped easily on her finger and sparkled in the light from the open window. How could she have felt tied down by such a beautiful thing?

While she was upstairs, away from Robin, she dialed Greg's cell. It rang a few times and went to voicemail. Not knowing what to say, she hung up. *Very mature, Maggie.* Oh, well, she'd try again later. Maybe dinner was a better idea anyway. Robin would understand.

Her clothes still hung in the closet. A handwritten note fluttered on the closet door.

Wash the clothes and hang them outside. You may have to wash them a few times to remove the smell, and there's no guarantee it will work. Unfortunately, dry cleaning won't touch it, so your dry-clean-only clothes are probably ruined.

Great. There were some nice things in there. "Robin?" she called down the stairs. "Can you help me get these in my car?" When Robin appeared at the bottom of the stairs, Maggie added, "I'm going to take them to Aunt Esther's and do them there."

They pulled everything washable out of the closet, her dresser, and her winter clothes storage, then retrieved sheets and towels from the blanket chest in her bedroom and stuffed her car full. "It's a good thing these have to be washed, so it doesn't matter how we put them in." Robin forced the trunk closed and worked to get it to latch. "We'd never get it all in if you had to worry about wrinkles."

Back inside, Robin helped her take measurements. "There isn't much I can do until the insurance company gets back to me, but I can at least start lining up what I want." Maggie let the tape measure slide closed with a snap. "Since I'm selling, I won't use the expensive stuff. Maybe insurance will cover everything."

They headed out to their cars.

Robin paused between the cars in the driveway. "Do you want me to come along and help you get the clothes out?"

"No, like you said I don't have to be neat. I'll get some baskets and haul them in one at a time." Maggie hugged her good-bye, tears forming in her eyes. "Thanks for everything. I don't know what I'd have done without you."

Robin sniffled, hugged her hard, wiped her eyes, and stepped back. "Since I have a free hour before I pick up Tony, I think I'll take my husband to lunch."

"Remember your promise," Maggie called after her.

Robin waved as she drove away.

At Aunt Esther's, Maggie parked in the driveway. Aunt Esther's white sedan was in still in the garage, so she'd have to either take the laundry through the front door or maneuver around the car. Maggie opened the front door and walked in. She was beginning to lose the feeling she should call out to Aunt Esther. Was it a good thing? Or did it mean she was starting to forget her aunt? Swallowing around a lump in her throat, she passed through the kitchen and the laundry room to the garage and hit the door opener.

Three empty baskets were stacked in the laundry room, and she carried them all out to her car and started loading up. Maybe she should have taken the clothes to a Laundromat. At least then, the baskets would have wheels. The flat four-wheel dolly in the garage caught her eye. Perfect! She filled the baskets and positioned them on the dolly, two on the bottom and one precariously on top. She pushed them to the door and tipped them over inside the laundry room. Good thing neatness didn't count.

After the second load, she began to wonder how many clothes one woman needed, anyway? Maybe it was time to pare down. After the third trip, she was considering calling the thrift store. But she would have to wash them anyway. Clothes this smelly couldn't even be given away.

She wiped her damp forehead with the back of her hand before shaking the last basketful of sheets onto the huge pile on the floor.

"Wow, that's a lot of laundry," a familiar voice sounded behind her.

She jumped, her heart pounding in her chest. "Edward, you scared me! I didn't hear you come in."

He smiled at her, but somehow she didn't feel relieved. There was something in his eyes — a watchfulness she hadn't seen before — and her heart didn't slow its frantic pace.

"The garage was open, so I came in," he said. "I hope you don't mind."

He stood next to Aunt Esther's car, effectively blocking her escape. Should she try to go out the front? Why was she afraid of him? He'd never done anything to make her afraid.

Except to cover up at least one murder and maybe two.

Another word popped unspoken in her brain — *Run!*

30

Greg suspected his patience was about to bear fruit.

"I want to deal," Grady said.

Greg stared across the table at Grady and Lyle Goodman. Neither one looked like they'd gotten much sleep. The guard said it was almost dawn by the time Goodman left the station. Greg glanced over, their signal for David to answer.

"We don't cut deals with murderers." He smirked.

Greg stifled a laugh.

"I didn't murder anybody!" Grady shouted. "I told you I wasn't there!"

Goodman placed his hand on Grady's arm. "My client feels he may have some information to help you find Mrs. Campbell's killer."

"Great! Let's have it." David's raised eyebrow displayed the same disbelief Greg was feeling.

Grady opened his mouth, but Goodman grabbed his arm before he could speak. "Not until we have an agreement."

"Mr. Goodman, you know we can't decide what charges are brought against Mr. Hayes or make any deals," David replied. "The Larimer County District Attorney makes those decisions."

"All I'm asking is for you to listen to him with an open mind and check out his story."

Grady nodded.

Greg leaned back in his chair. "OK, tell us what you know, and if what you say is true, we'll see what can be done to help you."

Grady glanced at Goodman, who nodded for him to begin. "We were watching the old lady's house, not because we wanted to steal, but because Cameron's girlfriend was in there, and he wanted to talk to her."

David rolled his eyes. "Yeah, right."

Grady glared at him and then spoke to Greg. "We saw someone go in the house. Then Cameron's girlfriend climbed out the window. She got in the old lady's car and took off. Cameron wanted to go after her, so we did." His hazel eyes pleaded for Greg to believe him. "I don't know what happened after, I swear. She wouldn't stop, even though we tried to get her to pull over.

We gave up halfway to Denver, because we were low on gas. Cameron was pretty mad. I told him she wasn't worth it, but he didn't want to hear it."

"What time did all this supposedly happen?" David's voice was sarcastic, but his stiffened posture told Greg he was more interested than he appeared.

"We quit chasing her around noon. I know because we decided to get something to eat."

"Where'd you go?"

"A pizza place off the highway with a gas station next door."

David scribbled some notes. "So did you pay for the gas or did Cameron?"

"It was Cam's truck, not mine. I'm not paying for gas to go chasing after some chick no matter how good looking she is." He laughed. "I'm smarter than that."

Greg peered at David's notes, trying not to show the excitement he felt. "So, what time did you leave Mrs. Campbell's?"

"Around ten thirty I guess. It took me and Bobby awhile to convince Cam to give up."

"So Bobby was with you?"

"Yeah. He didn't kill her either."

Greg exhaled. So far, they only had Bobby on burglary. If what Grady said was true, then burglary wasn't the motive. The killer would've had an hour and a half to kill Esther and bust the place up before Maggie showed up at noon. He pursed his lips. Tight, but possible. They'd have to check Cameron's credit card and verify Grady's story later. "So, Mr. Hayes, did you recognize the guy who went into Mrs. Campbell's house?"

"At the time, I didn't get a good look at him. We were down the street and saw his back as he got out of the car and walked up to the door. She knew him though. She opened it up before he even knocked."

"What did he look like?"

"He was older, his hair had some gray in it, but he still looked like you wouldn't want to mess with him, you know?"

"How tall was he?"

"Hard to tell from where we were parked, but I'd say he was pretty tall, maybe six feet or so. He was driving a black SUV, and he was taller than the vehicle."

"What kind of SUV?"

"I don't know the model, but it was expensive. And he looked like he had money. You know the type."

Greg wasn't sure what the type was exactly, but he continued, "So how does any of this help us?"

"I couldn't go home 'cause I knew you

322

were looking for me, so I holed up in the house near Maggie's. Cam was keeping an eye on Allie, so it seemed a good choice."

"So why did you burn Ms. Schreiber's house?" Greg tried to keep the anger out of his face and voice. He wanted to reach across the table and choke the life out of the little slug.

David glanced over, but didn't interrupt.

"Hey, man, I told you I didn't do that."

A hot wave of anger welled up from Greg's gut.

David put a restraining hand on his arm, and Goodman sat forward in his chair. Deep breaths — he needed to take some deep breaths or he would kill this kid.

"So," David spoke up, "you're admitting breaking and entering?"

Goodman kept his eyes on Greg, even as he answered David. "He's admitting to unlawful entry, yes. But he didn't commit arson." Goodman's posture remained tense.

Greg had been clenching his fists. He opened them and sat back, purposely relaxing his posture. "How about stalking?"

David watched Greg, even though he directed his words at Grady. "Mr. Hayes, you should know Detective Williams here is engaged to Ms. Schreiber." David let it sink in.

Grady's eyes widened, and his whole body tensed.

"However," David drawled, "I may be able to keep him from wrapping his hands around your throat if you give us something useful."

Grady's chair scraped as he stumbled back against the wall.

Goodman rose and stepped in front of him. "Are you threatening my client?"

David smiled his wolf smile. He was enjoying this. "Of course not, Counselor. I'm just giving you the facts." He paused. "Now why don't you both sit down and tell us what you know to help us take this killer off the streets?"

Goodman stayed in front of Grady and stared at Greg. "Not until you promise not to physically attack my client."

Heat tingled along his skin, but Greg forced his body to relax. He had to remain calm. "You have my word."

Goodman stepped aside, and Grady scooted his chair back to the table, lowering himself into it. But he positioned the chair farther away, out of reach. After searching Greg's face, Goodman sat as well. He leaned toward Grady. "Tell them what you know, son."

"I've seen him since then, and I saw him

when he set fire to Maggie's house. He's the guy who runs the construction company. You know who I mean? Edward Blake."

31

Maggie tried to remain calm. Edward stepped forward, watching her face the whole time. Was it obvious she was afraid of him? A glint flashed in his eye; a tick twitched in his jaw. She glanced toward the door to the backyard. Could she make it? She tensed, ready to spring.

He pulled a gun out of his pocket. "You won't make it, Maggie," he said softly. "I might not be able to run as fast as you, but I can shoot pretty well. Let's go inside where we can talk."

She edged past the washer and dryer, her eyes moving from the gun in his hand to his face. Her face hardened. "Was it you then? Did you murder Aunt Esther?" She couldn't help the rage welling up in her when she pictured the scene. "Tell me, did she trust you right to the end when she turned her back on you and you stuck a knife in it?"

He flinched as if she'd slapped him, but

he didn't stop. He shuffled into the laundry room and slammed the back door. "How did you find out? Did your sister tell you?"

Her sister? Had he arranged the attack on Allie?

Maggie tripped over a pile of clothes and righted herself. "No, why? She doesn't know anything. If she did, she would've told me already, and you wouldn't be standing here now." She continued to back up until he raised his gun. She froze.

"Where's your sister? I know she isn't here."

"How do you know she isn't upstairs?" Maybe if he went to check she could escape.

"If she was, you wouldn't have said that. I've had someone watching, and they say she hasn't been here." He waved his gun forward in a shooing motion. "Let's go into the kitchen, shall we? And you can tell me everything."

"I don't know where she is."

He raised his eyebrows. "You both need to disappear. You're so upset about your aunt and your house, you ran away."

"Both of us?" Maggie sidestepped into the kitchen, not wanting to take her eyes off him. "Greg will never believe it."

Edward pursued, the gun never wavering. "It doesn't matter what he believes — he won't be able to find you." He motioned her toward the kitchen table. "Sit down." She perched on the chair nearest the door, still facing him. "Eventually he'll understand you're gone, and he'll get on with his life."

She imagined Greg's face. "You're going to kill a cop's fiancée and expect him to just get over it? How stupid are you?"

His eyes glittered. "Fiancée, now, is it?"

She showed him her hand, the huge diamond flashing.

An ugly smile teased the corners of his mouth. "Does he know?"

The smile became bigger and chilled her. How did he know they'd broken up? She shuddered. "He won't stop. He'll keep hunting, keep at you until you make a mistake."

"It doesn't matter. It won't be soon enough to save you."

Getting him angry wasn't helping her. If she continued, he might shoot her right here. She lowered her eyes to break the standoff — to let him think he won. Maybe she could keep him talking.

He cleared his throat. "So how did you know it was me?"

"I wasn't sure. Aunt Esther said something in her diary. Nothing specific, but I realized she saw Jonathan the day his fiancée died. I

328

didn't connect it at first, and then I thought Jonathan killed both of them. But as you know he has an airtight alibi for the day Aunt Esther died." She wanted to say "for the day you murdered your friend," but it was better not to antagonize him further.

He kept his gun pointed at her and leaned against the counter. The ugliness of his expression vanished. He would've made a good politician. "Finally, tennis worked for him." He shrugged. "I didn't plan it. I helped Esther load her golf clubs, and she told me she'd seen him last Tuesday, but he left before she could say hello. She didn't know he shouldn't have been there. She was just making conversation. But I knew she'd put it together, and I panicked." He moved a box back from the edge of the counter and shifted his weight.

She had hoped he would sit down, but he didn't. He remained standing between her and the doors leading to the backyard and the garage. "I followed her home and rang the doorbell, telling her I needed to talk. She let me in and offered me lemonade." Sadness moistened his eyes. "I told her what happened, and she seemed to understand it was an accident. But I couldn't talk her out of telling the police. We argued, but she wouldn't budge. She picked up the phone, and I grabbed a knife from the block —"

"And stabbed her in the back." Maggie couldn't contain herself. It just popped out. She tensed in her chair. Maybe if she could stall him, she'd find a way to get free. Right now, her mind was blank. She relaxed her posture and evened out her voice. "What happened with Jonathan? Why did he kill Stephanie?"

"He didn't mean to." His eyes pleaded with her to understand, and the words spilled out. "He'd been telling people they were engaged, and he even got his great-grandmother's ring from Monica. It never occurred to him she might refuse, and when she did, it made him mad. All he could think of was how embarrassing it would be to tell all those people he'd been rejected. So he lost his temper and pushed her. She tripped over the rug and hit her head."

Maggie cleared her throat. "And then he called you. But how did he end up down the street where Aunt Esther saw him? And what about Carla and Ginger?"

"Who?" His face didn't change. "Esther must have seen him before he went inside. When I got there, we put the ring on her finger and washed the cup he'd been using. I didn't have to do much because our story was he'd been there the night before and asked her then." Edward stared at her, his face haggard. "I wish, for once in his life, I'd let him deal with the consequences. Or even before, when he was a kid and hurt the maid, I shouldn't have intervened. I used to say his mother spoiled him, and it was true — Francine adored the kid." He fingered the gun but didn't take his eyes from her face. "I realize I made it worse. I thought if he didn't get attention doing wrong things, he'd stop. The problem was Jonathan constantly did wrong things. It became a habit. Francine doted on him, and I ignored him."

The gun barrel drooped, and a faraway look glazed his eyes. "If I had just told Jonathan to go to the police, none of this would've happened. The push he gave Stephanie wasn't meant to kill her. Maybe we could have done something to reduce the sentence. He's my only son. There's no one else to take over the business."

Maggie saw her chance when the gun lowered again and his attention was diverted. She jumped out of the chair, shoving it in his direction. Expecting the gun to go off, she exploded through the swing door into the dining room.

The door swung back and thudded as he hit it when she was halfway through the living room. His footsteps pounded behind her.

Her phone rang in the kitchen, muffled inside her purse. She hesitated. No way could she reach it. She had to get outside. Could she make it? If she opened the front door, she could make enough noise to get someone's attention. She yanked at the knob, and it opened a sliver.

Edward crashed into her.

The door slammed shut, crushing her between it and Edward's body. She opened her mouth to scream when pain exploded in her head.

32

Greg and David approached the white board while a uniformed officer led Grady back to his cell.

David stared at the board. "So if Edward Blake killed Esther, who pushed Allie? Esther was his friend, and as far as we can tell, he didn't even know Allie." He wrote Edward Blake on the list. "And he doesn't fit the description Maggie gave us of Allie's attacker."

"Right," Greg agreed. "But what if Edward killed Esther, and Jonathan pushed Allie?"

David circled both names. "It would work as far as their alibis, but what motive would they have? Edward's a pretty powerful member of the community, to say nothing of his mother-in-law." He glanced at the door, and Greg followed his gaze.

Robin walked into the room, and Mark rose to greet her. She must be coming to take him to lunch.

Sadness speared through Greg. He wished it was Maggie walking through the door smiling.

"We'd better be sure before we tangle with the two of them," David continued.

Mark walked up, his arm around his wife.

Chief Donovan exited his office and joined them. "Tangle with whom?" he asked.

David pointed at the board. "Edward and Jonathan Blake. Our suspect identified Edward as being at Esther's house the morning she was killed, and he says he saw him start the fire at Maggie's. It fits the timeline we have for her murder, but we don't know if we can trust Grady's word. We were trying to figure out what their motive would be if Edward killed Esther and Jonathan pushed Allie."

Greg perched on the edge of the nearest desk, still staring at the board. "We know Jonathan has a temper. It's come up several times in our investigation. But why would he push Allie?" He turned to Donovan. "It would've made sense if he'd somehow killed Esther and then pushed Allie because she was there. But he has a solid alibi for Esther's murder."

David put the cap on the marker and moved over to his desk, staring at the board as if he could force it to give him the answer. "I can't imagine Edward Blake killing Esther Campbell. I mean they were on the same boards together, and Monica was Esther's friend. Why would he?"

"I can answer that." John Lister entered the room. "Maggie told me she thinks Esther saw Jonathan outside his fiancée's apartment the day she was killed."

"What? Why weren't we told about this?" Blood whooshed through Greg's ears as his face grew hot.

Lister strode forward until his puffed-out chest was inches from Greg's. "Hey, don't yell at me. I did the right thing. I sent the information straight to Denver."

Greg held his ground and tried to swallow his rage. If he smashed the smug jerk in the face like he wanted to, the chief would take him off the case.

Mark dropped his arm from Robin's shoulders and shifted in front of her, breaking Lister and Greg's staring match.

Robin's expression echoed Greg's fury, and he wasn't sure whether Mark was protecting his wife from a fight or keeping her from starting one.

"It's their case," Lister continued in a self-satisfied whine. "Besides, it was ruled an accident — why do you care whether he was there or not?"

Mark's hands clenched into fists, but he held them at his sides. "Because he lied. Jonathan told the police he was at his cousin's house in Wyoming, and the cousin verified it."

"OK." Donovan raised his hands, palms out. "Everybody calm down. John, catch us up on what's been done."

Lister stepped back. "I gave the information to the Denver police, and they said they would double check the alibi."

Mark relaxed his hands, but his face still showed the frustration Greg was feeling. "Have they gotten back to you?"

He checked his phone. "Not yet."

"Call them again." Donovan glanced at his watch. "We have enough to ask some questions, but, Greg, I don't want you involved." He stared directly at him. "I don't even want you here. You're too close, and Blake's lawyer will try to take advantage of it."

He was right. Even if he controlled his emotions, Blake's attorney would push him hard and twist anything he said.

The chief nodded to Peter. "Why don't you go and pick him up. Find out where he was when Esther was killed and tell him he was seen, but don't tell him by whom." He tapped the desk with his fingertips. "Grady isn't the best witness, and we want Blake to admit being there if we can." He smiled at Peter. "Use your natural charm and finesse him."

Peter grinned as he headed out the door. "OK, chief. I'll let you know what I find out." Everyone dispersed, and Mark motioned to Greg. "Since you have to leave, why don't you come to lunch with us?"

Robin tilted her head and smiled at him. "Unless you have other plans?"

Greg took his cell phone out of its holder. "No, but I wish there was something I could do. Let me check my messages, and I'll be right with you."

"Yes, by all means, check your messages first." Robin was almost beaming. What was up with her?

When he glanced at the screen, he knew. There was one from Maggie. He hit the Call button and glanced at Robin. "What's this about?"

"What's what about?" She had a frustrating, I-know-something-you-don't-know look on her face.

"There's a call from Maggie."

"Really? Why don't you call her back and see?"

No answer. He hung up. "What do you

know about this?"

"Nothing." She pivoted toward the doorway. "Let's go eat."

At the restaurant, Greg hit the *End Call* button on his cell phone again. Why didn't Maggie answer? He had to believe she'd called for a reason, and judging from Robin's smirk, it seemed positive. He couldn't get any information during lunch, even though he practically begged. Afterward, he climbed in their backseat and dialed the number again. Four rings, and it went to voicemail. He hung up, not wanting to leave a message.

"What are you doing?" Robin twisted in her seat. "Leave a message!"

"I don't want to sound desperate. If she wants to get back together, she knows where I am."

Mark found a space in the station lot and parked. "So calling her three times makes you look less desperate?"

Greg stared at the back of Mark's head. "I didn't think about that." He snugged the phone back on his belt.

"Oh, get over yourself," Mark shot over his shoulder. "Who cares whether she knows you're desperate . . . you are."

Robin elbowed her husband. "Why don't you go see her? She's at Esther's place."

Her voice was silk. "You can't go into the station yet anyway. Tell her you were worried about her." She opened her door and stepped out. "That should save your manly pride."

He climbed out, ran to his truck without answering, jumped in, and fired it up. Robin may not realize it, but he was worried. Maggie just had her house burned, for heaven's sake. He'd like to watch her 24/7, but it would border on stalking, even if he did have the best of intentions. What would he say when he got there? Then he had an idea. Perfect. Why hadn't he thought of it before? He would go home and get her dog.

33

Edward Blake stood over the crumpled form of a woman for the third time. Now what would he do? These erratic actions had to end now. Pistol whipping Maggie was spontaneous, but he had to admit it was brilliant. If he'd shot her, the neighbors might have heard it, to say nothing of the mess it would make.

He reached down and felt the base of her neck. A slow pulse thrummed against his fingertips. He went to the kitchen and searched until he found what he was looking for — duct tape. If she woke up, he didn't want her making a fuss and alerting the neighbors. He wrapped her wrists together and then her ankles, putting a piece over her mouth for good measure.

The new plan came to him quickly. He would take her to his cabin, wait until dark, and then push her and the car off the cliffs. Didn't Esther keep a set of keys hanging next to the back door? He remembered the many times he'd sat in her kitchen having coffee and a pastry. The last time flashed into his mind. Her body twisted after he'd stabbed her, and the look on her face before she fell haunted his dreams. Her eyes, he couldn't forget those eyes, sad and accusing, but not pleading. She never said a word, the breath catching in her throat, before she'd tumbled to the floor.

Pushing the disturbing thoughts out of his mind, he hurried to the kitchen. Sure enough, the keys were there, swinging from a wooden peg. He hit the button to close the garage door and cleared a path through the clothes. The trunk popped up with the remote. Slipping the keys into his pocket, he dashed into the kitchen. He'd have to move Maggie's car, too. Digging through her purse, he put her keys into his pocket with the others.

Back in the living room, he bent down, slipped his arms under her shoulders and knees, and heaved. Ooof, she was heavier than she looked. Her body bent at the waist, and she thudded to the floor. Man, he hoped the car wreck covered the bruising she would have. Bending down again, he placed her taped wrists behind his head. Lifting again, he was able to carry her. Backing into the kitchen, he maneuvered along the path through the clothes into the garage.

He eased around Esther's car and lowered Maggie into the trunk. Every emotion told him to throw her in and slam the lid, but her arms around his neck prevented it. Disengaging his head, he bumped it on something — the trunk release. If she woke during the drive, he didn't want her opening the trunk. After all, he didn't want her to hurt herself. He snickered as he slid out his pocketknife, cut the cord, and slammed the trunk. For the first time since he arrived, some relief oozed through him. *Don't relax now. There's a lot more to do.*

Taking Esther's car was a stroke of genius. If anyone came looking for Maggie, it would seem as if she'd gone somewhere in her aunt's car. He'd originally thought about hiding his in the garage but changed his mind. If someone did show up, it would be a dead giveaway. He'd park it on the street among all the others. A Mercedes would stand out more than he wanted, but there was nothing else to be done. He could move it before anyone came looking.

He parked Maggie's car in front of the house and his farther down the street. He walked back, head up, arms swinging, as though he didn't have a care in the world. If her neighbors glanced out, or heaven forbid came out, he'd tell them he was helping her sell the car. Hopefully, no one would even notice him.

Once inside, he retraced his steps. A smear of blood glistened on the floor by the front door, and his gun lay there with blood on the handle. He wiped the floor and his gun, then got another cloth and cleaned anywhere he might have touched. If he took the rags and the gun with him, he'd leave no trace of having been there. It was almost over. A couple of women were not ruining everything he'd taken his whole life to build.

Edward backed Esther's car out of the garage and searched for the right button on her sedan to close the overhead door. After three attempts, he found it and watched the door start down as he drove away. Once he got rid of Maggie, he'd be safe. *But what about Allie.* He pictured the pretty girl. At first, he thought she was upstairs while he killed Esther. But if she'd known anything, she would've told the police after her "accident." And she wouldn't have played tennis with his son.

He remembered waiting for his doorbell to ring the day Esther died, but nobody came to arrest him. It took all he had to appear normal the first time he saw Maggie, but it was obvious she didn't know anything. If only she would have left the diaries alone. Or if Jonathan had gotten them all the day of the funeral, none of this would have been necessary. But now they were destroyed, and Maggie was his last threat.

He shook his head and turned onto Park Road heading up the mountain. Too late to rethink it. After Maggie was gone, he could relax. Maybe he should consider selling the company. Even as the thought entered his mind, he knew it wouldn't happen. He didn't build it for some stranger to enjoy. It was his legacy — something he could leave for his grandchildren. Jonathan would have to learn to love it as he did. All those stupid dreams of becoming a tennis star. Yes, he was good, but a star? The boy couldn't even keep a job. He should have made him fend for himself when he got fired. Instead, he made allowances for him because his mother died. Well, so what? Lots of people die.

Maggie opened her eyes, but it was still dark. She opened them wider, but with no effect. She was lying on her side in a cramped space. Her heartbeat elevated, and she couldn't breathe. She tried to open her mouth, but something covered it, and the pain in her head pulsated with the rhythm of her heart. When she lifted her hand to investigate, the other came with it. Her eyes adjusted to the darkness, and she realized her wrists and ankles were taped together and tape covered her mouth. Terror surged through her, making her want to run. She struggled, fighting the tape on her wrists, the thought of suffocation making her dizzy.

Oxygen, she had to have more oxygen. She clawed at the tape on her mouth, scratched an end loose, and tugged. It hurt, but she jerked harder. Every movement thundered like a blow to her head. After she yanked at it a few times, it broke free. She sucked in huge gulps of air to relax. Panic wouldn't help. It made her head pound harder. She had to distract herself.

So, what was it with duct tape anyway? Previously, when Robin had tangled with a felon, duct tape was involved. Did every criminal drive around with it in their car? Was it in their secret handbook or something?

The floor rumbled beneath her, and the smell of exhaust permeated the confined space. A small amount of light filtered in, and she shifted to look around without jarring her pounding head. She was in the trunk of a moving car. Behind her a golf bag rested against the back of the seat. A latch held the seat in place. Must be like Esther's car where the seats folded down to allow transport of long items. She could enter the backseat, but the last thing she wanted was to get any closer to Edward. She pictured him flying after her. He must have hit her on the head with something. Where was he taking her? Probably out where he could kill her and bury her in the woods.

Something glimmered above her. The trunk release. She brought both hands up and pulled. Nothing happened. Great, he must have disabled it. The car hit a pothole, and she flew up, hit the trunk lid with her head, and slammed down, ramming her shoulder into something metal. She cried out, but no one would come to her rescue. The trunk was large as trunks go, but she struggled against the fear welling up and threatening to choke her.

Maggie lay still until the cacophony of pain in her body subsided slightly and then released the breath she'd been holding. Bringing her hands up to her face, she tried to bite through the tape on her wrists. It was much stronger than it looked. After repeated tries, she frayed the edges a little, but nowhere near enough to make a difference.

She hoisted herself on an elbow as far as she could and groped around the floor for the metal piece she'd landed on. A golf club — an iron. What could she do with a golf club? Could she wait until he opened the trunk and hit him with it? Her tied hands made the idea less than perfect. She was so clumsy she'd probably knock herself out instead.

Could she somehow pry the trunk open? Where could she wedge it? Her eyes settled on the taillights. A metal grid covered them, but if the club shaft fit, maybe she could force it through the plastic on the outside. A golf club sticking through the taillight might at least get noticed. She manipulated the iron above her head, holding the club about halfway down the shaft with her tied hands, trying to get the grip near the light. No such luck. It circled around and went everywhere except where she wanted it to go, while the club head swung dangerously near her face. She choked up higher on the shaft and tried again. Better. At least, she had more control. It slid through the grid when Edward hit another bump. The club stayed in place.

Pushing as hard as she could, she shoved the club into the outer plastic covering. Not enough leverage to force it through. Maybe if she used her knees. Should she take it out and put it in the other light? The thought of trying to get it into the small grid on the other side decided for her. She'd move her body around so her knees were in front of the light. Easier said than done. She got stuck and began to panic, the tightness of the trunk making her heart pound and her palms sweat.

She maneuvered to where her bent knees were in front of the club, and relief surged through her. She jerked, hitting the end of the club with one knee. The grip hit metal instead, sending a shooting pain up into her thigh. She shifted the club and tried again, connecting with the club — pfft. The plastic cracked. Twice more she hit it, her knee now throbbing, and then it slipped through. She pushed it all the way out until the club head met with the metal grate. She lay back, exhausted. If somebody doesn't see that, they weren't paying attention.

Maybe a policeman would pull him over. Then what would she do? If she could find another club, she could bang it against the trunk lid. The bag was behind her, but she could see no way to get a club out — the trunk was too small. She was lucky the first one was loose. It must be an extra. Not much hope of finding another one.

34

Esther's house was ahead on the right, and Greg still hadn't made up his mind what he should say beyond "Hey, here's your dog." The garage door was sliding up as he arrived out front. He passed Maggie's car, coasted past the driveway, and parked on the street. He waited for someone to pull either in or out, but nothing happened.

No sign of Maggie, so why was the garage door opening? The culprit became obvious when Greg got out and walked up the driveway. A leaf had blown in and disrupted the sensor, stopping the door from closing. He kicked it aside and entered the empty garage. Had Maggie taken Esther's car somewhere? Or had she sold it already, and the new owner was picking it up? He'd been out of the loop for a couple days, but he was pretty sure she hadn't sold anything yet. Instead of wasting more time, he jogged to his car, scooped Honey into his arms, and knocked on the back door. No answer. He twisted the knob and stuck his head in.

"Maggie? Are you here?"

He strained his ears. "Honey, where are you?" The dog squirmed in his arms until he put her down. She charged toward the swing door in the kitchen, barking nonstop. "I didn't mean you, Honey. What's the matter?"

The dog pushed through the swing door into the dining room, and it swung shut after her.

"Maggie?" He raised his voice to be heard over the constant barking. "Are you here?" Maybe she'd taken Esther's car after all. Queasiness settled in the pit of his stomach. Something wasn't right. Clothes were scattered everywhere, but Robin said she'd helped Maggie pack them in. Maybe she had to leave before she started the first load.

Calling her name again, he followed Honey. She jumped on the front door, barking. Maybe he should put her in a bedroom and leave Maggie a note. He bent to pick her up when he saw it. A smear of blood smudged the door.

"Honey, hush! I can't hear!" He scooped her in his arms, and she stopped barking. The whole house stood deadly quiet. He called Maggie's name again, but as before, no response. Could she have somehow fallen and hit her head? There'd been no blood on the door when they'd processed the scene. Dread dropped into his stomach, and his palms began to sweat. His long strides thundered through the rest of the house, but she was gone.

He shut the dog in a bedroom, and unclipping the phone from his belt, he dialed her cell again. The music of her ringtone sounded like it came from downstairs. The jingle increased down the stairs then stopped ringing and went to voicemail. He hit *end* and redialed, shoving through the kitchen door. It rang in her purse on the counter. No way would she have left without her purse, unless something was very wrong.

He ran out to his truck, hitting the garage door opener as he went. He ducked under the lowering door, while jumping over the sensor light. He dialed Mark as he sped away from her house.

"I think Maggie's in trouble."

"What happened?"

"Esther's car is missing, and Maggie's purse is on the counter. But she's not here. And there's blood on the inside of the front door. The garage door was obstructed, so it was coming back up when I got here. I must have just missed her."

He drove past a black Mercedes parked down the street. "Wait. There's a car here like Edward's." He backed up, stopped beside it, and read off the license number. "Does it belong to Edward?"

"Hold on a second. Let me check."

Greg continued down the street and around the corner, searching for Esther's car. After what seemed like forever, Mark came back on the line. "It's Edward's car all right. Why would he park it on her street?"

"Only if he didn't want it noticed."

"I'm putting out an APB. Hang on a second." Mark's muffled voice gave instruction to someone with the make, model, and license number of Esther's car. "Greg?" his voice came through strong. "Do you think he found out we're looking for him?"

"No. I think he tried to have her killed in a house fire, and now he's decided to do it himself. Where's Peter?"

"Peter says Edward's not at his office or at home. He's heading for the jobsite now."

"Tell him I'll meet him there." Greg disconnected and drove, praying God would lead him to Edward, and if he was on the wrong track, he would show him the right direction. Nothing came to him, but a rising tide of fear caused him to push harder on the accelerator.

He maneuvered through the traffic toward the construction site. Houses going up along the development's far edge would make a good place to hide a body. *Please let her be OK, Lord,* he prayed for the hundredth time since he'd gotten in his truck.

He took a sharp turn at the next corner and flew along the street toward the jobsite. As fast as he was going, he should have caught up with Edward by now if this was his destination. Based on the garage door, he must have just left. So he'd only had about a ten- or fifteen-minute head start while Greg searched the house. And he'd more than made up for that.

An American flag heralding the new development appeared ahead but still no sign of Edward. Maybe he went in the back way. Greg flew through the newly paved streets to the rear of the development where the skeletons of three new houses stood in various stages of framing. A couple workers clung to the top of the second one, nailing the plywood for the roof in place. Two vehicles waited at the curb but not a white sedan. He edged past, scanning the area for either the man or the car. Nothing.

Where could Edward have gone? He raced

back to the trailer and skidded to a stop, barely getting it into park before jumping out of the truck. He flew up the stairs and yanked on the trailer door.

Mike dropped the paper in his hand when he saw Greg's face. "What's wrong?"

"Where's Edward?"

"He's not here. I'm working today —"

"I know he's not here," Greg interrupted. "I need to find him. Now."

"I don't know." Mike held his hands up, palms out. "I swear, I don't know!"

"I have to find him. He might have Maggie."

"Do you think he's — ?"

"I don't know. I can't take the chance. Where does he go when he's not here?"

"He's working on a house for himself. Sometimes he takes a crew over there."

"Where?" Greg backed toward the door.

Mike yelled the cross streets at him.

Greg slammed out the door.

35

Edward glared at the steering wheel. What, no Bluetooth? Why did Esther have such an antiquated car? She had the money for a newer model. He eased his phone out of its holder and dialed Jonathan. "Where are you?"

The pause silencing the line meant he was about to lie.

"Where do you think? I'm working."

Edward pictured him at the club with a drink in his hand. "Meet me at the cabin, but don't tell anyone where you're going."

"The cabin? Why?"

"Don't ask questions. Just get there. I need a ride." He hung up, flipped the phone off, and slipped it into the cup holder. This road was hardly used during the day and deserted at night. He would have to wait several hours before it was safe to come back and finish the job. Had Maggie woken up yet? She must have by now. It would make getting her out of the trunk more difficult, unless he knocked her out again. At least, the trauma from the accident would cover any bruising. Amazing how easily his mind designed ways to kill now. It was true what they said — you do what you have to do.

A red SUV appeared in his rearview mirror, holding to a steady speed. The lights blinked and it sped up. He pushed down harder on the accelerator and achieved some distance between them. No way could anyone know what was in the trunk, so why was he jumpy? Prying his clenched fingers one at a time off the wheel, he flexed each hand, trying to calm himself. Not going to happen. The other vehicle fell back. Probably just a tourist, but he wanted to be alone.

He sped up a little more. Maybe the guy would pull off. He swerved onto Cliff Drive, watching the rearview mirror. The SUV followed. Great. His next street wasn't far, and he didn't want company. If he turned and the guy went straight, he could get him off his tail, but if not, he'd have nowhere to go but up the canyon. He didn't want anyone to see where he was going. Sweat beaded his brow.

At the last minute, he veered onto Canyon

Road. The other vehicle shot past. He exhaled, and his whole body relaxed. Of course, the guy wasn't chasing him. What a ridiculous idea. Wiping a hand over his forehead, he slowed onto a dirt road. All he wanted right now was to get this car out of sight. And a stiff drink, of course. Even though he rarely used the cabin, the liquor cabinet was stocked. He saw to it.

36

The radio chirped when Greg got in the truck, and he heard the chatter. Dispatch received a call about a white sedan with Esther's license plates, with a golf club sticking out of the taillight. Greg hit the mic button. "This is Detective Greg Williams. That's the car we're looking for. What's the location?"

"Park and Cliff Drive."

Greg startled. The huge ravine led to a rushing river. What was Edward planning to do, throw her over? Make it look like she fell? Greg skidded at the light and sped west, calling in reinforcements. Peter, pulling into the site as Greg flew out, hooked a U-turn, and followed.

A golf club through the taillight? It sounded like something Maggie would do.

Greg dialed the station.

Mark picked up. "Did you hear that?"

"Yeah, we're trying to get a location now.

A man called in saying he tried to warn the driver, but then he started driving erratically. The man said he turned onto Canyon Road heading up the mountain."

Greg's stomach twisted. Near the top, the canyon stretched for several miles, a thin guardrail the only separation between the road and death. He had no idea where Edward would go. He spoke into the phone. "Does Edward own any property up there?"

"Not that we can see. We're checking under Tate, too, in case it's Monica's. We're also picking up Jonathan. He may be able to help."

Greg flipped the siren off and left his grill lights on as he approached Park Street. He didn't want to spook Edward into doing something stupid. Although what was more stupid than kidnaping a policeman's fiancée? Ex-fiancée, he reminded himself. But she had called him. It had to mean something, didn't it? Unless she called to get her dog. He shook his head. Now was not the time to analyze their relationship. He had to ensure she was safe first.

He reached the intersection of Cliff Drive and Canyon Road sooner than he expected. He slowed his truck around the corner, seeing a police car ahead. The cruiser waited on the side of the road, his engine running.

Greg pulled alongside and rolled down the passenger window. "Stay here and block him in. If he tries to leave, stop him."

Peter parked his vehicle behind Greg's and hurried up to his window. "Let's split up and see if we can locate him."

Greg agreed and spoke to the other officer. "More backup should be here any minute. Whoever finds him first will radio it in, and we can build a net around this creep. He can't be allowed to escape."

The officer unlocked his gun rack and slid a rifle across his lap. "He won't get past me."

37

Maggie lay back, trying to still her pounding head. If she could rest it on something that didn't jar it every time the car hit a bump, maybe she could think. She leaned against the golf bag, trying to find a soft spot. Twisting her head, she saw the perfect thing. Club head covers. Esther had fuzzy club head covers; so was she in Esther's trunk? She maneuvered her hands up and around the driver cover and pulled. After a few tries, she dislodged it and dragged it under her head.

Ah, so much better. It wasn't thick enough, but it kept her head from smacking the bottom of the trunk at every pothole. Once the pounding settled to a dull ache, she was able to concentrate. There had to be a way out of here. Edward wouldn't drive forever, and she didn't want to face him trussed up like a pig ready for the spit. Once he stopped the car in some lonely spot, he'd have all the advantages. She had to get the tape off her wrists.

Maybe she could use the prongs of her ring to tear at the tape. She put the diamond in her mouth and eased it off her finger, then positioned it to where the diamond faced out. She scraped the ring repeatedly over the tape without catching, until it slipped out of her mouth and landed somewhere beneath her. She wanted to scream.

Laying her head back down, she surveyed the trunk and faced the golf bag again. Was there something in there she could use? She brought her hands up and worked at unzipping one of the pockets. Only golf balls in there, nothing to pry the sticky tape from her wrists. She unzipped another pocket, finding tees inside and what Esther had called a divot repair tool.

The U-shaped tool had a round logo at one end and two prongs at the other, which Esther had told her were used to pry up indented earth in the green. She clamped the logo in her mouth and tried to pierce the tape with the prongs. Either the tape was too strong or the prongs were too dull, but the tool swiveled in her mouth without doing any damage to the tape.

Spitting out the tool, she reached back into the bag and retrieved a tee. She bit down on the wooden stem and pushed hard against the tape. The resistance was strong, and just when she thought her teeth would break off, the tee pierced the tape. She moved it to another area and tried again, this time using the bottom of the trunk as leverage instead of her mouth. A few holes later, she ripped the tape and freed her hands. Now for her feet.

Unable to sit up, she raised her knees to her chest, stabbing and pushing at the tape with the tee until she'd made enough holes to free her feet. Now, at least if she got out of the trunk, she could run instead of hopping around helpless. Reaching under her, she felt around for her ring and slipped it back on her finger. If she died today, she wanted Greg to know she'd been wearing it.

38

At the station, Mark, along with David and Chief Donovan, watched two officers bring in Jonathan Blake. He'd been apprehended leaving the club. The officers held him lightly between them in handcuffs, so he must have resisted.

Officer Daniels steered him toward the trio. "He says he doesn't know where his dad is."

Jonathan saw the chief and tensed, pulling away from the hand on his arm. "I don't know what this is about," he jerked his chin up, "but I'm not staying here."

"Take him to a room," Donovan spoke to the officers. "We'll be there in a minute."

They led him away, and David rubbed his hands together. "Let me at the little puke. I'll wipe the arrogant smirk off his face."

Donovan nodded. "You and Mark question him, but, Mark, you take the lead. I don't want him to clam up."

Mark agreed.

David's hands dropped to his sides.

Donovan turned to him. "Don't worry. You'll get your chance if he doesn't cooperate."

David grinned. "Let's go."

Jonathan slumped in his chair, his hands on the table picking at the handcuffs.

Mark would have loved to let him stew awhile, but they needed an address fast. He moved into the room and pulled out the chair in front of Jonathan.

David eased into the seat next to him.

Mark glanced up at Daniels, leaning against the wall behind Jonathan. "Do we need the handcuffs?"

"He took a swing at me."

Mark shook his head. "Jonathan, assaulting an officer won't help you."

He didn't say anything, but his gaze darted to David and back to Mark.

"If I tell Officer Daniels to take off the cuffs, will you behave yourself?"

He nodded.

"Bert, will you, please?"

Daniels unlocked the cuffs and stood against the wall again.

Jonathan rubbed his wrists and stayed silent.

Mark kept picturing Maggie's face. Remaining calm demanded all his focus. "I need you to tell me the truth. Does your family have a cabin somewhere near Canyon Road?"

Jonathan raised his eyebrows. "Why?"

David sprang out of his seat. "Just answer the man!"

Jonathan jumped at David's intensity, and so did Mark.

David lowered himself into his chair, never shifting his gaze.

Mark couldn't blame him for the outburst. He wanted to slap the information out of the kid. Instead, he tried to keep his voice steady. "We need to know. It's important."

Jonathan leaned back in his chair. "Not until I get a phone call. My father won't appreciate the way I'm being treated."

Mark felt David tense next to him, and he nudged him with an elbow. "We believe your father has taken Maggie Schreiber hostage, and he's headed up Canyon Road. As of now, you're an accessory to kidnaping."

Jonathan's eyebrows popped up and he formed an O with his mouth.

Mark wanted to laugh. For the first time Daddy wouldn't be able to bail him out.

"Dad has Maggie?"

"We believe so, yes. And if you cooperate, we'll take kidnaping off the table."

It didn't even take a minute for Jonathan to respond. "He asked me to meet him at the cabin. Said he needed a ride."

"What cabin? We looked, and it doesn't appear your family owns one in the area."

"You wouldn't find it. It's under Blaszcyzyk — B-l-a-s-z-c-y-z-y-k." He gave the address, and David scribbled it down, then jumped from the table, and ran from the room.

"The cabin came from my grandfather on my dad's side. I never knew him, but Dad was ashamed of him or something. He said the man was nobody from nowhere, going no place. That's how he put it. Once he was old enough, Dad moved away and changed his name to Blake. Said he wanted a fresh start."

39

Maggie tensed when the car rolled to a stop and the engine shut off. She threaded the golf club back through the taillight, trying to make as little noise as possible. When he came to get her, he'd get a surprise. The car door slammed, and she grasped the club in both hands, ready to use it as a poker rather than swinging it like a bat. She squeezed the club and waited, listening hard.

Footsteps crunched away from the car. Soon another door slammed, and all went quiet. Could he have left her here? If so, now was her chance. Maybe the golf club would come in handy again. She moved to the rear of the trunk, as close to the seat as she could get with the golf bag blocking her way, and wedged the club head between the seat and the car frame, just above the latch. If she could get into the backseat, she had a chance of escaping before he returned. She forced the club sideways, not easy in the cramped space, and tugged. It slipped off. She tried again, and the latch bent slightly before the club head slipped out. On the third try the latch released and the left seat popped forward. Light streamed into the trunk. She could see into the car, and cool air touched her face.

Ignoring the thumping in her head, she pushed until the seat tilted forward. She scrambled over the golf clubs and onto the platform it made, feeling exposed. Slithering down onto the right seat, she exhaled and heaved the left one up again. The twisted fastener prevented it from locking into place, but it would appear normal from a distance.

Her legs would hardly straighten after being bent so long, and pins and needles raced along her nerve endings. Stretching as much as she could in the confined space, she flexed first one leg then another, hoping she'd be able to stand.

Keeping her head low, Maggie peered between the front seats. The car was parked in the middle of some aspen trees behind a two-story log cabin. Edward must have gone in there.

She ducked instinctively when he passed by a first-floor window. He didn't stop, so lying on her stomach, she eased open the door on the side farthest from the house. She peeked at the window again.

Being out of the car felt good, and fresh, pine-scented air renewed her lungs. Maggie stumbled behind the nearest aspen and evaluated her situation. A large deck with French doors led into the house on the lower level. A small balcony jutted from the second floor.

Hobbling to the safety of more aspens, she focused on the pinon pines beside the house. There was a section of open space, and she would have to run, but the pines afforded the best coverage. Her legs trembled, struggling to hold her weight.

She stretched her limbs and examined the house windows again. The upper ones reflected the sun, showing no sign whether anyone was behind them. Her mind screamed at her to stay put, but common sense argued she couldn't hide forever. When her legs seemed steady, she dashed to the shelter of the pines.

An explosion rang out. Something hit behind her, dirt spraying her jeans. She slid behind a large pinion and peered out.

Edward stood at the balcony edge, a rifle on his shoulder aimed straight at her.

Breath caught in her throat, everything inside begging her to run. She held her ground. The branches sheltered her, preventing him from getting a good shot.

The balcony ended at the edge of the house, and without outside stairs in the back, Edward would have to go through the house in order to get to her. She waited until he left the balcony and ran.

The cabin faced downhill, and the road wound below. The land had been cleared for several yards all around, probably to stop the spread of fire; but to reach her objective, she would have to leave the safety of the trees. That wouldn't work; she'd have to go around. Her feet slid on a patch of pine needles, and she nearly fell. Movies, where the poor little woman trips and the bad guy gets her, flashed through her mind. She couldn't allow herself to become the poor little woman. She slowed to regain her balance and continued to make her way forward.

Footsteps pounded on the front steps and paused. She stopped and held her breath. The wind whistled in the trees. He must be listening for her, so he didn't know which way she'd gone. Huddling behind a lodge pole pine, she waited for him to make the first move. The thin trunk with sparse branches didn't offer the best of hiding places. When she glanced down, she realized her white over shirt screamed her presence against the dark trees. She slipped it off as quietly as possible, appreciating Robin's choice of the dark green tank top underneath.

She paused again to listen. Where was he? Did he know which way she would go? Was he moving straight at her? She scanned the area for any indication of the direction he had taken. His boots crunched on gravel. He was in the cleared area. She couldn't see him, but she could hear him now, his feet sliding. He was going for the road. She rolled the shirt up, brushed dirt, leaves, and needles over it, and then, fighting her every instinct, she turned her back on him and started up the mountain.

40

Greg drove slowly, following each small road to a driveway where he could see the cars. What if it was parked in a garage? The mountain was huge. There had to be a hundred houses up here. They needed an army, not two guys driving around. They'd been at it for half an hour and hadn't seen a thing. Finding her would be a miracle.

There. Up ahead a white car sat in front of a log home. He slowed for a better look. Nope, it was the wrong model. On to the next house. The longer it took, the more frustrated he became, but it was better than doing nothing, waiting for backup. Maybe Peter was having more luck. Even knowing he would have heard if there was anything to report, Greg couldn't help himself. He picked up the mic. "Peter, you see anything?"

"Nothing yet. You?"

"No, and if it's in a garage, we may miss it."

"I know, but I didn't want to be the first to say it."

He clicked off the mic, frantic to race to her, not this crawl. The trouble was, he didn't know where to race. The radio buzzed alive again.

"Peter, Greg, you there?"

Greg grabbed the mic. "We're here, David."

"We've got Jonathan, and he's given us the address."

Finally, they were getting somewhere. "Let's have it."

The address crackled over the radio, and Greg didn't stop to answer. It was closer to Peter's location than his. He threw the mic in place and raced to catch up. A few minutes later, he rounded a curve and the house came into view. He flew up the driveway and skidded to a stop in front, right behind Peter's SUV. Peter jumped out. "You look for the car. I'll check the house."

Greg circled the house. The car waited semi-hidden in some trees. The doors were unlocked, and the backseat wasn't latched. He pulled it down and peered into the trunk. Nothing there. Where could Edward have taken her?

He raced to the front of the house, calling her name. Peter was already inside, and he hadn't called out, so he hadn't found them. Greg raced up the porch steps and into an open room. "Maggie!" he called. "Peter?"

"Up here!" Peter's voice. "He's not here now, but when he was, he discharged a weapon."

Greg flew up the stairs, through a bedroom, and out onto a deck, which gave the feeling of floating in space. Dizzy, he grasped the railing and focused on Peter. A spent shell casing teetered on the end of his pen.

"It's still warm."

"Do you think he shot her?" Greg's voice shook.

"Don't get too upset. I don't see any blood out there. Maybe she got away."

Greg surveyed the panorama. A cleared space surrounded them, and then a forest of aspens and pines closed in. Peter was trying to be reassuring, but a lack of visible blood in the clearing didn't mean Edward hadn't hit her.

Greg's stomach writhed. She could be lying out there, hidden in the trees, suffering. Or worse. The land climbed vertically and flattened out at a lake shimmering in the sunlight. He searched between the trees to catch a glimpse of either Maggie or Edward.

"Maggie!" His voice echoed through the canyon.

Silence was his answer.

41

Edward froze as two vehicles sped into his driveway. The cops? The fiancé, Greg. He shouldn't have brought her here. He should have killed her and left her at Esther's. Now he'd have to escape down the mountain unseen, and he couldn't use the road. Cops were never alone — they traveled in packs. Soon the mountain would be crawling with them.

He turned back. If he could reach the car while they searched for Maggie . . . but they knew the license number. He wouldn't get far. What about using her as a hostage? He'd have to find her first. How had they found the cabin? He winced and wanted to push the thought aside, but he couldn't. Jonathan. He must have given them the address. No one else knew about it — not even Monica. She knew he had a cabin, but had no idea where. Leaving it under Blaszcyzyk should have kept him safe. He tightened his grip on the rifle. After everything he'd done for the kid, this is how he repaid him? Betraying him to the police?

A voice echoed through the canyon, calling Maggie's name. So they hadn't picked her up yet. He listened for her response. Why didn't she answer? Afraid he'd find her first. And she should be.

Maggie heard the voice, and her heart leapt. Greg! He'd found her. Relief washed through her, and she almost called out. But wait, where was Edward? He'd started for the road, but wasn't far away. If he heard her, he might shoot just for spite.

She wiped a hand over her forehead. What if he got away? She and Allie would still be a threat. They were the only people who could send him to jail. Allie would be going away to college or traveling around playing in tournaments. She wouldn't be safe. The thought of him stalking her little sister brought the blood to Maggie's face. She couldn't allow it. He couldn't get away. She froze, straining to hear over her heartbeat.

The trees rustled in the wind. Wait. What was that crackle? Was it Edward or an animal? More sounds. Footsteps. Heading in the same direction she was, but off to the right. He must have decided the road was too dangerous. She peered into the trees, but they shielded him. How could she find him without being seen? A strategy formed in her mind. She would get him to betray his location to the police. She pivoted on her toes and started back the way she had come, moving as silently as she could. A few yards away lay the buried white shirt.

Lifting it from the ground, she shook the dirt and leaves from it, making as little noise as possible. She searched for some small rocks and slipped them into her pockets. Finding an aspen with limbs at the right position, she hung the shirt at the end of a shoulder-height branch and edged away, avoiding twigs and underbrush. This was the most dangerous part of her plan. If he saw it before she was ready . . .

She gazed around the forest as she tiptoed, and despite her caution, twigs snapped under her feet. She needed to find him without him seeing her. She gazed up at a tall pine. This would work. She left her trusty golf club at the bottom and climbed. Rough bark scraped her palms, and sap coated her hands with a sticky film. Pine needles poked at her, and a twig nearly stabbed her in the eye. A few feet farther, she'd lifted herself high enough to see, and there he was. The sight startled her, and she almost lost her balance. He must have heard the noise she made, because he changed direction.

She gauged the trajectory of his new course. He would pass too far away to see the shirt. She took a rock from her pocket and threw it toward an aspen near the one holding the shirt. It connected with a satisfying crack. He stopped. She tossed another one, and he turned to the clamor, lifting his rifle.

What was she thinking, leading him to her? She should have gotten farther away. He crept forward, one step at a time, sure-footed and quiet. Her palms began to sweat, and her body started to shake. *Come on. Fire at the shirt. Give yourself away.*

Other sounds rustled in the forest. Were Mark and Peter coming? She prayed Edward wouldn't shoot one of them if they got too close. There, he saw the shirt. He skulked closer, his hunting skills evident. She wouldn't have imagined a man his size could move so silently. He brought the rifle up and gazed through the scope.

This was a bad idea. She'd forgotten that he'd be able to see the shirt clearly in the scope, knowing she wasn't in it. He lowered the weapon and stalked until he stood next to the shirt. He gazed around and looked up, locking eyes with her. A smile spread across his face as he raised his weapon. Maggie screamed.

Crashing sounds of pounding feet drew near, but it was too late. She hid in the branches and prayed. At least, Allie would be OK. After he shot her, they would catch him, and Allie would be safe. He fired. Pain scorched her hand, and she lost her grip. She tried to grab the trunk, a branch, anything, to stop her fall, but her right hand wouldn't work. Several limbs hammered her body, and then mercifully, there was nothing.

42

"Mags? Are you OK?" Allie's tear-streaked face appeared above her when she opened her eyes.

Maggie squinted against the bright fluorescent lights, alive, and apparently, in the hospital. "Yeah, I'm OK." She struggled to sit up, her bandaged right hand making it difficult. "I'm feeling some déjà vu. Haven't we been here before?"

Allie helped her with the pillows, the tight lines in her face relaxing into a smile. "Yeah. One more visit and it's free."

"How long have I been in here? Did they catch Edward?"

The smile widened as she plopped into a chair next to the bed. "It all happened yesterday, and I flew in last night. And yeah, they got him. Once he shot at you, Greg shot him. He'll make it, but when he gets out of here, he's going to jail."

Maggie reached out with her good hand,

and Allie clutched it between hers. "You'll be OK. The bullet just grazed your hand. Then you fell and knocked yourself out. The doctor says you have a concussion."

A light knock sounded, and Greg filled the doorway. "May I come in?"

Allie gave her hand a squeeze, stretched for her crutches, and struggled to her feet. "I haven't had lunch, so I'll go get something to eat. Anybody hungry?"

Greg moved a second chair out of her way. "I'm good, thanks. Besides, you can't carry anything up here with those crutches."

"That's true. I guess I'll eat in the cafeteria." She hobbled toward the door and looked over her shoulder. "It should take me quite a while." With a final wink, she left them alone.

Greg smoothed the hair back from Maggie's forehead and leaned down, his lips brushing hers. "You scared me pretty bad, you know. I thought I'd lost you for good."

"Me, too."

He lowered himself into the chair Allie vacated. "They'll be in soon to take your statement, but for now, just tell me what happened."

She told him everything from the time she saw Edward in Aunt Esther's garage to when she fell out of the tree. "So it wasn't a burglary at all."

"Edward had heard about the robberies in the area, so he staged the crime scene to look like the others. Bobby, Grady, Cameron, and Cody were all part of the burglary ring. We're still seeking the brains behind it. Bobby isn't talking, and the others don't know who was calling the shots."

"What about Carla and Ginger? Edward acted like he didn't know who they were."

"I don't think he did. A kid came in with his parents and turned himself in for Carla's hit and run. So it was an accident, and he got scared and ran. Ginger just let her imagination run away with her."

Maggie played with the blanket, twisting it in her hand. "So it all came down to a man protecting his son."

"Not according to Jonathan. He says it was to protect the business. Evidently, Edward grew up with an alcoholic father who never wanted to work. They were very poor, and when he was sixteen, he was expected to work to support his dad. Edward left home, lied about his age, and got a job in construction. He thought Blake sounded classier than Blaszcyzyk, so he gave his employer that name. He never legally changed it, just bought fake documents. That's why we couldn't find the cabin."

She took a sip of water from the cup next to her bed. "So, what will happen to Jonathan? It sounded as though killing Stephanie was an accident."

"Yeah, but covering it up wasn't. He's facing a list of charges. Monica has him all lawyered up, so I imagine he'll be out on bail soon."

"Do you think he'll buckle down and work the construction business?"

"I doubt it. He says his father forced him to work even though he had no interest. My guess is Edward will have to sell to pay his legal fees. I have a feeling Monica will disown him. She's already making it clear that he's not a blood relative."

He grasped her hand, straightening the diamond on her finger. "Enough about them. Does this mean what I think it means?"

She grinned. "It means I'm taken."

"Blessed man."

The grin faded from her face. "I acted like an idiot. I don't know what came over me, but I got scared. I thought when you found out I wasn't like Aunt Esther, you'd leave. I couldn't handle that, so I left you first. Dumb, I know." She gazed into his eyes. "Can you forgive me? Do you still want to get married?"

His clear blue eyes swallowed her, and she felt like she could drown in them. "Of course, I still want to get married." He leaned over and gave her a long, slow kiss. "And not to an Esther clone." He sat back, capturing her hand in his. "Trust me. I know what I'm getting, and I want you."

Tears welled up in her eyes. She blinked them away. "I did a lot of thinking in the hotel, and I decided I want to fix my house and sell it. I'd like us to start someplace new."

He smiled. "Fine with me."

"Wait. There's more. I know how I can finish Aunt Esther's legacy and leave one of my own."

Greg stroked the back of her hand with his thumb. "How's that, sweetheart?"

"For Aunt Esther, I'll continue to support the school she loved so much. And for me, it's Allie. I know she doesn't need me the way I needed Esther, but I feel she needs me anyway."

The stroking paused, and Greg gazed into her eyes. "I agree. She needs a stable influence in her life."

"I want her to come and live with me. She can go to college wherever she wants and stay with me in between. Whenever she needs a place to land, I want her to be able to land with me." She watched Greg's face, looking for any sign of fear or withdrawal and saw none. "Is that something you would consider? Could she live with us when we're married?"

He smiled. "You don't even have to ask."

ABOUT THE AUTHOR

C. E. Waterman is an avid mystery reader. Starting with the Boxcar Children, followed by Nancy Drew and The Hardy Boys, on to Agatha Christie and then Mary Higgins Clark, she has always loved a good mystery. She lives in Colorado with her husband and her dog.

The employees of Thorndike Press hope you have enjoyed this Large Print book. All our Thorndike, Wheeler, and Kennebec Large Print titles are designed for easy reading, and all our books are made to last. Other Thorndike Press Large Print books are available at your library, through selected bookstores, or directly from us.

For information about titles, please call:
(800) 223-1244

or visit our website at:
gale.com/thorndike

To share your comments, please write:
Publisher
Thorndike Press
10 Water St., Suite 310
Waterville, ME 04901